THRAXAS AT WAR

BY
MARTIN SCOTT

THRAXAS AT WAR

Copyright © 2003 by Martin Scott. Published by permission of Orbit (Time Warner Books UK)

A Baen Book

Baen Publishing Enterprises
P.O. Box 1403
Riverdale, NY 10471
www.baen.com

ISBN 10: 1-4165-5513-7
ISBN 13: 978-1-4165-5513-1

Cover art by Tom Kidd

First Baen paperback printing, December 2007

Distributed by Simon & Schuster
1230 Avenue of the Americas
New York, NY 10020

Library of Congress Cataloging-in-Publication Data: 2005034213

Printed in the United States of America

10 9 8 7 6 5 4 3 2 1

CHAPTER ONE

I'm sitting at the bar in the Avenging Axe, a beer in one hand and a thazis stick in the other, trying to decide whether to have a glass of klee with my next beer. It's a difficult decision. There's a bottle of klee upstairs in my office. I could wait till I get there. But there's nothing quite like a glass of klee washed down by a flagon of Gurd's freshly drawn ale. Having examined my options for a while, studied the problem using the full weight of my experience, I decide on the klee. And another ale while I'm at it.

Dandelion, the idiot barmaid, looks as if she might be about to make some comment as to the wisdom of embarking on an ambitious drinking programme so early in the afternoon. I direct a stern glance in her direction. The last thing I need is a lecture about my drinking from Dandelion, a young woman who, while not working behind the bar, is generally to be found on the beach, talking to dolphins.

I frown. This tavern is really going downhill. It's bad enough having to put up with Makri and her moods without having to endure Dandelion's own particular brand of foolish behaviour. Worse, there's still no sign of Tanrose, the tavern's cook, coming back. I haven't had a decent meal for weeks. Life just gets worse.

Gurd, owner of the Avenging Axe and my oldest friend, sits down next to me. I'm about to launch into a complaint about the deteriorating quality of his barmaids but I bite back the words.

"No work, Thraxas?"

I shake my head.

"Things aren't so good. And you know why."

"The investigation?"

I nod. A few months back I was accused of cowardice in the face of the enemy. Throwing my shield away on the field of battle. This allegation, relating to the Battle of Sanasa, which took place around seventeen years ago, is so completely without foundation that it should never have been brought to court. Not when the man being accused has fought bravely for his city. Unfortunately Turai isn't a city that rewards a man for his past valour. Rather, it's a place that seeks to drag an honest man down, allowing advancement to the rich and corrupt at the expense of the poor but upright.

"Business has really gone downhill."

"No one believes it, Thraxas."

"Maybe not, but these things are lethal for a man's reputation. I'm tainted. I'm beginning to regret not killing Vadinex when he made the allegation. Would have got it over with quickly."

"And you'd be a fugitive by now," points out Gurd.

Vadinex fought at the Battle of Sanasa. Why he's now come up with this false accusation is something about which I'm still not certain.

I've spent the past weeks gathering evidence to defend myself in court. Plenty of men still living in Turai were at the Battle of Sanasa but it's not been easy finding many who were close at hand when the alleged events took place. Even for a professional Investigator like myself some of my old comrades took a lot of finding. It meant a lot of uncomfortable trudging round the city in the hot rainy season. Having found a few old comrades, I'm reasonably confident I'll win the case. Unless my enemies do a lot of serious bribery, which is always possible in this city. If that happens I'll kill my accuser and leave town. It's not like Turai is such a great place to live anyway.

I'd have run into money problems by now had it not been for a rather successful series of visits to the chariot races at the Stadium Superbius. I picked the winner of the Turas memorial race and went through the card very successfully, ending the week's racing with an extremely healthy profit and my reputation as a gambler somewhat restored after last year's debacle. But the races last year were fixed, of course. Everyone knows that Thraxas never makes losses like that in normal circumstances.

The tavern door flies open. An assortment of foul Orcish oaths heralds the arrival of Makri. The uttering of Orcish oaths is both taboo and illegal in Turai but Makri, in times of stress, tends to revert to the language of her youth. As she grew up in an Orcish gladiator pit, she has a wide variety of Orcish bad language to choose from.

Gurd frowns at her. Dandelion looks pained. Makri ignores them both.

"You know someone just insulted me in the street? I was minding my own business and then for no reason this man said, 'There goes that skinny Orc.'"

Makri reaches over and takes a thazis stick from me, igniting it from a candle and inhaling deeply.

"I hate this place," she says.

Makri is one quarter Orc. In a city where everyone hates Orcs, it can lead to trouble. Most people in Twelve Seas are used to her by now but she still runs into occasional hostility on the streets. Neither Gurd nor I take the trouble to ask what happened after the man insulted her. We already know.

"So aren't you going to ask what happened?" demands Makri.

I take a sip of my beer.

"Let me see. A stranger calls you a skinny Orc while you're walking down Quintessence Street. Now what could your response possibly be? You chuckle merrily and walk on? You congratulate him on a fine turn of phrase? No, don't tell me, I've got it. You punched him to the ground, then told him at sword point that if he ever bothered you again you'd kill him without mercy?"

Makri looks disappointed.

"Something like that," she says. "But you spoiled my story."

Makri lapses into silence. These past few weeks she hasn't been any more cheerful than me. Not just because of the hot rainy season and her aversion to the continual downpour. Even now, when we've reached autumn, one of the brief periods when climate in Turai could be considered pleasant, she's not happy. This summer was one of the high points of her life, when she scored top marks at the Guild College and sailed into her final year of study as number one student, but after the elation of that faded she got to remembering that her first romantic encounter seemed to have come to an untimely end. This encounter featured a young Elf on the Isle of Avula; a young Elf who has since neglected to get in touch with her. Avula is some weeks' sail from Turai, but, as Makri says, he could have sent a message. So Makri has spent the past month being about as miserable as a Niojan whore, much to the distress of the customers in the tavern.

There was a time when the sight of Makri, struggling to remain in her tiny chainmail bikini while bringing a tray of drinks, was enough to cheer up the most downhearted local dock worker. Makri's figure—unmatched, it's reckoned, in the entire city-state—was of such renown as to make people forget their prejudices against her. As old Parax the shoemaker says, you can't hold a little Orcish blood against a girl with a physique like that. And there have been plenty more comments in a similar vein, not just from Parax. But even the finest physique can't compensate for a waitress who bangs your drink on the table and looks like she'll knock your head off given the slightest excuse. When dockers, sailmakers and the like come to the Avenging Axe after a hard day's work, they're looking for a little light relaxation, and when Makri's angry, it's hard to relax.

She tosses a small bag in my direction. It contains various pastries from Morixa's bakery. Morixa took over the place from her mother Minarixa last year, after Minarixa unfortunately partook of too much dwa; a deadly mistake. The drug has claimed a lot of lives in this city. Most of them I don't care about but I miss my favourite baker. Morixa doesn't quite have her mother's skill at the pastry oven, but to give her her due, she's been improving recently. Which is a relief for me. The food in the Avenging Axe has suffered a sad decline in recent months. Without the bakery to keep me going I'd be in a sorry state. I'm a man with plenty of girth to maintain.

We have a new cook at the Avenging Axe, a woman by the name of Elsior. Not such a bad cook but not a match for Tanrose, peerless mistress of the venison stew, now estranged from Gurd and living with her mother in Pashish. When she and Gurd failed to sort out their romantic difficulties—their main difficulty being that Gurd finds it impossible to be romantic—I thought it would be no more than a temporary problem. Having come to rely utterly on Tanrose's stew, pies, pastries and desserts, I couldn't believe she'd be gone for long. I even went so far as to visit her to plead Gurd's case, not something that came easy to a man like myself, with a notably bad track record in matters of the heart. All to no avail. Tanrose remains outraged by Gurd's criticism of her book-keeping practices and refuses to return. My explanation that it was merely the rough Barbarian's way of showing affection came to naught. Tanrose is sulking in her tenement, and the patrons of the Avenging Axe are suffering.

I've marched all over the world with a sword in my hand. I've fought Orcs, men, dragons and trolls. I've seen friends butchered and cities in flames, but I can't think of anything to compare with the suffering caused by Minarixa's death and Tanrose's departure. Life without either of them doesn't bear thinking about.

Gurd takes a beer from Dandelion, though he rarely drinks during his working day. He isn't the most cheerful soul these days either. Tanrose's departure was a severe shock. It took him more than five years to even acknowledge his feelings towards her. Having got that far, the recalcitrant old warrior was actually on the point of proposing marriage when the blow fell. He's not a man to express his private emotions, even to his oldest friend, but I can tell he's suffering. Only last week I was telling the story of our notable victory over the Niojans to a group of young mercenaries. When I looked over to Gurd to support me in my claim—entirely truthful—that the two of us had put a whole squadron of Niojan guards to flight, Gurd just sat there with a blank expression on his face, mumbling that it was a long time ago and he couldn't remember it all that well. It completely ruined my story. I was flabbergasted. If Gurd won't join in with the old army stories, there's something seriously wrong.

We make for a sad trio, Gurd, Makri and I. I order another beer. In the circumstances, it's the only thing to do.

CHAPTER TWO

As afternoon turns into evening, Gurd leaves his place at my side to help serve the drinkers who begin to arrive in the tavern. After finishing their shifts in the local docks, warehouses, smithies or tanneries, many of them prefer to brace themselves with an ale or two before going home to the local tenements, which are generally poorly built, draughty and leaky. Not comfortable places, with a family crammed into a couple of small rooms and the local water supply never being quite sufficient.

Every year the King promises that conditions will improve for the poorer inhabitants of Turai. The Consul makes the same promise, with a fine speech in the Senate. Our local Prefect, Drinius, is proud to share their sentiments. But nothing ever seems to get better. Turai has certainly become richer in the past twenty years, but precious little of that wealth has ever found its way into Twelve Seas.

I take two beers and a plate of stew upstairs to my

room. Once more, the stew is a disappointment. Tanrose had a way with stew. It was a gift. Maybe a calling. The new cook has not yet found the art. Outside, the street is noisy. Vendors, taking advantage of the fine weather, are keen to sell their goods, hoping to make enough to get them through the harsh winter. Winter will be here in a month or so. Another reason not to rejoice. Winter in Turai is hell. Makri's right. It was a foolish place to build a city. A good harbour isn't everything.

There's a knock on my door, the one that leads via a staircase directly to the street outside. I consider answering it. I should. It might be a client. On the other hand, I'm tired and full of beer. Sleeping on my couch seems like a better option. Let them take their problems to the Civil Guard, it's what they're there for. The knocking continues and it's followed by a loud voice.

"Thraxas. Open this door. Official business."

I recognise the voice. Hansius, assistant to Deputy Consul Cicerius. Not a visitor I can ignore, unfortunately. I haul the door open and scowl at the young man.

"What do you want?"

"Official business."

"So what?"

I let him in. I've nothing against Hansius really, except that he's young, clean cut, and headed for a comfortable life as a Senator. I really hold that against him.

Hansius is clad in his official toga. He's a handsome young man and his teeth are a few shades whiter than you'd normally encounter in Twelve Seas.

"If Cicerius wants to hire me tell him he has to pay better this time."

"The Deputy Consul has paid you adequately for all services rendered," responds Hansius, curtly. He casts his eye briefly over the mess that clutters up my room. I feel annoyed.

"Want a beer?"

"No."

"Then what do you want?"

"Cicerius instructs me to summon you to a meeting tomorrow."

"Sorry. I'm right off the idea of attending meetings these days."

"And why would that be?"

"Because my plate of stew was really sub-standard. And I'm facing a charge of cowardice. So I'm not so keen on helping the city at this moment."

"It's an official summons," declares Hansius, as if that's an end to the matter.

"Is there going to be food?"

"I imagine there will be provisions on hand."

"Will you send a carriage?"

Hansius is a young man capable of tact and diplomacy. As aide to the Deputy Consul, he's already developed his political skills. But for some reason he starts to show signs of impatience.

"Are you unable to make the journey on your own?"

"I might be. Is Cicerius going to let the charges against me proceed?"

"The charges against you, Thraxas, are not the business of the Deputy Consul's office. Once the allegation has been made it must go before the courts, as you know."

"Sure I know. The fact that I risked my life a hundred

times for this lousy city has nothing to do with it. What does Cicerius want?"

"Everything will be explained at the conference."

"Conference? With other people? Cicerius isn't just hiring me to cover up some scandal one of his corrupt Senator buddies has got himself into?"

Hansius frowns. Now I'm annoying him. It makes me feel a little better.

"It is a formal meeting. At the Consul's office."

"The Consul's office?"

That's surprising. Cicerius, the Deputy Consul, has on occasion summoned me when he needed some help with a matter not suitable for investigation by the higher class of Investigators who work up-town, but it's rare for any common citizen to be summoned to the office of Consul Kalius, the city's highest official.

"Please be there at noon."

Having had enough of trading words with a large angry Investigator, Hansius abruptly departs. I head for the couch, but before I can lie down the door opens and Makri walks in.

"How many times have I told you to knock?"

Makri shrugs. She can't seem to get used to the civilised habit of knocking on doors. I shouldn't be surprised. After two years in the city, she's still not great with cutlery.

"What did Hansius want?"

I pick up my empty plate and brandish it.

"You see this stew? Deficient in every way. Taste, texture, presentation. All lacking. And you know why? I'll tell you why. Because Tanrose didn't cook it. And why is that? Because you advised her to leave the tavern."

Makri refuses to acknowledge the truth of this. She claims that her advice to Tanrose was simply to take a little time to herself to consider her relationship with Gurd. She wasn't expecting Tanrose to up and leave. Since then I've spent many a dissatisfied mealtime cursing the day that an axe-wielding Barbarian like Makri ever got the notion that she was qualified to give personal advice to anyone.

"Will you never stop complaining about that?" protests Makri. "I miss Tanrose too. It's bad enough that you and Gurd are continually going round as miserable as a pair of Niojan whores, but now I've got no one to discuss—"

I hold up my hand.

"Please. If this is going anywhere near the area of intimate female bodily functions, I don't want to hear it. I still haven't got over the last time."

"Fine," says Makri, sitting down on my only comfortable chair. "So what did Hansius want?"

There was a time, not too long ago, when I never discussed my affairs with anyone. As an Investigator it's necessary to be discreet. But in the two years or so since Makri arrived in the city I've found myself, almost without noticing, slipping into the habit of telling her about my business. I still balk at this occasionally but in general I don't mind. Makri is discreet, trustworthy and, more to the point, as lethal a fighter as ever set foot in Turai. Many times over the past two years I've been pleased to have her sword or axe at my side. Not that I'm going to admit it to her. Makri is always bragging about her exploits as champion gladiator and doesn't need any encouragement from me.

"Summoned me to a meeting. At the Consul's office, which is unusual."

"Are you in trouble?"

"Possibly. But I didn't really get that impression from Hansius."

"Maybe they're going to offer you another official position," suggests Makri.

"That's unlikely."

"You were a Tribune."

It's true, I was. Still am, technically. Last winter I was appointed Tribune of the People by Cicerius, as a convenient way of giving me the official status necessary to attend the Sorcerers Assemblage. And a Tribune of the People turned out to have a fair amount of power. On one occasion I prevented Praetor Capatius from evicting the tenants of one of his buildings in Twelve Seas. The Praetor is one of the richest men in Turai and he wasn't too pleased about it.

The appointment has now almost expired, and I can't say I'm sorry. The post wasn't exactly cushy. It was unpaid and any action I took always led to trouble. Politics is a dangerous game in this city, particularly for a man without a party to support him. I haven't used the Tribune's powers for any reason recently, and I don't intend to.

"I'm bored," says Makri.

"It beats being unhappy over an Elf."

"I'm also unhappy over an Elf. But I'm bored as well. My college is closed for a week. Some stupid holiday. What do they need a holiday for?"

"Probably to recover from teaching you. Don't you have books or scrolls to study?"

"I've read them all," says Makri.

Makri seems to be well in advance of her studies. The woman's energy can be quite disturbing. Reading scrolls, going to the Imperial Library, attending lectures, and working shifts in the Avenging Axe to pay for it all. And if it's not that it's weapons practice. At some point every day the back yard resounds with the noise of Makri knocking hell out of targets with her collection of swords, axes, knives, throwing stars and whatever else she has in her weapons chest. For a woman who can be ridiculously enthusiastic about some tedious old Elvish playwright, she still shows great dedication to her fighting skills.

Of course, I was a champion fighter myself, back in my younger days. And I didn't need to go around practising all the time. I just had a natural talent for it.

"Don't you have any criminals I could attack?"

"Well, technically, Makri, they're meant to commit a crime first. And business is quiet just now."

"Do you want to go back to the Fairy Glade?" asks Makri, unexpectedly.

"That's a long ride."

Makri and I did visit the Fairy Glade on one occasion, but we haven't had reason to go back since. Makri sighs. She liked it there, and the magical creatures of the glade certainly seemed to like her, even though no creature with Orcish blood is supposed to be able to enter. The fairies were all over her and she practically had to fight off the centaurs, who are lascivious creatures by nature.

Makri looks glum.

"I can't really take time off from the tavern just now. I need money to pay my fees at the library. You know, when

I killed all those Orcs and escaped to Turai to get an education, I never thought it would be so expensive."

It's true. Turai is famed for its scholarship but almost all of the students are the sons of the upper classes, whose fathers can afford the fees at the Imperial University. The Guild College Makri attends is less expensive, and the Federation of Guilds provides some help for the students, but even so, all of the scholars there are sons of relatively wealthy Guild members—merchants, goldsmiths, glass-makers and the like. I don't think there's anyone else there actually paying their own fees like Makri.

"Maybe I'll just take a walk outside the city walls tomorrow. You want to come?"

The idea of taking a walk outside the city walls for no apparent reason is so baffling I'm stuck for an immediate reply. Makri says she just feels like seeing something different.

"Could we at least look at the Fairy Glade?"

"You mean by sorcery?" I shake my head. A good Sorcerer like Lisutaris could open a seeing-window on the Fairy Glade without much effort, but my own sorcerous powers are so limited these days it would take too much expenditure of energy.

"Then I guess I'll have to make do with thazis," sighs Makri, lighting one of my thazis sticks. I pour a little beer for her, then pass her a glass of klee.

"The intoxicants of the poor."

I start setting up the pieces on my Niarit board. Niarit is a cunning game of skill and strategy at which Makri, despite her much-vaunted "I'm-top-of-the-class" intellect, has so far never defeated me. Only to be expected, really.

I'm the undisputed Niarit champion of Twelve Seas, and have in my time defeated lords, ladies, philosophers, Sorcerers and whoever else was foolish enough to challenge me. I take a hefty slug of klee and prepare for an infantry attack supported by elephants that will sweep Makri's forces from the board.

"This time you're dead," mutters Makri, and moves her Hero quickly into play. "And pass me the klee."

Makri shudders as the fiery spirit burns her throat. Top-quality klee, made by monks in the mountains. I let her Hero advance up the board, pretending to fall back with my troops, not even pushing up my Harper to increase the morale of my front line. Makri sends her heavy cavalry up my right flank, preparing, I imagine, for a pincer movement. Poor Makri. She might be number one chariot with a sword in her hand, and the smartest student in the Guild College, but she has a lot to learn about the art of war. Less than half an hour later Makri is looking glumly at the remnants of her army, now falling back in full retreat before the wave of elephants, infantry and light cavalry currently sweeping up the board as directed by Thraxas, unstoppable warlord.

True to her character, Makri refuses to surrender and plays the game to its bitter end. My troops place their siege tower next to her castle, swarm up the ladders, kill everyone inside and hoist a flag in triumph. Well, metaphorically anyway. There isn't actually a flag.

Makri stubs her thazis stick out in disgust.

"Why do you always beat me?"

"I'm smarter than you."

"Like hell you are. You've just been playing longer."

That's what Makri always says, generally with a angry scowl and occasionally with some implications of cheating on my part. She's a very poor loser. I ask her if she'd like another game. She shakes her head.

"I have to go out."

"Out? Where?"

"I'm teaching a class."

This is a surprise.

"At the college?"

"No, they wouldn't let me teach there. Not that I couldn't. My Elvish is far better than some of these professors. I'm going to Morixa's bakery to teach some women to read."

I'm still puzzled. Makri explains that she's been asked by the organiser of the local chapter of the Association of Gentlewomen if she'd like to teach reading to some women in the area.

"I didn't know you had a reading programme."

Makri notices the disapproving tone in my voice.

"You think it's a bad idea?"

"Not at all. A fine idea. If someone else was organising it."

"So who else is going to organise it in this city?"

Makri has a point. Very few women go to school in Turai. The wealthy classes often arrange private tuition for their daughters, but only a tiny proportion of women in a poor area like Twelve Seas have ever had any sort of schooling. Not that the men round here are exactly intellectual. I wouldn't disapprove at all if it wasn't for the involvement of the Association of Gentlewomen, a collection of malcontents, harridans and troublemakers who are quite rightly frowned upon by all honest citizens of Turai.

"Remember what happened last time you taught anything?"

Makri frowns.

"What's that supposed to mean?"

"I wouldn't say you were a patient tutor. You almost killed that young Elf on Avula."

Makri waves this away.

"An entirely different matter. I was teaching her to fight. A little rough treatment was necessary."

"A little rough treatment? I saw you kick her in the face."

"So? She learned how to fight, didn't she? She won the junior sword-fighting tournament. I regard the whole thing as a triumph."

"Well," I say, "if you start kicking the local women in the face, don't come complaining to me when they run you out of town."

"I won't," says Makri, and departs.

Later I see her leaving the tavern, on her way to her first teaching assignment. I notice that she has a sword at her hip and a knife in her boot. She's carrying a bag of scrolls, but from the way it bulges I'd guess she's got her short-handled axe in there as well. Makri never likes to go anywhere without some weapons to hand. I shake my head. As this enterprise involves both the totally incompetent Association of Gentlewomen and the fiery-tempered Makri, I have complete confidence that it will end in disaster.

CHAPTER THREE

The Consul's office is situated inside the Palace grounds. North of the river, and a long walk from Twelve Seas. Not feeling like a long walk, I take a landus. As the horse-drawn carriage trots up Moon and Stars Boulevard, working its way slowly through the heavy traffic, I wonder what they want me for. As far as I know, the city isn't gripped by any particular crisis at this moment, though when you a have a man like Prince Frisen-Akan as next in line to the King, there's always something scandalous likely to happen. If he drinks himself to death before succeeding to the throne he'll be doing the city a favour.

We turn left at Royal Way and travel through the wealthy suburb of Thamlin. I used to live here. When I worked as a Senior Investigator at the Palace. Before they threw me out on some pretext of drinking too much.

The Imperial Palace comes into view. Were I a man who was impressed by large buildings, I'd be impressed.

It outshines the palaces of many larger states than Turai. The entrance alone is enough to make visitors gaze in wonder—huge gates carved in the shape of twin lions, six times the height of a man. Inside are some of the most beautifully laid-out gardens in the whole of the Human lands. Long avenues of trees lead to contoured lawns, beds of flowers and gleaming fountains, all engineered by Afetha Ar Kyet, the great Elvish garden-maker. In one corner of the grounds is the Imperial Zoo, home to a collection of fabulous creatures, including, at one time, a dragon from the east, though that was killed a while ago. Killed by the King's daughter, Princess Du-Akai, actually, though it's not a story that was ever made public.

The Palace itself is a huge building, constructed of shining white marble topped by silver minarets. It's a fabulous place. I used to work here. Now I'm about as welcome as an Orc at an Elvish wedding. Seeing the luxury all around me does nothing but add to the general feeling of gloom I've had for the past few days.

Security at the Palace is tight. Civil Guards prevent anyone suspicious from coming too near, and inside the grounds officials from Palace Security are on patrol. If someone wanted to assassinate the King, they'd have to put in a lot of effort. You can't really blame the King for his security concerns. The city state of Turai contains some very talented assassins, and the King has enemies.

I'm searched when I enter the grounds and again when I approach the Consul's offices. I turn in my sword to a member of Palace Security while a Sorcerer checks that I'm not carrying any spells.

I'm deposited in a reception room. There's a tall man

there I don't recognise, staring out of the window. More importantly, there's an elegant trolley in the corner laden with food. My long journey has made me hungry, so I head straight for the trolley and get to work. The food provided for the Consul's guests is beautifully prepared, though I can't say I'm overimpressed by the size of the portions. There are some small pastries stuffed with venison, which, while tasting good enough to please the most demanding palate, are really not large enough to satisfy a man with a healthy appetite. I put one in my mouth, take another, grab a plate from under the trolley and load it with fifteen or so of the pastries. There's a carafe of wine on the table nearby which I use to wash down the pastries before moving on to the next dish, some sweet-tasting cakes delicately iced with sugar. Once more it's high-quality produce but somewhat on the small side. I fill up my plate with every cake on offer and retire to a chair in the corner, carafe of wine still in hand.

I've hardly sat down before my plate is empty. I catch the eye of my fellow guest, a dignified-looking individual in a green robe. Looks like a foreign priest, or maybe some sort of minor official.

"Not really generous portions, are they?" I say, affably. He turns back to the window without replying. Doesn't speak our language, probably. I saunter back over to the trolley, but apart from a plate of eggs there's nothing else on offer. I eat the eggs but really I'm not satisfied. If the Consul asks a man to a meeting at his office the least he can do is feed him properly. I look around hopefully, wondering where I might get some more food. At this moment the outside door opens and a woman in a long white dress comes in. Rather a fancy outfit for a waitress, but at the Palace they like their formal wear.

"Any chance of another trolley?" I ask, politely.

"Pardon?"

"More pastries. These ones seem to be finished. And maybe another tray or two of cakes? Hell, bring in more eggs if you want to get rid of them, I'm not too fussy. And do you think you could get this carafe filled up again?"

The waitress seems to be starring at me in an odd manner. Have I offended her? Palace etiquette can be tricky; even the servants need to be spoken to properly.

"Thraxas, guest of Consul Kalius," I announce. "Wondering if you might be able to bring me another platter of your fine cuisine?"

"I am the wife of the Juvalian ambassador," she replies, not looking too pleased.

"Oh . . . Sorry."

She sweeps past me with her nose in the air, and stands by the man in the window, who, from the outraged look on his face, is almost certainly the Juvalian ambassador. I'd no idea they wore green cloaks.

"Well, have you seen a waitress anywhere?" I ask, but they ignore me.

An inner door opens, a quiet word is spoken and the ambassador and his wife—no doubt a well-bred woman who has never worked as a waitress—are whisked inside to meet the Consul. I look around me with some dissatisfaction. I really need more to eat. The outside door opens and another young woman in a long white dress appears. I regard her dubiously.

"Are you an ambassador's wife?"

She shakes her head.

"A young relative of the royal family?"

"No. I serve food to the Consul's guests."

I can feel my face lighting up. This is exactly what's required. I point to the empty food trolley.

"Is there any chance of a bite to eat? There weren't more than a few crumbs left by the time I arrived. The Juvalian ambassador and his wife, they just ate like hogs."

The waitress smiles pleasantly, nods her head, and leaves the room. She's gone no more than a few minutes before reappearing with another trolley which is overflowing with food—pastries, sweetmeats, pies, cakes and other more exotic delicacies.

"Here you are," she says brightly.

I like this waitress. As she produces another carafe of wine I reflect that, even in an unfriendly city like Turai, you occasionally come across a person who's willing to help out a man in difficulty. The waitress departs and I get to work. With luck the Juvalian ambassador will take up a lot of the Consul's time. As I plough through the first tier of the trolley, with my eye already on the hearty provisions on the level below, I feel like I'm in no hurry.

Despite my best efforts I haven't quite finished all the food when the ambassador and his wife reappear. They pass out of the room without giving me so much as a look. An official summons me into the next room. Inside I find Consul Kalius, wearing the gold-rimmed toga that denotes his rank. He's sitting at an enormous wooden table in the company of Deputy Consul Cicerius, Lisutaris, Mistress of the Sky, head of the Sorcerers Guild, Old Hasius the Brilliant, Chief Sorcerer at the Palace,

Rittius, head of Palace Security, and Galwinius, Prefect of Thamlin. With them is General Pomius, the highest-ranking soldier in the state. A high-powered collection of Turai's finest. I'm still carrying the carafe of wine. I put it down casually on the table.

Kalius regards me somewhat coldly.

"Why did you ask the Juvalian ambassador's wife to bring you food?" he enquires.

"I thought she was a waitress."

Kalius shakes his head.

"The ambassador was insulted."

"It was a mistake anyone could have made."

"Surely, as a man who once worked at the Palace, you can tell the difference between a foreign dignitary and a waitress?"

"Thraxas was rarely sober while employed at the Palace," comments Rittius, who's always been an enemy of mine. "He probably has little recollection of his time here."

"I remember you well enough, Rittius,"

The Consul holds up his hand and looks stern. Consul Kalius, with his grey hair and sculpted features, can be impressive when he wants. While he's not exactly as sharp as an Elf's ear—and definitely no match for Cicerius in terms of intellect—he does always look the part. The city trusts him, almost, and he's remained reasonably popular throughout his term of office.

"Enough. We have not asked you here to discuss the lamentable history of your time at the Palace."

I'm prepared for some long-winded explanation of why exactly they have asked me here, particularly if any part of the explanation comes from Cicerius. Any time the Deputy

Consul has asked me to do something for him it's been proceeded by a long lecture on how vital it is to the welfare of the city, followed by another lecture on the patriotic duties of all Turanians. Kalius, however, does not dissemble.

"Lisutaris, Mistress of the Sky, believes that an attack from the Orcish Lands is imminent. For the past week we have been involved in meetings with all trustworthy elements in Turai with regard to the defence of the city. In your capacity as Tribune, you have a part to play in our preparations."

This wasn't what I was expecting. The last war with the Orcs was what—sixteen, seventeen years ago? We threw them back from the walls but it was the bloodiest struggle in the history of Turai and we were lucky to emerge as victors. If the Elvish army hadn't arrived when it did the city would have fallen. I always knew that I'd have to fight the Orcs again. But I hoped that maybe I wouldn't.

It's the first I've heard about this. In a city like Turai it's very hard to keep anything secret. If they've been having meetings for a week without word getting out they've obviously gone to a lot of trouble to keep things quiet.

Uninvited, I take a chair.

"Prince Amrag?"

Kalius nods. We've been hearing reports of Prince Amrag for some time now. He started off as a young rebel in the Orcish lands, and in what seemed like a very short time, he'd conquered his kingdom and started exerting his influence on those around him. It was to be expected that he might one day work himself into the position of war leader and overlord of all the Orc lands but it's come quicker than anyone anticipated.

The Orcs hate us as much as we hate them. The only thing that prevents them from attacking us constantly is their own internal feuding. Once someone comes along who's capable of uniting their nations, an attack on the west becomes inevitable.

"What do you want me to do?"

"Firstly," says Kalius, "you must speak of this to no one. We are not yet certain that the attack will happen."

"We are certain," states Lisutaris, flatly.

Old Hasius the Brilliant sniffs.

"I am not certain," he mutters.

Lisutaris is head of the Sorcerers Guild, not just for Turai, but for the whole of the west. She's a woman of immense power and as great intelligence. If she says it's going to happen, I believe her. Old Hasius is himself a mighty Sorcerer but he's well over a hundred years old, and I'm not certain he's as bright as he used to be.

"In your capacity as Tribune, we wish you to assist Prefect Drinius in various tasks in Twelve Seas. These include the checking of the southern part of the city walls, the inspection of the water supply, an account of all men of fighting age in the locality and the allocation of areas for the storing of weapons and other supplies."

"Consul Kalius, I'm willing to help, of course, but I'm not qualified or experienced in any of these things."

"We know. The Prefect has a staff of his own and he will be assigned additional men who are specialists in their fields. But we wish you to assist in the organisation. As Tribune you have the power to get things done, more power, in some ways, than the Prefect. Although it was not our intention to appoint any more Tribunes, we have now assigned one to each quadrant of the city. You will have a vital part to play in our defence."

I nod. It's going to mean working for Prefect Drinius, or Drinius Galwinius as he sometimes styles himself. He's a cousin of Galwinius, Prefect of Thamlin, and keen to play up the powerful connection. I've never got on too well with the local Prefect, but in the circumstances, I can't object.

"Please remember that you must be absolutely discreet. At this stage, the population of the city must not know of the threat. It will cause panic, and if it turns out to be a false alarm we will have panicked them unnecessarily."

Lisutaris frowns slightly.

"It is not a false alarm," she says. I get the impression she's been saying that a lot.

"How long do we have?"

"We're not sure," replies the Consul. "But even if the Orcs' preparations are as far advanced as Lisutaris believes, there are only three weeks left till winter sets in. We can be confident that they will not arrive before then, and of course, they cannot march from the east during winter. So we have five months at least."

I leave the meeting knowing far less than I'd like to. I didn't press for too much information. They're not going to tell me everything they know and they have other people to see. But I intend to visit Lisutaris as soon as I can. The head of the Sorcerers Guild owes me some favours. Enough favours to tell me what we're up against, I hope.

Once back at the Avenging Axe I hunt for Makri. She's out in the back yard, practising a complicated series of movements with her axe. I ask her to leave her weapons practice and come up to my room. Once upstairs I clear some junk off my floor and get out the very last of my supply of kuriya.

"What's happening?" asks Makri. "You have a case?"

The kuriya pool can produce magical pictures. An experienced practitioner of sorcery can use it to look almost anywhere, even back in time. I don't have the power to control it so well but I still remember enough from my Sorcerer's apprentice days to make it work, on occasion. I concentrate for a while and the air around the saucer of black liquid cools slightly.

"What's that?" asks Makri, as a picture starts to form in the pool.

"The Fairy Glade."

In the Fairy Glade everything is tranquil. Naiads swim lazily in pools. Fairies flutter gently around the bushes and centaurs rest under the trees. We watch for a long time. It's a peaceful scene, and quite magical. I don't think I ever really appreciated it before. After a while, my power and control over the liquid runs out and the pool goes black. I look round at Makri. She's smiling.

"That was good. What did you want to look at the Fairy Glade for?"

"Suddenly it didn't seem like such a bad idea. If I'd any time I might even go for that walk outside the city walls."

Makri frowns, knowing that something is wrong.

"What is it?"

"The Orcs. Prince Amrag is gathering his army and Lisutaris says they're going to attack. Probably as soon as winter is over. Once that happens, we're not going to have much time for anything peaceful."

CHAPTER FOUR

For the next week I'm busy checking the water supply in Twelve Seas and sending off reports about damaged aqueducts and blocked wells. It's not the most exciting job, but it's important. If the city comes under siege the infrastructure has to be able to support the population till help arrives. The Consul is doing his best to put Turai in some sort of order, though some things have been neglected for far too long to be easily repaired. Not that Kalius and his military advisers are anticipating a siege. Historically, the Human nations have united to face the Orcs on the battlefield. While I'm not party to any of the secret negotiations going on between nations at this moment, I've no doubt that frantic communications are being carried out at the highest levels. When the Orcs arrive from the east they'll find themselves confronted by a massive army drawn from all the Human lands, with an Elvish army at our side.

Working under the direction of Prefect Drinius isn't as onerous as I'd anticipated. He's too busy handing out tasks to his officials to remember that he doesn't like Investigators. I don't particularly mind that my task doesn't seem like the most important thing a man could be doing right now. When the time comes, I'll be in the thick of the fighting.

So far the population of Turai remains unaware of the threat. Prefect Drinius has put the story around that the King has increased the municipal grant given to Twelve Seas, and that his officials are busy taking stock of the needs of the area prior to extensive improvements. I find myself enthusiastically greeted by citizens who tell me it's about time their local well or aqueduct had some attention.

Arriving home after a hard day at the aqueducts I climb the stairs to my office, intending to dump my cloak before heading for the bar downstairs. It's a mild shock to find my office occupied by Makri and five other women. I can't say I'm pleased.

"What's going on?"

"Literacy class," says Makri, as if that explained anything.

"In my office?"

"We had a small crisis at the bakery," says another of the woman. It's Morixa, heir to the pastry empire of her late mother, Minarixa. Morixa explains that the back room they were using for their classes is currently full of the last shipment of wheat before winter sets in.

"So we came here instead," adds Makri.

"Why my office? What's wrong with your room?"

"It's too small."

I'm not pleased. No Investigator would be. A man's office is for working, drinking and sleeping on the couch. Maybe for thinking about an investigation. Not for reading classes taught by Makri. I'm about to speak a few harsh words when I remember how much the bakery means to me. Morixa might not have her mother's touch but she's making progress.

"Is this going to happen again?" I demand.

Makri shakes her head.

"We're just finishing. We'll be back in the bakery next time."

I decide to let it pass. No sense outraging the baker for no reason. The women, all inhabitants of Twelve Seas by their dress, thank Makri and file out of my office. I look at Makri. She looks at me.

"Don't start," says Makri.

"Start what?"

"Criticising and complaining."

"Wouldn't dream of it. After all, what can a man expect once the Association of Gentlewomen put their hands to anything? Chaos is bound to follow. If that's the worst I have to suffer I'll be getting off lightly. How are the classes going?"

"Okay," says Makri, but doesn't elaborate. "How are the war preparations?"

I've informed both Makri and Gurd about the impending arrival of the Orcs. Gurd took the news philosophically. He's sharpened his weapons and is ready to fight whenever required. As a resident alien in the city, he'll be called into the army. Makri won't. Already she's annoyed.

"You think I'm going to sit here while an Orc army marches up? Forget it. I'm joining up."

"Women can't join the army."

"Then I'll just have to tag along."

I know that Makri will join in the fighting. It would be pointless for anyone to try and dissuade her. She detests Orcs. She likes fighting. Nothing will keep her from the fray. However, I do point out to her that what we're about to face is unlike anything in her experience.

"You can beat just about anyone in close combat, Makri. I've seen you do it. But a battlefield isn't like the gladiatorial arena and it's not like fighting in the street either. There's no space to move, nowhere to go. You just stand there in a phalanx with a long spear in your hand, and the enemy phalanx charges towards you, and the strongest phalanx forces the other one back. You get trampled to death or stabbed by a spear held by someone you can't even get near. Fancy sword-play doesn't come into it, believe me. Most times you don't even get your sword out till the battle's half over."

Makri informs me testily that she is well aware of battle tactics, having read everything the Imperial Library has to offer on the subject. I wave this away.

"Books and scrolls can't tell you what it's like. I can tell you more than any military historian. I've been in the phalanx. I've mown down enemy divisions and I've run for my life after my own phalanx was broken. Back in the war with—"

I stop myself. Now that the Orcs are on their way I don't like my own war stories as much as I used to. Makri gathers up her scrolls and picks up a hefty-looking book.

"What's that?"

"Architecture. Advances in vaulted-arch construction in the last century. I'm learning it at college."

"What for?"

"What do you mean, what for?"

"Seems like a reasonable question, with the city about to be attacked by a vast Orcish horde. Who cares about vaulted-arch construction?"

"I do," says Makri. "And if the city gets destroyed and needs some new vaulted arches built, I'll be in a good position to help."

We head downstairs, me for some ale and Makri for her shift as barmaid. We're immediately confronted by Dandelion, who hurries out from behind the bar. She advances towards Makri, something which causes Makri to flinch, possibly fearing that she's about to be told all about today's encounter with the dolphins. Dandelion wears a long skirt embroidered with signs of the zodiac, and wanders around in bare feet. Possibly as a result of this, she seems unable to talk about anything sensible. To be fair to the young woman, she has, after a struggle, learned how to operate the beer taps. Apart from that, she's as bad as ever. It's largely Makri's fault that she's here. Any reasonable person would have thrown Dandelion out on her ear shortly after she arrived but Makri, showing a hitherto unsuspected soft streak, let her hang around till she became something of a fixture in the tavern, ending up eventually as a waitress and barmaid.

"You've got flowers!" blurts Dandelion, merrily. "I put them in water. Look, they're behind the bar!"

There are indeed flowers behind the bar. A very large

bunch, well presented in a blue vase. I glance at Makri's face and I can tell she's thinking that perhaps her Elf has finally got in touch. Pretending not to care, she strolls casually over.

"There's a card," says Dandelion. "But I can't read it. It must be Elvish!"

Makri almost smiles. She picks up the card and the moment she reads it her expression hardens.

"Is this someone's idea of a joke?" she snarls, looking round angrily.

"What's wrong?"

"This isn't Elvish. It's Orcish."

I hurry over to look.

"Orcish?"

Very few people in Turai speak any Orcish and even fewer can read it. Both Makri and I are fluent in the common Orc tongue. I gaze at the neatly written card.

"To Turai's finest flower. From Horm, Ruler of the Kingdom of Yal."

Makri looks baffled. I look baffled.

"Horm the Dead sent you flowers?"

"So it seems."

"Filthy Orc lord," snarls Makri, and sweeps the flowers on to the floor, vase and all.

"But they were nice," protests Dandelion.

"I don't take gifts from Orcs," says Makri, and storms off.

Horm, Lord of the Kingdom of Yal, or Horm the Dead as he's more commonly known, is actually half Orc, half Human, as far as I know. But he's an Orc lord all the same, as well as a fairly insane Sorcerer who's rumoured to have brought himself back from the dead in some ghastly ritual, thereby increasing his powers. A few months back he appeared in Turai, trying to steal a valuable item from Lisutaris, Mistress of the Sky. On encountering Makri, he was frankly impressed. Impressed enough to offer to save her life if Orcish troops happened to be sacking the city any time in the near future. Makri punched him in the face, which was quite a sight, and something that was long overdue. Horm has tried to destroy Turai and deserves a lot worse. He hates us bitterly. Why he was so attracted to Makri I couldn't quite fathom.

I'm glad his flowers met with a poor reception. For a fraction of a second I was worried Makri might have been pleased, because although few people would guess it, she is peculiarly susceptible to small gifts, particularly flowers. At various times in the past I've smoothed over some difficulties with a similar gift. Not something I'd have thought of myself of course, Makri being the mad axe-woman she is, and me not being the sort of man who goes around buying flowers, but Tanrose suggested it, and it worked well. Something to do with Makri growing up in a gladiator slave pit, and never getting any presents, or so Tanrose believes.

Thinking of Tanrose brings the painful realisation that I haven't eaten for hours. I purchase a large bowl of stew, which is again really not up to standard. This has gone on long enough. If I'm to fall on the battlefield I don't intend to meet my death looking like a man who hasn't had a proper meal for months. I rise to my feet.

"It's time to bring Tanrose back, and I'm not taking no for an answer!" I declare. "I'm practically skin and bone."

"You're slightly smaller than an elephant," says Makri.

"Exactly. I'm fading away. I'm getting Tanrose."

As I leave the tavern, I run into a small figure, dark-haired, pale-skinned, clad in the common grey garb of a market trader. It's Hanama, third in command of the Assassins Guild. A loathsome woman with a loathsome trade. I step back sharply, hand already on the hilt of my sword.

"What do you want?" I demand.

"Nothing that concerns you," replies Hanama.

As always, I find it hard to believe that this small, innocent and youthful-looking woman is such a notoriously efficient Assassin. She looks like she should be in school, not out killing people. But killing people she does, for the highest bidder. Even though I fought beside her one occasion, she's not a person I'm ever pleased to see.

"Everything around here concerns me. I'm the local Tribune."

Hanama almost smiles, though her eyes remain cold.

"An honorary appointment, I understand. And not one that ever had the power of preventing a free citizen from going about their business. Step aside. I'm here to visit Makri."

Makri does have some sort of friendship with this unpleasant woman. I scowl at her and walk on by, shaking my head at the deplorable state of affairs in the Avenging Axe these days,. Time was when it was an honest tavern where a hardworking man like myself could drink beer without interruption from undesirables. Look at it now. Makri, Dandelion, Hanama. A collection of women from hell. They should all go and live with Horm the Dead and pick flowers together.

Since leaving the Avenging Axe, Tanrose has been living with her elderly mother in a tenement in Pashish, just north of Twelve Seas. I make my way through the busy streets, then climb the stairs with a determined look on my face. Tanrose herself opens the door. She's pleased to see me and welcomes me in. Her mother doesn't seem to be around, so I get straight down to business.

"Tanrose, you have to—"

"Would you like something to eat?" says the kindly woman.

I nod eagerly. Business can wait. Tanrose leaves the room and bustles around in the kitchen for a while before returning with a large tray of food. After the unsatisfactory fare at the Avenging Axe, I attack the venison pie, yams and assorted vegetables like a dragon descending on a juicy flock of sheep.

"Would you like—"

I nod vigorously. Whatever it is, I want it. Tanrose brings me a second helping. When I'm finished I sigh with contentment. I feel ready for action. I haven't felt this good for months.

"Tanrose, you have to come back to the Avenging Axe. I know things are awkward between you and Gurd, but maybe you can sort it out, and if you can't sort it out, what the hell, you can just be mad at each other, I mean, who really cares? There are more important things in life. Should some slight personal difficulties keep you from your rightful place? You belong in the Avenging Axe. Personally I'm prepared to put up with any amount of bad feeling as long as you're back where you belong, dishing up the stew."

Tanrose frowns.

"Thraxas, is your stomach more important than my peace of mind?"

"Define *more important*."

"I really can't come back. Not while things are still awkward."

I rise to my feet in frustration.

"Please come back. I'm begging you."

"Sorry, I can't."

"I'm still a Tribune, you know. I order you to return."

Tanrose laughs.

"Thraxas. It's gratifying the way you miss me so much. Or at least miss my cooking. But really, you know I can't just walk back in without a lot of talking to Gurd first."

I slump into my chair, defeat staring me in the face. Things haven't looked so bleak since Gurd and I, employed as mercenaries in the Juvalian jungle, accidentally stumbled into the wrong camp after a night's drinking. I can still remember the look on the enemy commander's face as I clapped him heartily on the back and offered him a swig from my flagon. Fortunately, at that moment, the camp came under attack from the third army involved in the rather complicated war and Gurd and I made our escape in the confusion.

This time, however, there seems to be no escape. I'm trapped for ever with Elsior's inferior cooking. When the Orcs arrive I'll be lucky if I have the strength to pick up a sword. Suddenly inspiration strikes. Trying to inject some sincerity into my voice, I inform Tanrose that if she doesn't come back now she might never get the chance.

"What do you mean?"

"The Orcs are going to attack as soon as winter is over."

"Is this true?"

"It is. It's a state secret and I'm not supposed to tell anyone, but it'll be common knowledge soon enough. So if you want to sort things out with Gurd—and maybe cook a few pies and stews in the meantime—this might be your last chance."

Tanrose looks serious.

"Will we defeat the Orcs?"

"It's possible."

"And it's possible we won't?"

I nod. Tanrose needs only a few moments to make her decision.

"In that case, Thraxas, you're right. I'd better come back."

I leap to my feet in triumph. With the prospect of our treasured cook returning to the tavern, I'm now as happy as an Elf in a tree.

"You wouldn't believe how bad the tavern has become. Dandelion being insane, Makri being insane. Horm sending flowers."

"What?"

I inform Tanrose about the flower incident.

"Which was worrying, of course. You know what a sucker Makri is for flowers."

"So how did she take it?" asks Tanrose.

"Swept them to the floor with disgust. Quite right. The nerve of that Horm. What did he think he was going to achieve? Just because I can produce spectacular effects with flowers on the axe-wielding mistress of the bad temper doesn't mean he can. You know, the more I think about it the more convinced I am he stole the idea from me. Probably he was spying when I arrived home from the flower seller's. It's not the sort of thing Horm could ever have thought of himself."

"I remember you took a lot of persuading," says Tanrose. "I wouldn't worry. Makri is never going to fall for an Orc lord."

"Who's worried? Makri can do what she likes. I just don't like Horm stealing my ideas."

I leave the tenement, still as happy as an Elf in a tree. Okay, I had to tell Tanrose an important state secret to convince her to come back, but what the hell, it worked. Tanrose is very trustworthy. She won't tell anyone.

I pick up a landus in Pashish and instruct the driver to take me to Truth is Beauty Lane, home of Turai's Sorcerers. As the carriage runs along Royal Way I rest my hands on my stomach, appetite fully satisfied for the first time in weeks. Let the Orcs come. When they find a well-fed Thraxas leading a phalanx against them, they'll regret they ever made the journey.

CHAPTER FIVE

Successful Sorcerers in Turai usually become wealthy and their villas in Truth is Beauty Lane are luxurious dwellings with enough space for substantial gardens outside and a large contingent of household staff inside. There's nothing to show that the villas are occupied by Sorcerers, rather than Senators. Sorcerers are as worried about their status as the rest of Turai's upper classes, and it would be frowned upon to make any overt public display of their powers. While they might occasionally put on some fancy entertainment in their gardens, they wouldn't dream of lighting up the front of their houses with spells, or making any other sort of vulgar show. The highest class of family in Turai rarely goes in for sorcery, deeming it to be beneath them. Keen not to lend weight to this notion, Sorcerers are generally careful not to do anything that might be construed as common.

As I roll up to Lisutaris's villa I find signs of some serious activity, namely every top Sorcerer in the city state emerging from her house and climbing into their private carriages. Harmon Half Elf, Old Hasius the Brilliant, Melus the Fair, Lanius Suncatcher, Tirini Snake Smiter. Even Coranus the Grinder—famed for both his power and his bad temper—is there, and he very rarely visits the city, preferring to stay all year in his villa by the coast at Ferrias. As he strides to his four-horse carriage, younger Sorcerers like Capali Comet Rider and Anumaris Thunderbolt defer to him while lesser lights of the Sorcerers Guild such as Gorsius Starfinder and Patalix Rainmaker look on enviously.

Last to leave is Ovinian the True, who's helped into his guided carriage by a brace of liveried servants. Ovinian isn't all that powerful but he's Chief Sorcerous Adviser to the King, which gives him a lot of rank. In common with all Sorcerers in Turai, he's wearing a rainbow cloak. His is particularly bright. Lisutaris's cloak is rather more tasteful; well cut and more muted in colour. I'd say that the more powerful the Sorcerer, the more discreet is their cloak. Coranus's is mostly grey, with the rainbow motif only just visible around the collar. Tirini Snake Smiter is something of an exception. She's powerful, but not given to discretion in matters of fashion. She wears a very elegant cloak, silky and nearly transparent, to go with the elegant gown she wears under it, itself silky and close to transparent. Tirini is a great beauty, the most glamorous Sorcerer in the city state, and keen to never let anyone forget it. Her hair is dazzlingly blonde, and for a naturally dark-haired woman that takes a lot of herbal treatments and probably a spell or two. She caused a scandal last year by arriving at

Princess Du-Akai's birthday celebrations in a dress so clinging and diaphanous as to endanger the health of several elderly Senators who were present. Bishop Gzekius was so outraged he denounced her from the pulpit the very next day, much to the amusement of Tirini.

I studied sorcery when I was a youth, but I failed my studies and never accumulated more than a fraction of the power of these people. I draw back from the gate, letting them make their exit before approaching the house. Not that I think any Sorcerer is better than me. I just don't like to have my past failures pointed out.

After they've all departed I walk up the long garden path through the bushes and shrubs and knock on the door. It's answered by a servant who recognises me from my previous visits. She looks at me dubiously and informs me that the meeting has finished.

"I didn't come for the meeting. It's a private visit. Lisutaris will see me."

The servant, looking about as welcoming as the hounds that guard the gates of hell, is not at all convinced that Lisutaris will see me. She leaves me at the door. I wait for a long time. Eventually she returns with the message that her mistress is engaged and would I like to arrange to call another time.

"No," I say, and barge past her, using my considerable body weight to bat her out of the way, a tactic I've found very useful over the years. I know where Lisutaris will be. The Mistress of the Sky is a slave to thazis, ingesting it at a rate quite beyond the capacity of any other citizen. As she'll have been unable to indulge herself fully while conferring with her Sorcerer buddies, she'll now be ensconced in her comfortable room overlooking the gardens, sucking on her water pipe. I head for the back of the house, pursued by angry servants. We're wading through a carpet of quite astonishing luxuriousness. There's a lot of money in this house. The walls are hung with Elvish tapestries and the furniture, tastefully arranged and not too intrusive, is antique, mostly Elvish, and fantastically expensive. Lisutaris is one of the few Sorcerers who does originate from the very highest class of Turanian society, and she has a hefty fortune to play around with.

Suddenly the air around me cools. I'm gripped by a powerful force which renders me temporarily immobile. I'm wearing a good spell protection charm which will deflect most magic but Lisutaris, as head of the Sorcerers Guild, has spells in her possession which are not easily deflected.

"Lisutaris," I roar. "Get this spell off me and let me in. I know you're not busy in there, you're only smoking thazis."

I struggle against the spell, forcing myself forward a few inches at a time.

"I'm not going away. Let me in or I'll beat the door down!"

The spell abruptly ceases and I'm catapulted forward. The door opens and I end up in a heap on the floor. Lisutaris, sitting on a gold cushion in her favourite chair, looks down at me with idle disdain.

"Thraxas. If you ever try beating down one of my very expensive doors I'll explode your head," she says. "And what brings you here anyway? I have little time to spare these days."

Having only had a few minutes at her water pipe Lisutaris is not yet too intoxicated, but from the powerful aroma in the room and the lazy expression on her face she's not so far off. Lisutaris packs enough thazis into her water pipe to knock out a dragon. This is the woman who invented a new spell for making thazis plants grow faster.

"What brings me here, Lisutaris, is a desire for knowledge."

"Ah. Has Makri finally shamed you into bettering yourself?"

"Very amusing. I'm here to learn what's going on and how long I've got before I'm due on the battlefield, and anything else you know about the impending invasion. None of which anyone in government is going to tell me. Could you stop sucking on that thing for a second?"

An observer of this conversation might be surprised at my rather casual attitude towards Lisutaris. She is, after all, the head of the Sorcerers Guild, not to mention an aristocrat of the purest blood. However, in the past year or so I've rendered some sterling service to her. It was me who got her elected as head of the Guild, more or less single-handed, and only this summer I saved her reputation by locating a very important mystical jewel she'd carelessly lost at the race track. Besides, I've seen her keel over in my office from overindulgence in thazis. After that I figure there's no need to be too formal.

"You'd need something to calm you down if you'd had to spend time with these people. Harmon is a dreadful bore and both Lanius Suncatcher and Old Hasius doubt the accuracy of my observations."

"They do?"

Lanius is Chief Sorcerer at Palace Security. Hasius is Chief Sorcerer at the Abode of Justice. Lisutaris suddenly looks annoyed.

"They do indeed. It's a difficult business looking into the heart of the Orcish Lands, Thraxas. Even with the green jewel at my disposal and all the powers I command, it's almost impossible to get a clear picture. The Orcish Sorcerers Guild have been working hard at their own protection. I can't make a connection to Prince Amrag himself and I can't eavesdrop on his private meetings. But I can get close enough to learn what he's planning. And it involves a swift invasion, you can be sure of that. I've seen the troops gathering and the dragons massing."

"So why do they doubt you?"

Lisutaris shrugs, and draws on her pipe.

"Old Hasius the so-called Brilliant has always resented that I was elected head of the Guild. It clouds his judgement. That and his senility. It's high time they pensioned him off. As for Lanius, who knows? Palace Security are always looking out for their own interests. His boss Rittius has never been a friend of mine. Between them all they're proving to be a problem. It's a time for the city to be making preparations and forging alliances, not bickering about the precise meaning of what I've seen in the east. Naturally that oaf Ovinian the True reports their doubts back to the Palace. That man is a fool. How he ever became Chief Sorcerous Adviser to the King is beyond me."

I sympathise with her annoyance.

"It's often the way in this city. Worthy men are passed over in favour of some dolt who's good at flattery. Look at me. Thrown out of my job at the Palace. I was the only decent Investigator they had."

"You got drunk at Rittius's wedding and insulted his bride," says Lisutaris. "Right after you insulted Rittius. Which, as I remember, was almost immediately after you insulted Praetor Capatius."

"So what were you doing? Taking notes? These people deserved to be insulted. It's no wonder I was driven to drink. Is there any chance of a glass of wine?"

Lisutaris ignores my request, being too busy muttering about Ovinian.

"*He* had the nerve to suggest that my judgement may be clouded due to my annoyance over Herminis. As if I would let a domestic matter interfere with my war duties!"

I wonder if Lisutaris is going to lecture me about Herminis. I've already listened to several long diatribes from Makri on the subject, Herminis is the wife of a Senator, or was until a few months ago, when she stabbed him in the back with his own dagger. In court she claimed that her husband had violently abused her for all the ten years they were married. The court, feeling that this was not an adequate defence for a charge of murder—which legally it wasn't—sentenced her to death. She's currently languishing in prison awaiting execution. What's particularly annoying Makri, and probably Lisutaris, is that if the situation had been reversed and the Senator had killed his wife, he would have been given the option of exile from Turai. In all but the most exceptional of cases, members of the Turanian ruling classes are allowed to leave the city before execution. This option has not been extended to Herminis. Tough on the lady, but that's the way things work in Turai. Why Makri feels the need to berate me about it I've no idea. Fearing that Lisutaris may be working up to some berating of her own, I ask her how things stand in the matter of forging alliances.

"Quite well, fortunately. We've sent messengers all over the west and contacted the Elvish nations."

It's a strange thought that as we sit here, smoking thazis in this peaceful room, all over the west the first preparations are being made for the raising of a gigantic army.

"What sort of force can Prince Amrag muster?"

"Hard to say. He's been in a position of dominance for a relatively short time. Yet from my observations it seems as if the other Orc nations are answering his call. We're guessing that their army will be roughly the same size as last time."

"Who exactly is we?"

"The War Council. As organised by the Consul. I never had that much regard for Kalius, but at least he's got things moving quickly."

We sit in silence for a moment, both reflecting on the last war. After a lot of desperate fighting there came a point where we threw them back from the city walls, and at that moment I was, at it happened, standing next to Lisutaris. I saw her bring dragons down from the sky, and when her sorcerous power ran out I saw her pick up a sword and behead an Orc who made it to the top of the walls. Immediately after this the wall collapsed. I've no idea how any of us survived. We wouldn't have if the Elvish army hadn't arrived at that moment and taken the Orcish forces in the flank.

"Still, we beat them last time. We can beat them again."

"Perhaps," muses Lisutaris. "Though the armies of the Humans and the Elves are probably weaker these days. Not too much weaker, I hope. If they are, we're going to have to flee a long way west before we find a place to hide."

Lisutaris doesn't show any sign of summoning refreshments.

"Any chance of some refreshments?"

"I have no beer."

"But you do have a notably fine wine cellar. Nothing too fancy, a nice Elvish table wine will hit the spot."

Lisutaris pulls the bell rope, summoning a servant. She's not such a bad woman, really. Smokes far too much thazis and spends a lot of money on clothes, hair styling and the like, but she's served the city well. We're about the same age, though you'd hardly know it. She's preserved her looks a lot better than me. Of course, she had more looks to preserve. And my life has been a good deal harder.

I take a glass of wine.

"Good wine. Maybe you ought to spend the next four months enjoying the contents of your wine cellar."

"If we have four months," says Lisutaris.

"What do you mean?"

"I suspect the Orcs may march earlier."

I'm puzzled.

"Earlier? Winter is only a week or two away. They can't cross the wastelands in winter."

Lisutaris looks thoughtful.

"So everyone says. And they never have before. But I picked up a message from Amrag to another Orc lord that seemed to imply they might be planning it this time."

I'm sceptical about this. Campaigns are rarely launched in winter; the weather is far too fierce for marching.

"I can't believe Amrag would do that. What would it benefit him?"

"He'd get here before the Elves could. They can't sail in winter. If he can bring his army over here before they arrive, he'll have already avoided half the opposition."

"But think of the logistics. Marching in winter? Orcs aren't that much hardier than Humans. They'd never get here. Neither would their dragons, they get sluggish in the cold. They couldn't fly all the way here in winter. And their navy couldn't support them on the coast."

"That's what the War Council thinks," says Lisutaris. "Old Hasius went so far as to suggest I'd intercepted a message that Prince Amrag had planted deliberately to confuse us."

She shrugs.

"Possibly I did. The Orcish Sorcerers Guild is a lot more powerful than they used to be, and possibly a lot more subtle. Some of the mystical defences they've set up in the past few years have surprised me with their complexity. It's not impossible I've been misled. Nonetheless, I'm worried."

"Has any other Sorcerer reached the same conclusions as you?"

Lisutaris admits they haven't. No other Sorcerer thinks there is any chance of the Orcs attacking before winter is through. According to Lisutaris, several foreign Sorcerers are doubtful that the Orcs are planning to invade at all. Personally, I don't doubt Lisutaris for a second. Few Sorcerers can equal her in terms of power and knowledge.

Few in the west, and none in the east. The Mistress of the Sky has a matchless talent. Apart from when she's too wrecked on thazis to work her spells. That's not too often.

"Could you pull that bell rope for me?" she asks. "I can't seem to lift my arms."

I frown at her.

"No thought of giving up thazis for the duration of the war?"

"Why?"

"So you can lead the forces of western sorcery in a last-ditch attempt to save humanity?"

Lisutaris starts to giggle.

"Save humanity," she says, several times, and laughs out loud. Her laughter subsides to a chuckle before she sticks the water pipe back in her mouth.

The last piece of information I learn from her is that there's a meeting of the War Council tomorrow, followed by a meeting of the Lesser War Council, at which I will be expected to attend. As I leave the room she's slumped on her chair, puffing thazis, still laughing about the amusing notion of saving humanity. Her servants follow me to the front door.

"The mistress should not allow you in this house," says the servant I barged past at the door.

"You're right. She shouldn't. I'm a bad element."

She glares at me with loathing in her eyes. That happens to me a lot.

CHAPTER SIX

The meeting of the Lesser War Council is chaired by Cicerius, assisted by Hansius. Thirty people are gathered in the conference room, many of whom I've never encountered before. Prefects from each part of the city, their assistants, the Praetors who normally answer only to the Consul, the newly created Tribunes, plus officials from the Palace, the Civil Guards and the military. I'm surprised to see that Senator Lodius is here. Lodius is the head of the opposition Populares party. He's the main opponent of the Consul in the Senate and a bitter critic of the Traditionals. His reforming, anti-monarchy party has been enjoying increasing support in Turai in the past few years. In consequence, the city's rulers hate him. I can only presume he's here as some sort of attempt at national unity in the face of a crisis.

I'm not exactly keen on Lodius myself. He's always going on about the need to distribute the city state's wealth more fairly. I could do with some wealth being distributed in my direction, but he's always struck me as a man who'd say anything in order to gain power for himself. I have the strong feeling that if he ever did come to power, all talk of democratic reform would be quietly forgotten about. Apart from this, he blackmailed me into helping him last year, and I resent being blackmailed. Lodius is accompanied by Rittius, a political ally of his. Rittius hates me more than anyone in the city.

Being at such a meeting is a strange experience. I've had little to do with officialdom in any capacity and have never served on a committee before. It goes against the grain. Due to the urgency of the situation and the danger we're all facing, I've managed so far to forget my natural mistrust of the city authorities. I've even managed to take orders from Prefect Drinius without abusing him to his face, but as I sit in the room listening to Prefect Resius drone on about the capacity for grain storage in Jade Temple Fields, I find myself impatiently wishing the meeting to be over. The organisation of the city's defence is important but it's starting to get on my nerves.

While Prefect Drinius is giving a report on the available stock of raw material for weapon making—which will be followed by another report on the capacity of the royal armoury—I find myself nodding off and have to concentrate to stay awake. I'm looking forward to a break for food. By my calculations lunch should be served any time now. Unfortunately, Cicerius seems dissatisfied with some elements of Prefect Drinius's report and begins a long series of questions which Drinius responds to with equally long answers. I sigh. When I fought in the last war I had no involvement in its planning. I didn't realise it was so tedious.

I start daydreaming about the possible food on offer. It will, I understand through some determined questioning of the catering staff, be delivered through the back door on a series of trolleys. Will it be a proper meal with platters of beef and venison? Or just a collection of those small fancy pastries they seem so fond of in the Consul's offices? I'm hoping for something more substantial. Not that there's anything wrong with the pastries—they're made by a fine hand in the kitchen—but they're not really enough to sustain a man. Not when he's faced with several hours of talk about aqueducts. I look suspiciously round, wondering who else might be planning a sudden dash towards the food. It could be I've made something of a tactical error in sitting in the middle of the room. When the victuals arrive I might miss out. Prefect Galwinius, right at the back, is a notable eater, as is his assistant. They both have a hungry look about them and they're well placed for a sudden dash to the trolleys. If they get to the food first there'll be precious little left for latecomers. I curse myself for my carelessness and start edging my chair backwards. If Prefect Galwinius thinks he's having it all his own way with the provisions he can think again. I've outsmarted better men than him at the pastry cart.

"By this time next month there must be at least one hundred tons of raw iron ore at the—"

The Deputy Consul is interrupted by the clattering noise of food trolleys appearing through the door. I'm on my feet and halfway to the back before anyone else has moved. Galwinius sees me coming and makes a brave effort at hauling himself out of his chair, but I knock him out of the way and tread on his assistant's foot as I pass, leaving them reeling in confusion. I make it to the trolleys first and start hacking a thick slice off a slab of venison before grabbing a handful of yams and loading them on to my tray, followed by as much as everything else as I can lay my hands on.

"You ill-mannered oaf," hisses Galwinius, appearing at the rear.

"Wartime," I reply. "A man needs to be quickly into action."

All in all, it's a successful mission and I'm moving away from the trolleys with a heavy tray of food while the stragglers are still making their first approach. It's the sort of fast and deadly assault which made me such a force on the battlefield. I find myself next to Deputy Consul Cicerius and greet him affably.

"You did not take long to avail yourself of the Consul's hospitality," he says, drily.

"When it comes to a crisis I know how to act."

Cicerius eyes me with distaste.

"I was in the middle of a speech."

"And very interesting it was too. I count it an honour to be in your service."

I excuse myself and make for my chair, head down, ignoring the crowd. In truth, the crowd are pretty much ignoring me. I'm out of my social class here, and well aware of it. Most of those at the meeting belong to Turai's aristocracy and are clad in togas. My dull tunic is shabby in comparison. Their hair is short, neatly styled. Mine hangs long down my back. Their voices are more refined and their manners far better. Even my name, Thraxas, gives me away as low-born. It's an odd quirk of fate, really, that I've ended up in this position. Had Cicerius known he was going to be stuck with me as a city official when he made me a Tribune, he might have thought twice about it.

The venison is excellent and the yams are cooked to perfection. Whoever takes care of the cooking for the Consul's office really knows his business. The man is a credit to his city. So fine is the food that it's a positive shock to the system when I bite into a sweet pastry and find it's not been baked quite properly. Inside it's doughy, as if it's not been in the oven for long enough. I shrug, and push it to the side of my plate. Even the greatest chef can have an off moment, I suppose. Maybe one of his assistants was responsible. The next pastry is well up to the usual standard and I forget my disappointment, particularly when I see Cicerius and Hansius standing at the trolleys looking like two men who've arrived late at the party. There's nothing left except a yam or two. Cicerius, always keen to maintain his dignity, pretends he doesn't care, but I can tell he'd have liked a slice of venison, or maybe some grilled fish. The grilled fish was quite superb, and I speak as a man who doesn't eat a lot of fish as a rule. When you're in a stranger's house you just have to take what you can get.

I'm about to ask one of the catering staff if there might be any beer on offer when the Consul himself walks into the room and I'm obliged to stand as a mark of respect. The city Prefects who are here—Galwinius, Drinius, Resius—gather around him. There's a moment's awkwardness when the Consul turns round and finds himself face to face with Senator Lodius. In the spirit of national unity the Consul greets him courteously. Given some of the things Lodius has accused the Consul of in the Senate this year, this must take some effort. Senator Lodius, probably keen not to be seen doing anything which might rock the boat at such a perilous time, returns the Consul's greeting, equally courteously. The Consul steps away to talk to Cicerius, leaving the Prefects still in the company of Lodius. Galwinius and Drinius are both opponents of Lodius, though Prefect Resius has been suspected in the past of having some sympathy for the Populares. Again there's some awkwardness. Galwinius fiddles with a scroll he's carrying and Resius scratches his head. Despite this, they manage to carry on with their show of civility. No one wants to be seen causing dissension, not even Lodius and Galwinius, who are due to face each other in court soon in a messy fraud case. In an effort to be civil, Senator Lodius even goes so far as to raise the silver platter he holds in his hand, offering Galwinius a choice of food. The Prefect accepts his offer, taking a small pastry from the plate. I'm impressed. National unity is going over big in all quarters.

Prefect Galwinius turns to speak to Senator Bevarius, the Consul's assistant. Before he can complete his sentence, his face goes red and he puts his hand to his throat, as if choking. There's a sudden deathly silence in the room as all eyes turn to the Prefect. Drinius reaches out to support him as he sags to the ground.

By this time I've hurried over, because I've got a good idea that Galwinius is not just choking on his food. It's hard to see through the clutter of Prefects and Praetors, but from the way his face is turning green and his eyes are bulging I'd say Galwinius has been poisoned. People cry out in alarm and yell for a doctor. I force my way through. Galwinius is already in his death throes. He shivers for only a few seconds more, then goes still. He isn't going to be needing a doctor. The Prefect is dead.

Chaos erupts in the room. Some people are yelling for assistance while others struggle to get closer to the prone body as if somehow their presence will help. Unable to carry out any sort of examination, I let myself be forced back from the body. I look around. The only person who's standing quite still is Senator Lodius, the man who handed the food to the Prefect. I cross over to him and look him right in the eye. From the blank way he stares through me I'd say that he was profoundly shocked. Or possibly horrified by what he's just done.

"Lodius. What do you know about this?"

Lodius looks blank. I shake him by the shoulder and he manages to focus on me.

"Lodius. Where did you get that bowl from?"

"Get your hands off me!" he snarls.

Before I can respond, two uniformed Civil Guards get between us. The room is filling up with Guards, which is only adding to the confusion. Finally a commanding voice rises about the babble of the crowd. Cicerius, the finest orator in the city, speaks in such an authoritative manner that the room falls silent.

"Make room for the doctor," he says. "And everyone in this room remain where you are until the Consul orders otherwise."

This causes some consternation. The high-ranking Senators and Praetors in the crowd aren't used to being treated like suspects in a murder case. I am. I've been in the slammer more times than I can count. While others are still milling around, I take a chair and sit down to wait. There are going to be a lot of questions asked and I'll be here for a long time.

CHAPTER SEVEN

Turai has been in chaos before. We've suffered riots, plague, sorcerous attack and drought, not to mention the civic unrest that erupts every couple of years when elections roll around. In the past few years crime has exploded with the mushrooming of the trade in dwa, the evil drug that has the city in its grasp, adding to the turmoil. But in my long experience, the city has rarely been gripped by fever in the way it is now.

Perfects have died in battle or died from illness but no one can remember one expiring from poison. As Prefect of the richest part of the city, Galwinius was a very important official, ranking almost as highly as the Praetors. More influential in some ways, given the wealth of his constituents. His murder comes as a shocking blow to the population. It doesn't take long for the truth to come out about the reason behind the meeting. Soon the whole city knows that the Consul had gathered his officials together to plan for the defence of Turai against the Orcs. Panic erupts on all sides. The news-sheets hardly know which terrible story merits more prominence. Crowds gather on the streets and the common opinion is that it's the end of the world as we know it. Which it might well be.

It was ten hours before I was allowed to leave the consular buildings. Though I had to answer a lot of routine questions, for once in my life I'm not a suspect. That was three days ago, since when I've once more applied myself to the task of checking aqueducts. Figuring that if the world is about to end there's no sense in wasting beer, I make a brief report to Prefect Drinius before heading back to the Avenging Axe. It's been a hard day and the weather is turning cold. I cheer myself up with the thought of the bottle of klee that's waiting for me in my office.

Also waiting in my office are Makri, eight other women, a lot of scrolls and a powerful aroma of thazis.

"We're just finishing," says Makri.

"Finishing? What are you doing here?"

"Reading."

"How dare you read in my office! Didn't you say this wouldn't happen again?"

"The bakery is still full."

I inform the assembled women that I don't care how full the bakery is, they can't use my office for their classes. I spy an empty bottle of klee on the table.

"Is that my klee? Did you drink my klee?"

Makri is unapologetic.

"Just being hospitable to my guests."

"With my klee? Were you thinking of paying for it? Where are my pastries? Did you eat them?"

I realise that everyone is looking at me in a particularly disapproving manner. Morixa the baker turns to me and speaks quite sternly.

"The women of Twelve Seas do not exist merely to cook pastries for you, Investigator. We have our own aspirations. And we will pursue our aspirations despite your continual harassment."

"Harassment? I'm the one who's being—"

"He reminds me of my father," says a young prostitute to her companion. "Drove my mother into an early grave. Makri, if this man threatens you in any way, send a message. I'll bring my guild round to protect you immediately."

The women collect their belongings and begin to file out of my room. Makri bids them all a polite farewell and shuts the door behind them.

"Was I just threatened by the Prostitutes Guild?"

"I think so. You better watch out, they know how to look after themselves."

"Makri, this has got to stop. I demand you never teach women to read in my office again."

Makri shrugs.

"Okay. We'll go somewhere else. Not that it's such a big inconvenience. You might be a little more supportive. You know I need the money. I expect I'd earn more as a waitress if it wasn't for all the times I've helped you investigate. And of course I had to pay for having my axe sharpened after I blunted it saving you from—"

I hold up my hand.

"Spare me the moral blackmail. Just find another place. After checking aqueducts all day, I need my space."

Makri lights another thazis stick. The room reeks of the stuff.

"I thought you'd be busy investigating the Prefect's murder."

"No one's asked me to."

"But you were right there in the room."

Makri still has some difficulty in understanding that I don't investigate for fun. I do it for a living.

"No one is going to hire me to investigate Galwinius. Palace Security and the Civil Guards are all over it."

"I'm still confused as to why there are two Galwiniuses," says Makri. "Isn't the Prefect of Twelve Seas called Galwinius as well?"

"That's Drinius Galwinius. Cousin of the murdered man. These aristocrats, they're all related. Inbred, probably."

"Everyone says Lodius did it. Is that true?"

I admit I don't know.

"You saw him hand over the food."

I did. But I don't know if Senator Lodius meant to poison the Consul. If he did, I'd have expected him to be more circumspect about it. While I don't normally have that much confidence in the investigative powers of either Palace Security or the Civil Guards, I'm fairly sure they'll sort this one out, if only because for an affair of this magnitude they'll be employing the talents of every Sorcerer in Turai. Sorcerers can on occasion look back in time, and though it's a tricky business I can't see the combined talents of Lisutaris, Hasius and Lanius failing to come up with a culprit.

"It's been three days now," points out Makri. "And they haven't arrested anyone."

"True. I wouldn't mind joining in the investigation, because I'm offended that anyone could be murdered while I'm in the same room. But they're not going to call on my services and that's that."

There are two popular theories currently circulating. The first is that Senator Lodius, tired of years of political strife with the Traditionals, had decided to move things along by taking some direct action. But even the most ardent supporter of the Traditionals can see problems with that one. Lodius isn't stupid. And a man would have to be fairly stupid to hand over a poisoned pastry in full view of thirty or so Senators and expect to get away with it.

The other popular theory is that the murder is the work of the Orcs, seeking to destabilise the city before they attack. I'm dubious. Orcs are low, despicable creatures, but they've never poisoned any Human official before and I can't see why they'd start now.

Consul Kalius has insisted that war preparations must go on uninterrupted. It's hard to concentrate in the hubbub, and not as easy to go about my business anymore. People were glad to see officials ostensibly preparing improvements for the city, but now that news of the Orcs has got out, any official soon finds himself surrounded by anxious citizens asking for news, demanding to know how long we have till the Orcs start marching.

There's a coldness in the air that says winter is no more than a week away, maybe less. When winter comes the city would normally grind to a halt. This time, we'll have to keep going. Many things have to be done before the spring. Lisutaris has given warning that the birth rate of dragons has gone up dramatically in the past few years, something which the Orcish Sorcerers have until now managed to conceal.

"So let them come on their dragons," says Makri as we walk downstairs to the bar. "I've killed dragons before."

"You killed one dragon."

"Well, if another one had come along I'd have killed that too."

"We didn't kill that dragon in the Fairy Glade," I remind her.

"That was a hefty beast," admits Makri. "But I chased it off."

"What do you mean, you chased it off? I was there too."

"You were ogling the naiads in the water."

"Very humorous, Makri. I was chopping up a squadron of Orcs so you could get to the commander."

The door of the Avenging Axe swings open and a messenger struggles in weighed down by an enormous bunch of flowers. He places them on the counter.

"Delivery for Makri."

The messenger departs. Makri looks at the card. She scowls, then sweeps the flowers on to the floor.

"Horm again?" says Gurd, appearing from the storeroom. Makri nods, and looks annoyed. Gurd is troubled. When the Orcs are about to attack, no tavern owner wants to be receiving bunches of flowers from one of their leaders. People could get the wrong impression.

"Why does he keep sending you flowers?" asks Gurd. Makri shrugs.

"Did you encourage him in some way?"

Makri is offended.

"Of course I didn't encourage him! Thraxas, did I encourage Horm the Dead to send me flowers?"

"Of course not. No encouragement at all. Though you did wander into my offices wearing your chainmail bikini while he was there. Maybe if you'd covered yourself up a bit better . . ."

"Ah," says Gurd, nodding his head. "The chainmail bikini."

"Which has been getting smaller and smaller in recent months . . ."

"I need to earn tips!" exclaims Makri. "You know how much it costs at the College!"

"I suppose there's some truth in that. Though it doesn't entirely explain why you were flaunting yourself at a foreign Sorcerer who was not, as far as I remember, buying drinks at the time."

"This is outrageous," says Makri. "I was not flaunting myself."

"Well, you know," I say, "a mad half-Orc Sorcerer spends all his time in the wastelands surrounded by stone-faced troll-girls and when he arrives in Turai the first thing he sees is you sauntering around practically naked, it's bound to have an effect. He'd only met you for about a minute when he was offering you a position."

Gurd laughs.

"What position was that?"

"Captain of his Armies," says Makri, not sounding at all amused.

"And he called you the finest flower in all of Turai, I remember. Which might explain the flower motif. Probably since he left Turai he's spent all his time languishing in his mountain palace or wherever he lives, thinking about you."

Having now had enough of this, Makri turns on her heel and departs in a bad mood, leaving a few Orcish curses in her wake. I'm just taking a jar of ale from Gurd when the door opens again and Tanrose walks in. I'm about to rush and embrace her—something I can't remember doing for a good many years—but Gurd beats me to it.

Thinking it best to leave them in peace, I pause only long enough to mention to Tanrose that I really would enjoy one of her substantial venison pies for dinner tonight, and maybe a lemon tart for dessert, before heading upstairs to my office. I sweep some junk off the couch prior to lying down for an afternoon sleep. Unfortunately, as is so often the case when I'm headed for the couch, some damned client knocks on the door. I haul it open and make ready to repel visitors. I'm faced with a plump, well-dressed middle-aged woman who's accompanied by a brawny young man, a servant from his attire.

"May I come in?" asks the woman in a voice so refined she could cut glass with it.

"If you must."

I welcome them in, if allowing them to find their way through the mess on the floor while scowling roundly at them could be called a welcome. What does this Senator's wife want with me? She settles down quite gracefully on the chair in front of my desk.

"I wish to hire you," she says.

"What for?"

"To clear my husband's name."

"What's he accused of?"

"Murdering Prefect Galwinius."

There's a brief pause while I digest this.

"And your husband is?"

"Senator Lodius."

I rise to my feet and point to the door.

"Can't do it. Try the Venarius agency uptown. They're more your sort of people."

The woman remains seated. She looks unruffled, which makes me feel foolish.

"You are an Investigator for hire, are you not?"

"I am. And your husband blackmailed me last year. And called me a low-life piece of scum."

"Did he really say that? It doesn't sound like my husband."

I admit he might not have used those exact words.

"But he implied it."

She wrinkles her brow just a little.

"Oh. I see. When you were recommended to me as a competent Investigator—and a man who'd fought in the war—I did not expect you to be so sensitive."

"I'm not sensitive. I'm insulted. And I'm sensitive. Thanks to your husband I had to prevent an eviction."

"Prevent an eviction? Was this unjust?"

"Well—"

I halt. I sit down.

"Possibly not, from the tenants' point of view. But it meant going against Praetor Capatius and it got me in a load of trouble."

Trouble which hasn't gone away yet. That was the start of the accusations against me. It's fatal to become embroiled in the politics of Turai. Lodius forced me into it.

"Has he been arrested?"

"He will be very shortly. I received a message."

"And Senator Lodius sent you here to hire me?"

She shakes her head. It wasn't her husband who suggested it.

"Deputy Consul Cicerius recommended you. It was he who sent the message."

This takes me by surprise. I've done some good work for the Deputy Consul in the past year. He's never shown much sign of appreciating it. I didn't know I'd risen enough in his estimation for him to be recommending me. And it's doubly strange, because Cicerius is also a bitter enemy of Lodius.

"Cicerius? Why would he try to help your husband?"

She shakes her head. She doesn't know.

"What did he say? Try Thraxas, he's a drunken disgrace to the city but he doesn't mind getting his hands dirty?"

"He was a good deal politer than that."

The woman's facade slips a little, though she's not exactly close to tears. Upper-class women rarely cry about important matters; it would show bad breeding. On the other hand, they may weep profusely if the hairdresser is late.

I don't want to take on the case. Not only do I dislike Senator Lodius, I've a lot on my plate right now. Besides, with the Orcs planning an attack, the city's liable to be razed to the ground in a few months' time. Then who's going to care who killed the Prefect? Still, I hate to see a murderer go unpunished. If the Civil Guards and Palace Security fail to catch the killer, he'll be walking around free, and that never sits right. If I take on the case and clear

Lodius, it'll probably mean finding the real murderer. That, I suppose, would be good. But then I'd find myself on the wrong side of the city authorities and the King, who despise Lodius. That would be bad. I try to weigh things up but I'm drowsy from beer and tired from walking round Twelve Seas.

"I saw your husband hand food to Galwinius. Right after that Galwinius dropped down dead. It doesn't look so good for him."

"My husband did not kill the Prefect," says his wife, emphatically. "No matter what the Sorcerers at Palace Security say."

"The Sorcerers say he did?"

"I believe they are about to. An arrest warrant is being written as we speak."

"Then Lodius is doomed."

"My husband is not doomed."

"He is. If the Sorcerers have fingered him, he's doomed. Sorry, lady, just because he's a rich Senator doesn't mean he doesn't have to suffer for his crimes."

The woman looks at me coldly. She rises to her feet and speaks to her servant.

"Come. This man is not the person to help us. Deputy Consul Cicerius has misinformed us about his abilities."

She turns away in a dignified manner.

"I'm sorry to have wasted your time."

They walk to the door and leave via the staircase to the street below. I let them go, then take a hefty slug from my new bottle of klee. I'm annoyed. Usually when I give the brush-off to some unwanted client, they rant for a while, and insult me. Call me fat, or drunk, or cowardly,

or something. They don't just apologise for wasting my
time and walk out in a dignified manner. The more I think
about it, the more annoying it becomes. Who does that
woman think she is to just walk in here, be insulted by me,
then leave in a dignified manner?

I cross swiftly to the door and haul it open again. At the
foot of the stairs the servant is still helping his mistress
into the carriage.

"Okay, I'll take the damned case," I yell at her.

She raises her eyes towards me.

"Good," she says, simply. "Would you like to visit my
house to learn more of the matter? Perhaps later this
evening?"

I nod, then slam the door. Makri chooses this moment
to walk in.

"So you're taking the case?" she says. "Is Lodius innocent?"

"How do you know so much about it?"

"I was listening at the door. So? Is he innocent?"

"I've no idea. But now I have to find out. Damn it, I
didn't want to have to work for Senator Lodius. I hate
Lodius."

"Then why did you take it on?"

"His wife tricked me by behaving in a dignified manner."

"The calculating bitch," says Makri. "There's no way
you could stand up to that."

"You said it. Now I'm going to be defending the person
the whole city will think murdered Galwinius. Probably at
the instigation of the Orcs. The news-sheets will be down
on me like a bad spell. Why is it I always get the really bad
cases?"

"Well," says Makri, thoughtfully. "You live in quite a bad part of town. Probably most of the better cases go to the high-class Investigators in Thamlin. And you drink a lot, which might put some of the more respectable clients off, and you're known to have a really bad temper, which again is off-putting for a lot of people. Also you've got quite a serious gambling problem so I suppose some people might think you're not really a trustworthy person to give money to. You've been thrown in prison quite a few times, you were denounced in the Senate and you've been regularly criticised in the news-sheets, including one really comprehensive report which included not only the time you were hauled before a magistrate for stealing a loaf of bread but also the time you tried to steal wine from the church in Quintessence Lane. You were sacked from your job at the Palace, your wife ran off, and you sometimes turn up to meet clients after smoking far too much thazis, which hardly gives a good impression, and didn't you once—"

"Makri, will you shut up. It was a rhetorical question."

"I'm just explaining why—"

"Fine. I get the picture. Why don't you go downstairs and see if any Orc Sorcerers have been sending you flowers? I need to sleep."

"Also, you sleep on the couch when you should be working."

Makri departs. To hell with her. One day that woman will push my endurance past its limit. I drink more klee and fall asleep.

CHAPTER EIGHT

I waken to the notion that I should be getting on with something. I've forgotten what. I'm splashing water on my face when I remember I've just been hired by the wife of Senator Lodius. It's one of the biggest criminal cases in the history of Turai. I guess I should be pleased to be involved. I'm not, and not just because I'm going to have to miss out on Tanrose's cooking for another few hours.

I curse out loud. Of all the assorted aristocrats who've ever looked down their noses at me, Lodius is one of the worst. In normal circumstances he wouldn't let me in his house. No doubt he laughed when I was booted out of my job at the Palace. The senatorial class have always had it in for me. Senators, Prefects, Consuls, I loathe them all. I put my life on the line for this city. What did they do in the Orc War? Hid in their villas, probably, while poor men like me did all the fighting. And did we get any thanks after the war? We didn't. I detest them.

I put my sword on my hip, place a spell in my memory in case of emergencies, and head downstairs for a final beer before setting off. Makri has finished her shift and wants to know where I'm going.

"To see Lodius's wife."

"I want to come."

"Why?"

"Gurd and Tanrose are having this intense conversation and it's making me uncomfortable. And Dandelion is being really irritatingly happy about them getting back together. She's talking about the stars smiling in the heavens and I can't take it anymore."

I'm about to tell Makri that she can't accompany me because I'm about to visit the house of a Senator and Makri, with her Orcish blood, won't really be welcome, but I stop myself. Why should I put myself out just to please some Senator's wife? Apart from when she's being the most aggravating person in the city, Makri's my friend. One of the very few friends I have. She can come if she wants. Do them good in Thamlin to see how the other half lives. I pick up another bottle of klee from behind the bar. Dandelion hands it over with a frown. She's possibly the only barmaid in Turai who doesn't really approve of drinking. Makri puts on her man's tunic, fits two swords at her hips, a knife in her boot and wonders if she should bring her axe.

"We're not going to fight a dragon, we're going to interview a Senator's wife."

"That's what you always say. And then something bad happens and I really need my axe."

"Believe me, no axe is necessary."

Makri looks a little unhappy.

"You just don't like walking down the street with a woman with an axe."

It's not long till nightfall. Unless we want to walk to Thamlin, we'll have to catch a landus quickly. Riding is forbidden in Turai after dark. We find one at the foot of Moon and Stars Boulevard. I tell the driver our destination and sip from my bottle of klee as we trot over the river. Makri lights a thazis stick. Thazis is still technically illegal, but with the influx of dwa, a much more serious drug, the authorities have given up caring about it. The driver wants to talk about the imminent attack from the Orcs. We remain silent but it doesn't put him off.

"The end for Turai, I reckon," he says. "We can't fight them again. Where's our army going to come from? Half the young men in the city are off their heads on dwa. Half the Senators too. I heard that General Lamisius got thrown out of the army last week for selling the stuff to his men. And there's nothing in the armoury; the Brotherhood and the Society of Friends sold all our weapons long ago. And who's going to come to our assistance? The Simnians? No chance. They'll sit at home while we get butchered. And I can't see the Elves sailing up again. Why would they? They've got problems of their own, and anyway, I don't think the Elves have really got the stomach for another war. What does that leave us with? Nioj? There's no way they're going to help us; those northern pigs would probably laugh if the Orcs destroyed us. Which leaves us the League of City States, and what's that worth these days? The League's been in chaos longer than anyone can remember. You think they're going to be able to raise an army? That's about as likely as sunshine in the underworld. We're doomed and everyone knows it. As soon as winter's over I'm taking the family and heading west. See if we can go far enough so the Orcs won't find us."

I try to ignore him. I've got enough on my mind without the relentless pessimism of a landus driver. Besides, there's more truth in what he says than I want to acknowledge.

Senator Lodius's villa is guarded by four uniformed men from the Securitas Guild. I'm expecting trouble gaining entry, but when I announce myself they wave me right through. Makri gets a few curious glances but they don't raise any objections. The servant who answers the door seems a little surprised, but even so she welcomes us in. She deposits us in a waiting room, where I look morosely at a small bust of Saint Quatinius which I recognise as coming from the workshop of Drantaax, one of Turai's most famous sculptors. Or he was, till he was murdered last year. I investigated the case. Another sorry affair full of malice and greed.

We wait for what seems like a long time. Makri wonders out loud if my clients always take this long to appear.

"Only the wealthy ones. Senators, Prefects, they never treat a man right. And their wives are worse. When she gets here she'll demand I clear her husband in the space of a couple of hours and probably add on a lecture about my public duty into the bargain. As if any of these people ever did their public duty."

I take another drink of klee and belch noisily.

"Why did she hire you?" says Makri.

"Number one chariot at investigating," I reply.

The Senator's wife, Ivaris, appears in the room, accompanied by a young female servant. She apologises for keeping us waiting, citing a crisis in the kitchen as an excuse.

"I was hoping you'd change your mind," she says. "And you are . . . ?" She looks towards Makri.

"Makri. I help Thraxas with the fighting."

Ivaris smiles politely. I'm half expecting her to throw us out on the spot, but even Makri's pointy ears, male attire and twin swords don't seem to upset her.

"I do hope you can help my husband. It would be a terrible tragedy were he to be unjustly convicted of such a crime."

"Yes, he's a fine man. It's an honour to work for him."

"I do not believe you like him at all," responds Ivaris.

"I don't. But I'm taking the case. No one poisons a man when I'm in the room and gets away with it. Especially when I've been eating the food."

"You find that particularly offensive?"

"I do. Tampering with food is a serious crime. I charge thirty gurans a day plus expenses. But when you hire me I'm in charge of the case. So don't get it into your head that you can start telling me how to do my job."

Ivaris looks a little puzzled.

"I wouldn't dream of it."

She's so polite. It's annoying.

"Where's Lodius?"

"At the Abode of Justice. Ostensibly he is helping with their inquiries but in reality they're not letting him out of their sight. He'll be arrested and charged any time now. It might already have happened."

The Senator's wife again manages to conceal her emotions, though it must be hurting. I wonder if I should dislike her a little less. Being so wealthy, plump and clean she doesn't look like she's got an ounce of strength in her, but she probably has. She's the daughter of a Senator, from one of Turai's oldest families, naturally. Came with a lot of money, I expect, from her father's interests in the gold mines, and his shipping concerns.

Lodius himself is equally well born, though he's not above styling himself a man of the people when it suits him, because his family were originally farmers outside the city. But they made a lot of money by buying up land from families impoverished by the wars in the last century and I doubt if anyone in the family has touched a plough in the past fifty years. He's an aristocrat through and through, which might not save his neck this time. Even though the male aristocracy are, unlike the unfortunate Herminis, generally allowed to go into exile if convicted of a serious crime, I doubt that option will be offered in this instance. Public opinion wouldn't allow it, not for the killer of Prefect Galwinius. And if public opinion did allow it, the Palace wouldn't. Lodius is facing execution. The King will be delighted at an excuse to get rid of him.

"Do you have any idea what the evidence is? Apart from being the person who handed over the poisoned food?"

Ivaris shakes her head.

"It all came as a terrible shock. I have no idea why anyone would accuse my husband. He cannot possibly have done such a thing."

"Your husband spends his life berating the Traditionals. Galwinius was a very important Traditional. They were hardly the best of friends."

"That is simply the way things are done in the Senate. My husband would never condone any act of violence."

This isn't true. When the elections come round there's plenty of violence, condoned by anyone who wins votes as a result. I let it pass, but point out that being an opponent of the Consul might easily be enough to land Lodius in serious trouble.

"It wouldn't be the first false accusation of murder made in this city for political ends. I'm suffering a false accusation myself. Which Lodius and his Populares weren't falling over themselves to help me with, now I think about it."

Ivaris looks upset. I move the conversation on.

"What about this court case? Galwinius was reported to be suing your husband."

"A dispute over a will," says Ivaris. "But I do not know the details."

I doubt that's true. Ivaris doesn't seem like a woman who's entirely ignorant of her husband's affairs. I let it pass. I can find out the details elsewhere. But already it's obvious that things aren't looking good for Lodius. He's just handed over a poisoned pastry to a man who was about to sue him. A man who was already his enemy.

"Did Cicerius say he'd get me access to your husband?"

"Yes. Can you go immediately? Or rather, as soon as Sabav is over."

"Pardon?"

"Evening prayers. It's almost time."

It's a legal requirement for all citizens of Turai to pray three times a day. The more devout among the population go to church, though that's not required by law. Anywhere will do. If I'm in my own room I ignore the call for prayer. Any time I'm unlucky enough to be caught outside I generally just kneel down in the street with the other unfortunates and doze off for a few minutes while they go through their routine. As for Makri, she has no affinity whatsoever with Turanian religious practices and generally makes sure she's well out of sight at prayer times. But now Ivaris is actually offering us the use of her family's prayer temple. I don't want to accept. Suddenly I'm painfully aware that I reek of klee. Though I'm not what you'd call a religious man, you never know. Entering a private chapel while stinking of alcohol might lead to problems. I've often felt I was cursed by the Gods. No point making things worse. I start to make an excuse but Ivaris waves it away. Makri is shuffling round uncomfortably and looks very unhappy about the whole idea. As Ivaris leads us towards the courtyard temple in the centre of the house, Makri whispers in my ear quite urgently.

"Will I have to say anything?"

"No," I whisper back. "Just nod at the right places. And don't sing any Orcish hymns or anything."

"I don't sing Orcish hymns," hisses Makri. "I only curse in Orcish."

"Well don't do that either."

"Why would I?" says Makri.

"Who knows? I've never understood anything you do."

"Are you accusing me of being an Orc?" demands Makri, quite loudly.

"Not at all."

"You were implying it."

"So what?"

Makri looks angry.

"Why don't you just admit you think one day my Orc blood is going to take over and I'll start slaughtering Humans?"

I shake my head.

"You see, Makri, this is why I never bring you on cases. The slightest thing and you start getting upset and waving your swords about."

"I'm not waving my swords."

"You're close to it. Just calm down."

"Calm down?" shouts Makri. "I'm just minding my own business and you suddenly start accusing me of singing Orcish hymns. I don't know any Orcish hymns. Well, maybe one or two. But that's not the point."

"Will you stop shouting? I bring you to a Senator's house and you just don't know how to act civilised."

"Civilised? You're taking this woman's money and you said you hate the Senator and everyone like him, you cusux!"

"You see? Orcish curses just come naturally to you. I knew you couldn't get through Human prayers without reverting to type. We'll be lucky if you don't sacrifice someone."

Ivaris coughs gently. We turn round to find about twenty or so members of the household looking at us rather nervously. A few of the brawnier servants seem to be preparing to defend their mistress.

"It's time for prayers," says Ivaris, calmly.

"We're ready," I mutter, and we troop shamefacedly into the courtyard temple.

I can't remember when I was last in a place like this. Probably not since I burgled the Niojan attaché's house. It's clean, white and peaceful. Ivy climbs the walls. A wisp of smoke from an incense burner trails lazily towards the sky, just enough to provide a delicate aroma in the open-air space. The evening is still warm. It's so quiet in here you could forget you were in the city. Stick a decent-sized couch down somewhere and it would be the perfect place for an after-dinner sleep.

The family has its own Pontifex to lead them in their prayers, an old, grey-haired man who's probably retired from his official church duties. As he intones the words I have to struggle to stay awake. Kneeling beside me, Makri is fidgeting. She's probably worried that they might go on for hours. I'm feeling quite peaceful. I forget about the Orcish hordes gathering to attack us. I'm almost sorry when the prayers end.

I haul myself to my feet. The household disperses. Ivaris thanks the Pontifex. Makri backs out of the shrine as quickly as she can but I wait to say a polite farewell to the Senator's wife. I'd like to thank her for inviting us to share the family prayers but I can't quite find the words to do it. I look at her awkwardly.

"I'll clear your husband's name," I say, eventually, and turn round smartly, picking up Makri on my way to the door. Our landus is waiting outside. Makri complains for a while about my rudeness towards her then falls silent as we continue towards the Abode of Justice. On arrival we're intercepted by Cicerius's assistant Hansius.

"The Deputy Consul has been expecting you."

We're taken along a corridor and dumped in some sort of waiting room.

"Trouble already," I mutter to Makri. "The authorities are not going to like it that I've taken on Lodius as a client."

I'm already feeling uncomfortable because I know that the decision to prosecute Lodius must have come from the top, which means the Palace. I really could be walking into a lot of trouble here. Damn Lodius's wife for being so polite and hospitable.

Cicerius—thin, grey and even more austere-looking than usual—enters briskly. As ever, he's clad in his green-rimmed toga, the mark of his rank. Our Deputy Consul is an unusual mixture of honesty, hard work, and over-whelming vanity. He's been strutting round all summer trying not to look too pleased at the new statue of himself that's just been erected outside the Senate, "In appreciation of his sterling service to the city," as the Consul said at the unveiling ceremony. Cicerius, while publicly deploring the use of public funds for such a reason, is in reality as pleased as a man can be. It's rumoured he instigated the campaign to have the statue erected in the first place. On the plinth there's a quotation from one of his speeches: "The true mark of a man is not what he achieves, but what he strives for." Good advice, maybe. Cicerius has been striving for that statue for a long time.

"You are investigating on behalf of Senator Lodius?"

I nod. Cicerius looks thoughtful, and remains silent for a long time.

"The King himself has authorised the prosecution," he says, eventually.

"I imagined that was the case."

"It means you'll find a lot of difficulties put in your way. The King and Consul Kalius both wish to see justice done swiftly. No official in Turai is going to offer any help."

"They never do," I say. "If you're trying to put me off, Cicerius, you're wasting your time."

"I am not trying to put you off. It was I who recommended you to the Senator's wife."

"I'd have expected you to be cheering on the prosecution, not helping with the defence,"

"I do not intend to help with the defence," says Cicerius, sharply. "But I wish to ensure that the matter is properly investigated."

"Are you telling me that Lodius is facing a phony charge and your conscience is bothering you?"

Cicerius glares at me. He's seconds away from giving me a lecture about my manners but he restrains himself, probably because he has more important things to be getting on with.

"No. There is some evidence against the Senator. How strong it is, I'm not certain. If he's guilty I won't be displeased to be rid of him. Senator Lodius is a disgrace to the city and has caused us great harm over the years. Now, with the enemy practically at the gates, he's a disruptive force we could well do without. Yet . . ."

Cicerius lets the next sentence hang in the air. I catch his drift. The Deputy Consul is one of the few politicians in the city with any real integrity. He might be rather too keen to see himself publicly honoured, but he's never taken a bribe. Even though it would suit him to have Lodius out of the way, he can't bring himself to see an injustice done.

"My assistant Hansius will apprise you of the details. After which you will be permitted to visit Senator Lodius. Meanwhile, I think it best if you step down from the Lesser War Council. Everyone is appalled at the tragic events of the last meeting. It may be awkward if one of the members were to be involved in defending the perpetrator of the crime."

"Alleged perpetrator."

"As you say. Alleged perpetrator."

Cicerius nods, and strides out of the room. Off to admire his new statue, I expect. He doesn't wish me luck.

CHAPTER NINE

The evidence against Senator Lodius isn't especially strong but it might be strong enough to hang him if a better suspect doesn't come along. According to Hansius, information from the government's Sorcerers is inconclusive. The alignment of the moons has allowed them to look back in time but the results are murky. There were just too many people around to allow for a clear sight of every action. No one can say for sure if Lodius put poison in the food. Old Hasius the Brilliant is a master of examining the past but even his best efforts haven't managed to locate the precise moment when the pastry was poisoned. Too many people passed by the food and even the best sorcery can't pick up every detail of every movement by every person in a crowded room. If Lodius did slip something into the pastry it can't be proved by sorcery.

Hasius has examined the remains of the pastry. Of course he's picked up the aura of Lodius from it but that doesn't prove anything. Lodius isn't claiming he never touched the poisoned food. He admits handing it to Prefect Galwinius, but claims he simply picked it up from the food trolley, not knowing it was poisoned. Also on the pastry were the auras of the kitchen staff, Lodius's assistant, Galwinius, a Senator who picked up the pastry before changing his mind and putting it back on the trolley, and various others who have not yet been identified. It's surprising how many people touched that pastry before it was eaten. Given the enthusiastic way I attacked the food trolleys, it's fortunate I didn't pick it up myself.

According to Hansius, no one at the Abode of Justice believes that Lodius picked up the pastry by chance. If that were true it would seem to imply that an item of food was randomly poisoned and left on the food trolley for anyone to take. This doesn't make sense, unless the kitchen staff were feeling particularly murderous that day, but then these things generally don't make sense until you dig a little deeper. Just because there isn't another good suspect in view doesn't mean my client is guilty.

I point out to Hansius that the natural conclusion a person might draw from Senator Lodius ending up with a poisoned pastry on his plate is that someone was trying to poison the Senator. Hansius is shocked, or pretends to be.

"The Traditionals do not poison their political opponents."

That's true, as far as I know, though I wouldn't swear they haven't had a few of them assassinated by other means.

The poison used was carasin, which is rare in these parts. It comes from a plant that grows far south of here, and ingestion is always fatal. It only has one other use, as far as anyone knows, which is as a binding agent in the manufacture of coloured vellum, the sort of thing ladies might use for writing fancy messages to their lovers.

"That looks very bad for Senator Lodius."

"Why?"

"Because he owns the only workshop in Turai which manufactures coloured vellum. It is the source of much of his wealth."

"So? Anyone could have got hold of carasin."

Hansius doesn't think so. Senator Lodius's family holds the exclusive licence for the import of the substance. The licence was granted to Lodius's father back in the days when the family hadn't taken sides against the Traditionals. Hansius is impressed with this as evidence. I'm not.

"So Lodius is the only legal importer of carasin into Turai. A pastry poisoned with carasin ends up killing Galwinius. That sounds like someone is trying to frame my client."

"Your client handed over the pastry. And he's the only importer."

"Then it's a good frame. But it isn't proof of his guilt. What's his motive?"

"The enormous law suit Galwinius was bringing against him," says Hansius, quite smugly.

I purse my lips. There is, of course, the enormous law suit.

"You are familiar with the details?" asks Hansius.

"Run it by me again."

"Prefect Galwinius was about to prosecute Senator Lodius for forging a will. The deceased, Comosius, died in

Abelasi last year, leaving a large fortune. Comosius was a cousin of Prefect Galwinius, and as he died without issue the Prefect, as head of the family, had expected to inherit the estate. However, Senator Lodius produced a will which purported to show that Comosius left his entire estate to him. The Prefect alleged the will was a forgery, made in Abelasi at the behest of Senator Lodius. The case was about to be put to the courts and in the mean time the money has been frozen. The court case ends with the death of Galwinius, which means that Lodius now inherits the money. You must admit that this is a strong motive and gives credence to the charge of murder."

I admit it's a motive of sorts. The forging of wills, particularly of people who die abroad, is a long-standing problem. Prefect Galwinius wouldn't have been the first one to have been cheated out of money in this manner. But it seems unlikely to me that Senator Lodius would involve himself in an affair like this. He must know that the authorities have it in for him. Why run the risk? He's a wealthy man.

"Senator Lodius's political campaigns have eaten deep into his family fortune in the past years," says Hansius. "And investigations by the Abode of Justice reveal him to be short of the money he needs to carry on."

I leave with a lot to think about. Makri meets me at the gate and we climb back into the landus. She doesn't seem to mind that she's been waiting. She's been studying the architecture around her.

"Vaulted arches?"

"A few. And a lot of other things. It's strange how the palace and all the buildings around it are so fine and

Twelve Seas is such a dump. Why does the population still like the King?"

"That's a hard question to answer. Because they always have, I suppose. And he's a symbol of the nation."

"He keeps himself very comfortable."

"That's what kings do."

"What did you learn from Hansius?"

"Sorcerous evidence is inconclusive but Prefect Galwinius was killed with a poison which only Lodius imports into Turai. Galwinius was about to prosecute Lodius for forging a will to get his hands on a lot of money. Lodius needs the money because he's broke. Now Galwinius is dead he gets to keep the money."

"Strong motives," says Makri.

"Maybe."

"You think he's innocent?"

"Of course he's innocent. He's my client."

Makri says there's some backwards logic going on here. I ignore this. Logic is for her philosophy classes. When it comes to a client, I go on my intuition.

"And my intuition is telling me Lodius is innocent."

Makri looks me in the eyes.

"You're lying."

I'm shocked. Makri isn't sophisticated enough to know when I'm lying.

"I am not lying."

"You are. After careful observation I can read the signs."

"Rubbish. You've a lot to learn about lying in the civilised world. My intuition tells me that Lodius is innocent."

Makri shrugs.

"Okay."

My intuition isn't telling me a thing. For all I know, Lodius could have packed the pastry with carasin and fed it to Galwinius with a smile on his face. I hope he didn't. I hate it when my clients turn out to be murderers. It makes things awkward.

On the journey home the air is noticeably colder. I shiver and draw my cloak around me. As I climb the stairs to my office, the first flake of snow settles gently on my sleeve. Winter is here. Tomorrow I'll have to put a warming spell on my cloak before I visit Senator Lodius.

In deference to his rank, the Senator will not be held in jail while he awaits trial. He's been placed under house arrest. Humiliating for a man of his class, but not as bad as languishing for months in a cell with common criminals. Justice in Turai can move painfully slowly and there's little prospect of Lodius coming in front of a judge before the winter is over. The preliminary hearings normally wouldn't start till the weather improved. It's possible, I suppose, that the Consul might call a special session earlier in an attempt to get the matter over with quickly. Lodius has a lot of support in Turai and his party aren't going to take kindly to these events. The Consul will be hoping that the oncoming bad weather and the impending attack by the Orcs will keep the lid on any civil unrest, but he can't be sure of it.

Reflecting that, in the circumstances, an early trial isn't that unlikely, I drag myself out of bed the next morning a good deal earlier than I'd like to. I set about placing the warming spell on my cloak. This is one of the few sorcerous acts I'm still able to perform, and with the Turanian winter being so grim, it's proved to be a life-saver in recent years. Then I head out into the first day of winter to clear the name of Senator Lodius, archenemy of the Consul.

At such an early hour there's no sign of a landus and I have to walk a long way up Moon and Stars Boulevard before I can find anyone to take me to Thamlin. The streets are busy with early activity as the city's traders try to make the best of the last few weeks in which they can trade. When winter really sets in, little business can be done. Ships are already hurrying into the docks, their captains relieved to have made it home safely before the storms arrive. The last wagons carrying goods from the south will soon be rolling in through the city gates. Both land and sea around Turai will soon be impassable. If the weather is particularly severe, the city itself is difficult to move around in. It's my ambition every winter to have enough money saved to enable me to avoid work completely, spending my time in front of the roaring fire at the Avenging Axe with a beer in one hand and a tray of food in the other. It rarely works out that way.

For someone facing a charge of murder, Senator Lodius doesn't seem particularly pleased to see the man who's about to investigate on his behalf. He's far less hospitable than his wife, and informs me that he's not certain I'm the right man for the job.

"This matter is obviously part of some plot by the Traditionals to discredit me and you don't have the right connections among the senatorial classes to investigate it properly. Furthermore, I do not approve of you bringing a woman with Orcish blood into this house. My shrine is at this moment being purified as a result of her presence."

Like many of Turai's democratic politicians, Lodius is a terrible snob. With his short grey hair and perfectly folded toga he's every inch the Senator, and his manner strongly suggests that he'd rather not be spending his time in my company.

"I didn't approve of you blackmailing me last winter. So we're even. Maybe you want to tell me some facts about the case?"

"I understand you were recommended to my wife by Deputy Consul Cicerius? Hardly a recommendation she should have taken, one would have thought, given the man's antipathy towards me. Are you in his pay?"

I'm rapidly becoming annoyed by his attitude. I don't expect my clients to love me, but no Investigator likes being branded a spy. Remembering that his wife was very polite to me, I persevere.

"No."

"So you say."

"What are you insinuating?"

"That the Deputy Consul would be pleased to have an informer in my household as he prepares his case against me."

"Senator Lodius, no amount of money would induce me to spy on a client."

"You are claiming to be an honest man?" The Senator chuckles. "And yet when I needed your services last winter, it did not seem so difficult to make you do as I wished."

I'm now struggling to avoid abusing Lodius. I've taken his wife's money. He's my client. I make a final attempt.

"Perhaps you could tell me some details of the matter

of the will? The one which Galwinius was about to prosecute you for?"

Lodius's face hardens.

"You will not investigate that matter."

"I'll have to. It's part of the case."

"I repeat. You will not investigate it."

"I have to. You're facing a murder charge, Senator Lodius. If I'm going to get to the bottom of it I can't miss out on parts of the story."

"No doubt the Deputy Consul will be pleased to hear all the details of my affairs you may learn from me," sneers Lodius.

I'm grossly insulted by the notion that I might be secretly working for the Deputy Consul.

"Lodius, you're a fool. You're going to hang and I'm the one person in the city who might prevent it."

"What you are," says Senator Lodius, "is a man who's facing a charge of throwing away his shield and deserting the battlefield."

"What?"

"Which would be an excellent reason for you to work for Cicerius. No doubt he has promised to drop the charges in return for spying on me."

I take three steps towards Lodius then push him, using all my weight. The Senator flies into the far wall and slumps to the ground. He's on his feet quickly, an expression of fury on his face.

"How dare you lay a hand on me!"

"Consider yourself lucky. If you weren't my client I'd have punched your head off."

I march out of the room and head for home. I'm madder

than a mad dragon. When I find myself in dispute with a wool merchant over a landus in Moon and Stars Boulevard I bounce him out of the way without mercy. I can't believe I've just been accused of such a vile piece of treachery. Lodius is fortunate I didn't run him through. I pull my warm cloak around me and stare through the window of the landus. Snow is falling lightly. The wind's blowing in from the east. For the first time I can almost sense the Orcish troops massing. My sorcerous powers were never great, but the training left me with my intuition enhanced, or so I like to think. I can feel the Orcs marshalling their armies.

I wonder if there's any equivalent to an Investigator in Prince Amrag's kingdom, maybe tramping the streets trying to clear some Orcish aristocrat of murder. I doubt it. Makri, one of the only people in Turai with any real experience of Orcish society, claims their level of civilisation is not so primitive as we Humans like to think. Maybe she's right. Even so, I've never heard of an Orcish Investigator. If such a creature does exist, he has my sympathy.

"How were things with the Senator?" enquires Gurd, as I reach the bar and hold my hand out for a refreshing tankard of ale.

"I knocked him over."

"No, I mean your client."

"That's who I'm talking about."

Gurd looks puzzled.

"I didn't think you were meant to do that."

"Well, it's not recommended," I admit. "But some clients, you have to beat them into shape."

"We didn't have Investigators in the north," says Gurd. "But we didn't have much crime. Maybe someone stole seal blubber from a neighbouring village every now and then."

Gurd sighs.

"I don't suppose I'll ever see the old village again."

"Why not?"

"Come on, Thraxas. What're the chances of anyone surviving this war?"

Makri appears in the bar wearing her normal garb, a man's short tunic. She's accompanied by Hanama and another woman I don't recognise. They walk up the staircase without acknowledging us.

"Were they being furtive?" I ask Gurd.

"I don't think so."

"They looked furtive to me. I don't trust Hanama. Any time she's with Makri something bad is going to happen."

"You mean an assassination?"

I shake my head.

"No. Hanama wouldn't share her guild work with anyone. But something bad."

Gurd nods.

"Where I come from, a woman like Hanama wouldn't be running around assassinating people. She'd be at home, cooking seal blubber."

"And a good thing too. The city of Turai could learn a lot from your village, Gurd."

I wonder what Makri is up to. I know she isn't teaching Hanama to read. The diminutive assassin is already an educated woman. Ever since the Senator's wife Herminis was sentenced to death, Makri's been acting strangely.

"Do you think they might be collecting money for an appeal?"

"Who?"

"The Association of Gentlewomen."

The very mention of the name causes Gurd to frown.

"She'd better not collect money for that organisation in this tavern."

Few men in Turai have any sympathy for the Association of Gentlewomen. The King doesn't like them, the Consul doesn't like them, and nor does the Senate. Tavern owners and Investigators likewise have very little sympathy.

"Herminis killed her husband," I point out. "What do they expect the city to do? Give her a medal?"

"Scandalous," agrees Gurd, shaking his head. "She deserves to be hanged."

"Of course she does."

"But only last month Senator Divanius was allowed to go into exile after he pushed his wife downstairs," says Tanrose, appearing unexpectedly at our side.

"That was completely different," I say. "Divanius was a war hero."

"So?"

"You can't go executing war heroes. It's bad for the city. Especially with the Orcs at the door."

"It's shocking hypocrisy," says Tanrose, transferring her gaze to Gurd.

"That's just what I was telling Thraxas," agrees Gurd. "Back in my village, we treated women better."

I'm shocked, rendered speechless by Gurd's base treachery. Tanrose puts her arm round his shoulders.

"Thraxas, you should learn from Gurd. You're too stuck in your old ways. The city's changing."

Having had more than enough of this, I take my beer to the table in front of the fire and sit down to ruminate on my investigation. It's a very comfortable chair. After some moments' rumination, I drift off to sleep.

CHAPTER TEN

Two weeks later winter has the city in its grip. Snow is lying on the ground and the wind from the northeast is bitterly cold. It promises to be a hard season. This might not be such a bad thing. The Orcs certainly can't march till it's over, something that Lisutaris is apparently still concerned about. No other Sorcerer or politician believes this to be at all likely, or so I understand. Now that my services are no longer required on the Lesser War Council, I don't hear all the latest talk. What snippets of sorcerous gossip I do hear come mainly from Astrath Triple Moon. My old friend Astrath is in permanent disgrace due to some indiscretions on his part when he was the official Sorcerer at the Stadium Superbius—Astrath not proving to be as incorruptible as the position demanded—but as he wasn't actually expelled from the Sorcerers Guild he still hears some of the news.

I think old Astrath might actually be looking forward to

the war. He's bound to be called into action and might well get the chance to redeem himself, if he can bring down a dragon or two. Sorcerers are too valuable in wartime for any to be left out. There's even talk of Kemlath Orc Slayer being recalled. He's in exile for murder at this moment, but he was a tremendous asset during the last war.

According to Astrath, Lisutaris is out on a limb with her theory that Prince Amrag might march in the winter. Apparently it's led to a lessening of her influence on the War Council. Ovinian the True has reported adversely on her performance to the King. Prince Dees-Akan, in overall command of the Council, has been heard to say in private that perhaps the head of the Sorcerers Guild is losing her grip.

As for war preparations, they're proceeding reasonably well. The entire west is in a state of alert and the response to the call hasn't been as poor as the more pessimistic among us feared. Simnia, the large state to the west of Turai, will send an army as soon as winter breaks. The League of City States has managed to put aside some of its differences and each of the small member states is making preparations. The League will assemble an army under the control of the Abelasian General Hiffier, who's respected far and wide for his endeavours in the last war. Troops from further west—Hadassa, Kamara and others—should be arriving not long after the Simnians. Even Nioj seems to be co-operating. The eastern borders of Nioj aren't too far from the Orcish Lands but they're protected by a mountainous barrier which no army can penetrate. However, if the Orcs march into Turai, there's nothing to stop them from turning north and heading into Nioj from the south. That being the case, the Niojans would rather make a first defence on Turanian soil than their own.

The Elves have sent word that they'll sail up from the south as soon as the seas are calm enough. Turai has good relations with most of the Elvish nations and we can depend on them. All over the west and south, states are arming themselves for war. Which is good news for Turai. Turai is the natural focus of any attack from the east. Once through the narrow stretch of land which makes up the city state of Turai, the Orcs could flood into the rest of the west, which is why even the Simnians, who don't like us, are prepared to defend the line here. Thanks to Lisutaris's early warning, we might yet throw the enemy back.

The standing army of the city state of Turai is very small. At times of national crisis all able-bodied men are obliged to enlist. If weather allows, there will be training in phalanx manoeuvring outside the city walls. This is something which has been unfortunately neglected in recent years, though most men in Turai have seen military service of some sort. Any man over thirty, no matter what his position now, will at one time have picked up his sword and spear and marched into battle. Most of them will have been expecting to do it again, some day.

To bolster our forces, mercenaries are being recruited and the city's population is starting to swell. Mostly they arrive either singly or in small companies, but the King has managed to hire a large contingent several thousand strong, from Sumark, far to the north. They marched in before winter set in and are quartered at the Stadium Superbius, just outside the city walls.

With so many mercenaries in the city, Makri is permanently busy at the tables, which prevents her from complaining too much about her college being closed for winter. Instead she complains about the mercenaries' manners. After a few early skirmishes, they've now learned to respect her. The Avenging Axe is doing a fine trade. This pleases Gurd, as do his frequent encounters with old companions he's fought with in the past. When they recognise their former comrade now employed as a landlord, they laugh, bang their fists on the tables and demand to know what an old soldier is doing serving beer for a living.

"Doing well, you dogs," bellows Gurd. "And don't worry about me, when the Orcs arrive I'll be cutting them down while you weaklings are still in your beds."

Gurd picks up his axe from behind the bar and brandishes it to show he's lost none of his prowess. The mercenaries roar with laughter, drink heavily, and ogle Makri. Makri has a purse slung round her neck in which she puts her tips, and I'd say she was doing better than she has for a while. The war is good business, at least for the taverns and the brothels.

Tanrose and Gurd seem to be reconciled. Maybe not in immediate danger of getting married but at least friendly again. As a result of this—and the upturn in business—Gurd ceases to be as miserable as a Niojan whore and once more becomes the cheerful Barbarian with whom I marched all over the world. It's a welcome change. As is the return of Tanrose to the kitchen. For the first time in months I'm well fed. Facing extra demands for food, Tanrose has retained the services of Elsior and is teaching her the proper art of cooking. A commendable idea, as I point out to Makri. If Tanrose gets killed in the war I'll still be able to get a decent plate of stew.

"Are you going to be a troop commander or anything?" Makri enquires.

"A commander? Me? I doubt it."

"But you're a Tribune. You're on the Lesser War Council. And you've got wartime experience."

"All good points," I agree. "Except I got thrown off the Council. And the rest doesn't count for much in this city. All the commanders come from the senatorial class. No one with 'ax' or 'ox' in his name ever got promoted in the Turanian army. Anyway, since I took on the defence of Senator Lodius I've been frozen out. I'm about as welcome as an Orc at an Elvish wedding up in Thamlin. I've spent three weeks investigating the case, and I've hardly learned a thing."

"Why are you still on the case? Lodius doesn't want you."

"I was hired by his wife. I took her money. Lodius is my client whether he likes it or not."

That's the theory anyway. In practice I'm making little progress. My investigation has been blocked on all sides. Any official I want to talk to is either busy or not available. The city authorities are keen to pin the murder on Lodius and it's not hard to see why. Lodius has so much support from all parts of the disaffected population that they haven't dared to move against him before. Now, with the Orcs practically at the gates and the population rallying round the flag, it's the one really good opportunity the King and his party will get to put Lodius away. If the

Traditionals had tried to pin a murder on Lodius at any other time, the city would've been torn apart by rioting. But now, they might just get away with it.

"So let him hang," says Makri.

"I can't. Not if he's innocent."

Makri shrugs. Any time Makri suspects I might be following some sort of ethical code she laughs, and points out the numerous occasions on which I've acted with a notable lack of ethics. I don't know if she means it. She's an ethical woman herself, in her way.

"You're not really so bothered by that, are you? I mean, whether he's innocent or not? You just hate to give up on a client."

"Maybe."

"I can understand that," says Makri. "Sometimes in the arena they sent me in with a partner. I never liked it when they got killed. I used to protect them. Kill their opponents for them. Sometimes, anyway. But maybe that was just because I liked killing."

"You liked killing?"

"Of course."

"You must be looking forward to the war."

"I am."

"We're quite likely to get killed ourselves," I point out.

Makri shrugs. She doesn't care about dying, as long as she has the opportunity to kill a lot of Orcs. Makri's hatred for Orcs is very intense.

I'm pondering my next step in the investigation. Thanks to Astrath Triple Moon, I've seen the best pictures available to the Sorcerers Guild when they tried looking into the past. We didn't fare much better than Old Hasius the

Brilliant. There are too many people around and nothing is really clear. Astrath is slightly puzzled. By his calculations, the alignments of the moons at the time of the crime should allow for better sorcerous examination.

"Is something blocking it?"

Astrath doesn't think so.

"The pictures aren't as clear as I'd expect, but sometimes that just happens. Sorcerers can't explain everything."

Astrath Triple Moon's pictures do tell me more than Hansius did. Lodius spent some time hanging round in the corridor before the meeting, which looks bad for him. But there was plenty of movement in that corridor: Senators walking this way and that, engrossed in private discussions; Praetor Capatius engaged in some sort of debate with Prefect Drinius, and joined by Cicerius and Hansius; Consul Kalius and his assistant Bevarius talking to Rittius. There's no sign of anything suspicious, however, and none of them entered the kitchen, as far as can be seen.

With official avenues blocked, I've been visiting supporters of Lodius, trying to make some sort of break-through from a different angle, but even that's proving difficult. Lodius's supporters are themselves suspicious of me. They know that the Senator doesn't trust me.

I did manage to speak to the man responsible for cooking the pastry which killed Prefect Galwinius. And in some ways my visit to the consular kitchens was very rewarding. Erisox, the man in charge, is a master chef and not too stingy at dishing out samples. From the moment I first tasted his food I recognised him as great man and it was a pleasure to meet him. We talked of pastry, venison, fish, yams, and other items of interest. He enjoys all aspects of food, and just because he spends a lot of time making fancy little dishes for the Consul's guests doesn't mean he disregards the importance of a hearty bowl of stew in winter.

Unfortunately, great man or not, he couldn't tell me anything about the murder. He swore that no stranger had entered his kitchen. I questioned him fairly intensely on the matter but he was adamant. No one had disturbed him as he prepared the food and he hadn't left the kitchen for any reason.

I'm inclined to believe him. I trust a man with such a great talent for food preparation. But of course Erisox couldn't see what happened to his pastries after they left the kitchen. The food was taken out on trolleys, some of which were left in the corridor for a space of time before being brought into the meeting room. I wish that Lodius hadn't been hanging round in the corridor, without a good explanation for why he was there.

I tried following up the carasin angle, attempting to find out who else might have brought some of the poison into the city, but the trail led nowhere. I've learned quite a lot about the manufacture of vellum, but other than that, nothing. It's the sort of task which really requires the services of a large body like the Civil Guard, but that's not going to happen. Guardsman Jevox, one of my few contacts in the force, told me at once that I was wasting my time nosing round the Guards. No Civil Guard is helping me on this one.

The one aspect of the case I've made progress on is the matter of Galwinius's law suit against Lodius over the matter of the forged will. Officials at the Abode of Justice weren't shy about handing over details of that and it looks bad for Lodius. Statements taken in Abelasi and a Sorcerer's report on the will both suggest that there was an attempt to defraud Galwinius. Given that the beneficiary of the fraud was Lodius, he would have had a hard time explaining the matter to a judge. But again, the Traditionals had it in for Lodius. Who's to say Galwinius wasn't participating in some plot cooked up in the Palace to discredit him? Till I've made more investigations, I'm keeping an open mind on the matter.

One straw I've succeeded in clutching is that there are several other people in Turai who might well have been pleased to see Prefect Galwinius dead. The Society of Friends, for instance. They control all organised crime in the north of the city and Galwinius had just closed down two houses of ill repute which bordered on Thamlin. It's possible the Society might have taken revenge. Organised crime hasn't previously dared to assassinate such a senior politician but as their wealth has grown, so has their ruthlessness. I don't really think that they'd risk murdering a Prefect, but it's a sign of the confusion in the city that there are people who are prepared to believe it might be true. Just like there are people prepared to believe that the Association of Gentlewoman organised Galwinius's murder because he refused to commute Herminis's death sentence.

Whilst mulling this over with a beer in one hand and a venison pie in the other, I'm suddenly struck on the back by a blow which sends me thudding into the bar and causes me to drop my pie. I turn round angrily with my hand on the hilt of my sword to find myself confronted by a huge man with long blond hair, a bushy grey beard and a scar on his face from temple to chin.

"Viriggax!"

"Thraxas, you dog! Come to sign up for the fight?"

"Worse. I live here."

"You live here?"

"That's not all," I add. "Gurd's the landlord!"

"The landlord?"

Viriggax howls with laughter and pounds me another friendly blow on the shoulder. I pound him back.

"It's good to see you!"

Viriggax is a mercenary from some godforsaken island in the frozen north. I've fought many a battle in his company. I haven't seen him for twelve years or so but he doesn't seem to have changed, apart from maybe growing a little in every direction. He's got an axe strapped to his back that could chop a horse in half and a great iron shield slung casually over his shoulder. When he spots Gurd he lets out a roar that can be heard over the din in the tavern. Gurd looks round. His face breaks into a joyous, craggy smile and he hurries over.

"You run this hostelry?" demands Viriggax.

"I do," replies Gurd.

"Then where's the beer?" roars Viriggax, who, I remember, never likes to talk quietly.

Viriggax looks towards the bar. His brow wrinkles as he sights Dandelion, who today has chosen to weave a circlet of leaves in her hair, defying both fashion and common sense.

"What is that?"

"One of my barmaids," admits Gurd, apologetically, and winces as Dandelion steps out from the bar, revealing her lack of foot attire. Before Viriggax can comment, Makri waltzes past in her tiny chainmail bikini with a tray of drinks on her arm. Viriggax's jaw sags as he takes in her copper-coloured skin and pointed ears.

"Have the Orcs got here already?"

"Just another of my staff," explains Gurd, uncomfortably.

"By the northern Gods, this is an odd place you have here, Gurd. Girls with no shoes and Orcs with no clothes!" Viriggax slaps his thigh and laughs mightily.

"That's what you get for living in the city! No life for a man! Now where's the beer, I've got a powerful thirst from travelling!"

Gurd calls for beer from Dandelion, clears us a table and we sit down to talk about the war and catch up on old times. Three or four ales later we're deep into a series of reminiscences.

"You remember those Juvalians who tried to cheat us at cards? We showed them a thing or two!"

"Or what about the time Thraxas fell into a ravine and we couldn't find him for two days?"

"He didn't want to shout for help because he had all the food with him. I swear he was happy to stay in that hole till the supplies ran out!"

"It was safer down there than up at the front with you! Viriggax, you're lagging behind. You northerners never could hold your ale."

"What?" bawls Viriggax, emptying his tankard and banging it down on the table. "I'll show you how a northerner can drink! More ale!"

Some hours later I've forgotten all about Senator Lodius. In fact I've forgotten about most things and am as happy as an Elf in a tree. I launch into a powerful rendition of the Turanian bowmen's drinking song—not that I was ever a bowman, but it's a fine song with a strong melody, and a chorus that requires a lot of banging of tankards on tables. I'm just getting to the verse where the enemy dragons are brought crashing from the sky, cut down by our mighty arrows, when the door of the tavern swings open and a messenger enters with an even more extravagant bunch of flowers than was previously delivered.

"Makri? Delivery for Makri?"

Makri is at the bar getting her tray loaded up so Gurd calls the messenger over and takes the flowers on to our table, something which I can sense is a bad mistake. Gurd has a lot of ale inside him and may not be thinking that clearly.

"What's this?" demands Viriggax, who's looking rather bloated around the face after consuming enough beer to float a trireme. He fingers the card that accompanies the enormous bunch of flowers.

"Orcish writing?"

"From Horm, I expect," sighs Gurd.

Viriggax looks puzzled as he tries to work out exactly what this means. Makri, meanwhile, having been alerted by Dandelion, is hurrying over. She arrives just as it dawns on Viriggax who Makri is, and who Horm is.

"Your barmaid receives flowers from an Orc lord?" he cries, and stands up abruptly, pushing back his chair. "What sort of traitorous establishment are you running here?"

"Traitorous?" yells Gurd, and leaps to his feet, or tries to. Actually his legs get tangled under the table and he's a little slow from alcohol so it takes him a while to get vertical. But once he's up, he's a formidable sight.

"That's what I think of Orcish flowers!" bellows Viriggax, sweeping them on to the floor.

"Hey, those were mine!" yells Makri.

"How dare you abuse my barmaid's flowers!" shouts Gurd.

"I'm getting completely fed up with Horm sending you flowers." I tell Makri. "It's really starting to get on my nerves."

"I never asked for them!" protests Makri, before turning swiftly back to Viriggax and abusing him roundly for daring to touch her property.

A band of northern mercenaries are gathering behind Viriggax in case he needs some assistance. Viriggax is temporarily stunned by the ferocity of Makri's abuse but it doesn't take long for him to recover his voice. In no time a series of grim mercenary and Orcish curses are flying over the table.

"Excuse me," says Dandelion, arriving at this moment and dropping to her knees to scramble round on the floor. "I think I can still rescue the flowers if I get them into a vase of water."

"I don't want them rescued!" screams Makri. "I hate the flowers!"

"Sure, that's what you say now," I shout. "But I'm starting to think you're quite pleased to be getting them."

"I am not!"

"The woman is a traitor!" roars Viriggax.

"Don't you call my barmaid a traitor!" roars back Gurd. "I never thought I'd see the day when Gurd of the North took the side of an Orcish bitch!"

There's only about half a second before the tavern explodes but in that half a second I have time to mentally sigh, clap my hand to my forehead and wonder why it is that my life has brought me to this. Now I have to fight my old comrade Viriggax, just because Makri has an unreasonable dislike of being called an Orcish bitch. As soon as the words are out of Viriggax's mouth Makri leaps on the table and kicks him in the chest with such force that Viriggax is sent sprawling back into his companions. After that, the tavern erupts into a bar-room brawl the like of which I haven't seen since the Brotherhood and the Society of Friends went head to head for control of the Blind Horse in Kushni. Viriggax's companions pile in on top of Makri, I pile in on top of them, Gurd joins in, and the rest of the mercenaries in the tavern, not wishing to miss a good fight, pick sides at random and weigh in with their fists.

Shouts, screams, battle-cries and oaths come from every direction as the bar degenerates into a heaving mass of struggling bodies. Chairs and tables are picked up as weapons and splinters of wood fly over our heads. I pound my fist on the back of some monstrous mercenary who's attempting to attack Makri from behind and am immediately brought down by a blow from a table leg that causes me to sag at the knees. My assailant attempts to bring the lump of wood down on my head but is halted by Makri, who spins round and strikes him a blow on the temple that drops him to the floor. Gurd uses his mighty fists to beat a path through to us and the next thing we find ourselves surrounded by a solid circle of angry-looking northerners, all long blond hair, beards, and muscular arms.

"Get back, you scum!" I yell, picking up a chair and brandishing it fiercely. "The first man to move gets—"

A shuddering assault on my left flank prevents me from completing the sentence. I wince, then hit my attacker with the chair.

"Ah!" yells Gurd, with relish. "Like the old days!" Gurd is brawling with such enthusiasm that's he's forgotten it's his furniture that's being reduced to matchwood. He disappears under three mercenaries. There's a moment's heaving, then, like a volcano suddenly erupting, the three northerners find themselves tossed into the air as Gurd wrenches himself free and weighs in again with his fists.

After this, things get worse. I find myself next to a mercenary from the south who's decided to take our side and we use our combined body weight to good effect until three northerners drive a wedge between us with the remains of a table and I'm forced back against the wall, punching furiously in every direction. Makri, at something of a disadvantage in the close struggle due to her lack of weight, nonetheless proves her worth, leaping, twisting and turning to keep herself out of trouble while lashing out with the sort of blows she learned during her years as a gladiator. Undefeated champion between the ages of thirteen and nineteen, as she's fond of saying. Unfortunately she finds herself trapped in a corner, and when I see her hand flicker towards her boot, where she generally keeps a knife, I know that things are about to go too far. It's against the unwritten rules to use weapons in a bar-room brawl such as this, but Makri has little regard for rules when it comes to fighting. She'll quite certainly kill her opponent before conceding defeat. I'm considering using my sleep spell to settle things, though this does go against the grain. A good bar-room brawl shouldn't be settled by magic. The decision is taken out of my hands as shrill whistles sound outside and the Civil Guards start pouring into the room. The fight gradually subsides as the uniformed men fill up the bar, separating the combatants and waving their batons.

Captain Rallee steps forward. He briefly surveys the wreckage. All over the room bodies lie groaning on the floor and there's hardly a person standing who's not bruised and bleeding.

"What's this all about?" demands the Captain, looking towards Gurd. Gurd shrugs. Though he's normally on good terms with the Captain, he's not going to start complaining to the Civil Guards about a fight in his tavern, not when the fight could be classified as a small dispute among friends. The Captain turns his gaze towards me. We also used to be on good terms, though it's waned in recent years.

"Did you start this?"

"Me? I was hardly involved at all."

Captain Rallee looks uncertain. He doesn't like trouble on his beat but the Avenging Axe isn't an establishment that generally causes him trouble. He's not sure whether to let it go or start rounding us all up.

Suddenly Viriggax steps forward, grinning effusively.

"A small dispute among friends, Captain," he says, loudly. "Nothing more."

"What sort of small dispute?"

"We were discussing flowers."

As Viriggax says this, his companions burst into raucous laughter, and Viriggax himself howls with delight. Northern mercenaries are not entirely lacking a sense of the ridiculous. Makri is looking on suspiciously from the side of the room. Viriggax strides over to her, throws one extremely brawny arm around her shoulders and turns towards the Captain.

"This young woman and I were simply discussing the merits of various floral arrangements when things got out of hand."

The enormous northerner, towering over Makri, beams down at her. Obviously, having been kicked across the room by her, he now considers her a worthy companion.

Captain Rallee glares at Makri.

"I might have known you'd be involved. If you want to stay in the city, keep out of trouble."

He turns to Gurd.

"And if you want to keep your licence, no more fights. We've got enough to do round here without you making it worse."

Captain Rallee signals to his men and they depart as abruptly as they arrived. It's true that the Captain does have a lot to do. With the huge increase in crime in the past few years, the Guards are stretched, particularly in a bad area like Twelve Seas. As the city is now full of mercenaries, things are worse than ever.

Having had a good fight, Viriggax is now as happy as a drunken mercenary. Which, of course, he is. He pulls out a fat purse from his tunic.

"Drinks for everyone!" he yells. "Now we've shaken the dust from our feet, we'll show those Orcish dogs a thing or two if they dare to attack this city!"

CHAPTER ELEVEN

Next day I wake with the sort of hangover that makes a man realise the foolishness of all alcoholic beverages. I stumble from my bedroom to my office and grope for my supply of lesada leaves, which are carefully wrapped in silk in the bottom drawer of my desk. I place one of the small leaves in my mouth, wash it down with water and sit motionless, waiting for it to do its work.

The lesada plant grows only on the Elvish Isles. The Elves use it as a healing herb. Since I discovered its properties for curing hangovers I've had reason to bless its existence. It's possibly the finest thing ever to come from the Elvish Isles. Certainly more useful than their epic poetry.

My head is still pounding and it takes me a little while to realise there's a feeble sort of scratching noise at my door. I make my way gingerly over and pull it open. It all seems like a lot of effort and makes me nauseous, a feeling which isn't improved by the sight of Makri trying to crawl into my room, groaning and whimpering pathetically as she inches her way blindly forward. I shake my head sadly. She's not a great drinker. Last night's celebrations were very extensive, and she shouldn't have tried to keep up. By now the lesada leaf I swallowed is doing its work, allowing me to regard Makri with some pity.

"It's strange really," I say, looking down at the back of her head as she crawls past. "Your peculiar mixture of Orcish, Elvish and Human blood seems to let you do most things well. Fine swordswoman, clever student, excellent with languages. And you're not bad with your axe either, though I've seen better. But for some reason it just doesn't seem to let you drink very much."

"Shut up and give me a lesada leaf, you cusux," croaks Makri.

"Of course, you're far too skinny, which probably explains some of it. Even so, with all your other attributes it's strange you're such a lightweight. Probably it would be best if you stuck to the weaker brews the women and children drink at public celebrations."

Makri promises to kill me if I don't stop talking and give her a leaf. Fearing that she's about to vomit on my floor— something about which she would have no qualms—I make with the leaf. Makri swallows it whole, then lies on the floor groaning and trembling. All in all, it's a shameful performance.

As the leaf does its work, her colour returns to normal.

"I thought I was going to die," she says. "What happened last night?"

"Last night? Not a great deal. A drinking competition

between myself and some of the more optimistic members of Viriggax's troop. I put them soundly in their place, naturally."

"Did I participate?"

I laugh, rather mockingly.

"You? In a drinking contest? That's hardly likely. You passed out the fourth time the klee went round. If Gurd hadn't hauled you up to your room you'd still be lying there like a sack of yams."

Makri scowls, but rises to her feet gracefully. The lesada leaf works quickly on her athletic frame, and after splashing water from my sink over her face and shoulders she declares herself fit for action.

"Another day serving the mercenary hordes. I'm making more money than I have done all year. Are you investigating?"

I shake my head.

"I can't. Today is the first day of troop practice. Weather permitting, my phalanx will be doing manoeuvres."

"You have a phalanx?"

"Yes. Turanian phalanx number seven. We haven't met each other yet. Me and four hundred and ninety-nine others are going to be drilled in close formation work."

Makri is interested, as she always is when it comes to fighting.

"Are these all experienced men? You don't have a lot of time to learn manoeuvres."

"About half will be experienced. The young men won't be. It's up to us to show them the ropes. And you're right, we don't have a lot of time."

Up till about ten years ago the whole male population

used to do this sort of thing every year, but the city has let it slide recently.

"I think it was Consul Sebernius who stopped the regular drills, after the Honourable Merchants Association complained it was taking men away from their work and costing them money. It's a few years since I've even held a long spear in my hand. I expect it will come back soon enough."

I pick up a long candle and start brandishing it enthusiastically, demonstrating to Makri how I held back the Orcs at the Battle of Gorox River.

"Forced them into the river then slaughtered every one of them."

"You outnumbered them two to one," says Makri, who's been reading up on her military history.

"So? You don't stop to count heads when the Orcs are coming at you in a phalanx with thirty-foot spears pointing in every direction. My phalanx did a fine job that day. Stayed rock solid, pushed them back and broke their ranks in two."

I advance across the office with some gusto. The candle slips from my grasp and falls to the floor. I look at it rather ruefully.

"I expect it will all come back with practice."

I hope it does. It's no easy task manoeuvring a phalanx of five hundred men, keeping everybody in the correct position during advance or retreat. You have to be able to run over rough terrain without breaking formation. A good phalanx will crash into the enemy in an unstoppable wave, or repulse an attack like an immovable wall, but it takes a lot of practice. I'm hoping that we have a competent commander. If it turns out to be some Senator's son who's never seen action, we'll be in trouble.

"What am I going to do in the war?" asks Makri "They're not going to let me join the army. You know I'm going to fight anyway. Will I just have to walk out there on my own?"

"Difficult, Makri. Apart from Sorcerers, no Turanian women fight. Not officially anyway. I remember one woman joined up last time the Orcs attacked. She dressed in men's clothes and fought in the light infantry and no one knew till she was killed and it was time to bury her."

"Should I do that?"

"I don't think you'd get away with it. She was quite a brawny girl, passed for a man easily enough. You wouldn't. It's difficult. I don't really see where you might fit in."

As well as the citizens' phalanxes, Senators' cavalry companies and mercenary squadrons there are various brigades of light troops—archers, crossbowmen, light cavalry and such like—but every one is commanded by someone from the senatorial class.

"They're just not going to let you join. But you know, if we suffer defeat in the field and the city comes under siege, no one's going to stop you defending the walls."

"I'm not waiting till then," states Makri, emphatically.

I promise to see what I can do. Maybe I can think of some way for Makri to enlist in the army. Really I'd prefer that she didn't. In a full-scale war with the Orcs, casualties will be very heavy. I'd rather Makri was safe in the city. If we both enter the battle, it's very unlikely that we'll both survive it. I know from experience. When the last Orc War started I was a young man with a assortment of drinking

buddies that could fill a tavern. When it ended I hardly
had enough friends to fit round a table. You can't replace
the companions of your youth. I still miss them, sometimes.

Winter is not the time for troop practice. It's going to be
difficult finding many days that are mild enough to permit
it. The authorities shouldn't have allowed this to happen.
We're ill prepared. Turai has grown richer in the last
decade but it has come at the expense of our defences.
Now we're going to suffer for it.

Outside the snow has stopped but it's very cold.
Fortunately I have my magic warm cloak which should
last for half the day at least. I set off for the area around
the Stadium Superbius, outside the city walls to the east,
where the military training grounds are. Despite the bad
weather, the imminent danger, and the frustrations of my
current investigation, I'm feeling surprisingly good.
Something about being a soldier again makes me feel
alive. As I make my way through the Varquinius Gate I'm
almost cheerful. When I find myself in the company of
others I've fought with in the past, some of them men I
haven't seen for fifteen years, I start to think that if I have
to die in the upcoming war, it's not such a bad way to go.
Maybe better than growing old and dying poor in Twelve
Seas.

On reaching the appointed place, just south of the
stadium, I join with the five hundred men of phalanx
number seven. Some talk to their friends, some look
thoughtful. Most just look cold. My feeling of well-being
is enhanced when I recognise the tall figure of Senator
Marius standing with his aide on a small knoll nearby.

Senator Marius was a young commander of a phalanx in the last war. He did well and was commended for his bravery. If he's our commandeer, I'll be pleased. We could have fared a lot worse.

All around the stadium, other phalanxes have gathered for practice. Further away I can see a group of cross-bowmen practising with targets. Beyond them a company of light cavalry are wheeling in formation. I notice a few faces looking down at us from the walls of the Stadium Superbius. The mercenary army is quartered inside. Probably they're amused by the antics of the amateur citizen soldierly they're watching.

"We'll show them a thing or two," I say, to the man next to me.

"Silence!" roars Senator Marius, right in my ear. "Didn't you hear my order?"

Unfortunately I didn't. The Senator wrinkles his nose and looks at me suspiciously.

"I know you."

"I don't think so . . ."

"You're Thraxas. You were in my uncle's regiment in the last war."

"Really? I didn't know he was—"

"Silence!" roars Marius.

Marius is an unusually tall man and he stares down at me with distaste.

"I remember him talking about you. Half the time you were too drunk to hold your spear."

This really is an injustice. It's the sort of wartime story that gets hopelessly exaggerated. Maybe it happened once or twice.

"Well there'll be no drinking on duty in my phalanx," growls the Senator. "Turn up drunk and you'll be sorry. Gravius, keep an eye on this man."

Centurion Gravius stares at me fiercely. I start to remember why life in the army wasn't so great. At this moment I'm under military discipline and the Senator has the power to lock me up for disobedience if he so wishes. Once you're in the ranks, even as a citizen soldier, your legal rights seem to vanish.

Marius still isn't satisfied. He reaches out a hand to finger my cloak.

"What's this? It's warm. You have a spell on your cloak?"

Under the gaze of the entire phalanx I'm feeling very uncomfortable.

"What sort of a man turns up for military duty with a magic warm cloak?" roars Senator Marius. "Is this a regiment of women? Does the cold weather upset you?"

He stoops to place his face close to mine.

"You'll have a lot more to worry about than a little cold weather, you overweight excuse for a soldier! Now take that cloak off!"

I take it off, meanwhile cursing the bad fortune that has brought me into Marius's phalanx. The man is a petty dictator and a disgrace to the army. I wonder if I can pull some strings to get a transfer.

We start going through manoeuvres. The young men in the phalanx do everything wrong. They drop their long spears when advancing and get their shields tangled when retreating. The temperature drops. Senator Marius barks orders at us, liberally sprinkled with abuse. He keeps us at it even when the snow starts falling from the overcast sky.

I'm as cold as the Ice Queen's grave. The whole day is a nightmare. I always hated being in the army.

When manoeuvres finally come to an end the afternoon light is fading. I'm chilled to the bone. I wrap my cloak around me but all the heat is gone. The men are silent as we trudge away from the field. The older soldiers are probably thinking much the same as me—as a phalanx we're hopeless, and we don't have enough time to get better. Probably these youngsters will break and run at the first sign of danger, leaving me to be mown down by an enemy dragon. What a pointless way to go.

Between the Stadium and the city walls I pass by the retinue of Consul Kalius. He's here to check on today's progress. I smell the pleasant aroma of cooking coming from a small tent. I swiftly duck inside and find Erisox the chef laying out some warm pastries on a silver platter, fresh from the small field oven he's brought with him. Trust Consul Kalius not to travel without some home comforts.

The chef recognises me, and grins.

"Still carrying on my investigation," I lie. "Been busy with the Consul."

Erisox probably knows I'm lying but he doesn't try to prevent me as I scoop up several pastries.

"Best not let the Consul catch you," he says, but he's still smiling. I depart quickly, eating as I join the throng re-entering the city through the East Gate. Excellent pastries, it has to be said. The Consul's chef can really turn them out, even in adverse conditions.

With so many men heading south there's no chance of finding a landus. I'm about to start off on the long walk home when I catch sight of Praetor Samilius's official carriage parked just inside the city gates. Praetor Samilius is head of the Civil Guard. I've been trying for two weeks to make an appointment to see him at the Abode of Justice. I'm quite certain the Praetor would have some interesting things to tell me regarding Lodius's arrest, but, in line with every other official in Turai, he has been unwilling to see me.

"It's your unlucky day, Samilius," I mutter. "When Thraxas wants to see you, you get seen, one way or another."

I can hear voices inside the wagon as I reach for the door handle. I'm well aware that the Praetor is going to be furious when I barge unannounced into his carriage and start interrogating him, but I'm so cold, fed up and frustrated at recent events that I'll welcome a confrontation with authority. I wrench open the door and haul myself in.

"Don't bother protesting, Samilius. I've got some questions for you and you're going to answer them whether you like it or not. Resistance is futile—"

I stop. Inside the carriage—a luxurious eight-seater—there doesn't seem to be any sign of a Praetor. No Prefects or Senators either. Not a single high-ranking official, in fact. Just Makri, Morixa, Hanama, Lisutaris and four other women huddled over some scrolls and a basket of food.

"What the—?"

"Thraxas!" exclaims Makri. "What are you doing here?"

"How dare you disturb us in this manner!" says Lisutaris.

"He keeps doing this!" says Makri, agitated. "Every time I get my reading group going he bursts in and interrupts us."

Lisutaris regards me with a quite frigid stare.

"Do you have some objection to Makri's tutoring the women of Turai?"

"Tutoring? In the Praetor's carriage?"

"The Praetor and I were examining troop manoeuvres," explains Lisutaris. "I am looking after it for him while he is still on the field. We simply took advantage of the space while he was gone, not that it's any business of yours."

"So get the hell out," adds Makri.

"But you already know how to read," I say to Lisutaris, rather weakly.

"I have no objection to aiding Makri in her patriotic endeavours. Morixa, you've spelled *Samsarina* incorrectly again."

With the carriage already occupied by eight women and a large Investigator there's not a lot of room left inside. When someone opens the door behind me and tries to climb in there's a good deal of confusion accompanied by some raised voices.

"What is the meaning of this?" demands Praetor Samilius, forcing his way into his carriage. "Who are all these people?"

"All right, that's enough for today," says Makri, and leaves briskly by the other door. She's swiftly followed out of the carriage by six women, leaving me and Lisutaris facing an angry Praetor.

"Were the troop manoeuvres satisfactory?" enquires Lisutaris.

"Never mind that," replies Samilius. "Who were all those people?"

"Some guests of mine," answers Lisutaris smoothly. "I

took the liberty of showing them your official carriage. They were most impressed by the upholstery. It does you great credit."

"They said that?"

"Certainly. Most impressive."

The Praetor seems pleased. He nods, then looks at me.

"Is he one of your guests?"

"No," says Lisutaris. "I really don't know why he's here."

By now I'm no longer in the same belligerent mood I was when I hoisted myself into the carriage. Makri and her damned reading group has completely taken the wind out of my sails. When I tell the Praetor I'm here to ask a few questions it comes out in a very awkward manner, far removed from the merciless interrogation I had in mind. The Praetor informs me that I've got three seconds to get the hell out of his official carriage before he instructs his guards to haul me off to a cell at the Abode of Justice. I look to Lisutaris for support.

"We do have important war business to discuss," says the Mistress of the Sky.

I give up. My taste for interrogating has vanished. I get the hell out of the carriage. As I take the long walk through the still-falling snow back to the Avenging Axe I rehearse a few harsh words to say to Makri. The woman's craziness has now reached new heights and has started to severely interfere with my work. I can't believe her reading group had the audacity to invade the official carriage of Praetor Samilius. It's among the most uncivilised acts I've ever heard of.

I march through the doors and head straight for the bar.

Or what I believe is the bar. It's hard to tell. It appears to be covered with flowers. I'm puzzled. Up till now, Gurd has never been big on floral decorations. He's usually stuck with a more manly motif. A few axes on the wall, that sort of thing.

Makri appears.

"What's this?" I demand.

"Toraggax, mainly."

"What?"

"Toraggax. Viriggax's nephew. He brought me flowers. To apologise for his uncle ruining the bunch Horm sent me."

"But you didn't want the bunch from Horm."

"That doesn't mean anyone was free to destroy it," says Makri. "Anyway, I thought it was a nice gesture."

"This is starting to make me ill."

Makri shrugs.

"How were the manoeuvres?"

"Never mind how the manoeuvres were. What's the idea of infesting Samilius's carriage when I wanted to talk to him?"

"Reading group," says Makri, as if that explains everything.

"But why there?"

"Lisutaris invited us in."

"I mean why that part of the city?"

"It was convenient. Morixa had food to sell at the troop manoeuvres."

"This all sounds very strange. Why were there Senators' wives there?"

"You think I shouldn't teach Senators' wives?"

"I think you should teach in a place where I'm not investigating."

"Is that right?" says Makri. "You've already tried to chase us out of Twelve Seas. Is there anywhere you'd approve of? Maybe I should take the group to Samsarina?"

"An excellent idea."

I'd prolong the argument but find myself in urgent need of a beer, so I let it drop. Makri hands over a tankard. I drink it in one and take a swift refill.

"So how were the manoeuvres? Is the army in good shape?"

I shake my head.

"The phrase 'ignominious defeat' springs to mind."

"That bad?"

"Terrible. Phalanx number seven couldn't manoeuvre its way along Quintessence Street. Though we weren't quite as bad as phalanx number eight, who managed to crash into the Stadium Superbius. At least the mercenaries in the stadium had a good laugh. More beer. It's been a bad day. And how is a man supposed to enjoy his beer when he can't see over the bar for flowers? How many bunches are there? What did Toraggax do, loot the city?"

Makri leans over the bar to whisper.

"I think he's sweet on me."

"Right. So he's an imbecile," I grunt. "Inbred in his northern village, I expect."

"Everyone's inbred according to you," says Makri. "Senators. Northern Barbarians. The entire population of Simnia."

"Damn right they are. I wouldn't worry about Toraggax.

When his uncle Viriggax finds out his nephew's been prancing round Twelve Seas buying flowers he'll soon sort him out."

"Viriggax also brought a small bunch."

I stare at Makri.

"You're lying."

"No I'm not."

Maybe Tanrose is right. Perhaps times are changing. But I still find it hard to believe that old Viriggax, hardened mercenary, survivor of a hundred battles and feared all over the world, has been wandering around Twelve Seas looking for winter blooms. It defies common sense. Suddenly in a worse mood than ever, I take my beer upstairs, where I find that my office is freezing. I get out my grimoire, and make a determined effort to relearn the spell for lighting a fire.

CHAPTER TWELVE

Next day I take in a large breakfast. I'm going to need my strength because I'm about to visit Rittius. Rittius and I have a long history, all of it bad. I'm still far from certain that he isn't behind the charge of cowardice that's still hanging over me.

As head of Palace Security, Rittius has been largely responsible for investigating the death of Galwinius, because the murder happened inside the Palace grounds. Praetor Samilius, head of the Civil Guards, has also been investigating. Probably this has led to some tensions and it might even have hindered the investigation. Palace Security and the Civil Guards never like working together.

It's taken me a lot of effort to get this interview, and I'm not sure why. Officialdom in Turai has been closing its doors to me but I wasn't expecting Rittius to go along with officialdom so readily on this one, because Rittius is a supporter of the Populares, as led by Senator Lodius. I might have expected him to lend some help to a man who was investigating on behalf of his own party leader.

Tanrose is in good spirits as she ladles food on to my plate. With a man like myself as a customer, she always feels appreciated. I'm not certain how things stand between her and Gurd but at least they haven't been arguing. With so many mercenaries needing service, they're too busy to do much else except hand over the food and drink. Gurd is looking at his most profitable winter season ever. He'll be well set up for the next year or two, unless we all die in battle and the city is burnt to the ground.

"It's bad," I say, in between mouthfuls of bread. Tanrose bakes bread with herbs and olives. It's a fine product.

"What, your investigation?"

"No, it's bad the way everyone keeps giving Makri flowers. I mean, what's got into them all? I never saw a bunch of flowers from one year to the next in this place and now a man can't move without bumping into a vase of winter blooms. It's not as if the crazed axewoman even likes them all that much. She's just pleased when anyone gives her a present."

"So what's wrong with that?" asks Tanrose.

"What's wrong with it is that now everyone's started doing it, it won't work for me any more. You know it was your suggestion in the first place that I smoothed things out with a bunch of flowers when Makri was annoyed for some trivial reason—"

"Like when you called her a pointy-eared Orc freak?"

"That sort of thing. I still don't see why she was so upset. It's a reasonably accurate description. And I have to admit your suggestion worked well. But now she's getting spoiled. If the whole of Twelve Seas keeps marching into the Avenging Axe with flowers, where does that leave me? Next time she's upset at some imagined slight she'll get mad and stay mad and make my life hell."

"It's not the whole of Twelve Seas, Thraxas. Just an Orc lord from the wastelands and some mercenaries from the north."

"But where will it all end? It was bad enough with Horm the Dead playing the lovesick suitor. Now this idiot nephew of Viriggax is joining in."

"I wouldn't say he was an idiot nephew," says Tanrose. "Maybe not as sharp as an Elf's ear, but smart enough. Good-looking too. A lot of golden hair, and muscular."

"Spare me the eulogy. He's obviously a man of limited intelligence or he wouldn't be wasting his time with flowers. The city is doomed. We need fighting men to protect us, not some effeminate youth whose jaw goes slack at the first sight of a chainmail bikini."

Tanrose smiles.

"I suppose the bikini helps. But there's more to it than that. People just seem to take to her. Maybe you should join in," she suggests.

"What do you mean?"

"Bring Makri flowers."

"But we're not arguing just now."

"Well, just bring them as a present."

I stare at Tanrose.

"As a present? For no reason? Why?"

"As a nice gesture to a friend?"

"A nice gesture to a friend? You haven't noticed I'm a large, bad-tempered Investigator who isn't given to nice gestures?"

"I noticed. Maybe it's time you changed your ways."

I shudder.

"Just hand over another bowl of stew, Tanrose. I stopped making nice gestures when my wife left."

"You never made a single nice gesture in all the time she was here."

"Is there some problem with the stew? Can a man get any food around here?"

Tanrose ladles more stew into my bowl. Not desiring any more personal advice, I take it over to a table in front of the fire and consider what to say to Rittius. I've no leads and no inspiration. The deeper I get into the case the worse it looks for Lodius. I've done a fair amount of digging into the matter of the forged will, and as far as I can see, Prefect Galwinius had a case. It's quite possible that Senator Lodius defrauded him. I've asked a lawyer to look at the papers and give me his expert opinion but I'm not optimistic about the result. If Lodius really was caught out by Galwinius attempting to defraud the Prefect, he had every reason to kill him. The meeting of the Lesser War Council wasn't the greatest time to do it, but maybe he just saw an opportunity and took it.

Once more I wish that I wasn't involved. Too late now. There's nothing for it but to place a warming spell on my cloak and hunt for some answers. And if the answers don't come out the way I want, tip off Lodius and advise him to flee the city. After praying in his temple, I figure I owe him

that much, or owe it to his wife at least. As I'm leaving the
Avenging Axe I again run into Hanama.

"Come to brush up on your reading skills?"

Hanama strides past me without replying. Assassins are
never great with small talk.

The interview with Rittius is exactly as unpleasant as I'd
anticipated. Sensing that I'm stuck with a losing hand, the
head of Palace Security wastes no opportunity to rub it in.

"Please, ask me anything you wish," he says. "I'm eager
to co-operate. Seeing you struggle hopelessly to clear the
name of a guilty man is reward in itself."

"Lodius is not a guilty man."

"And on what do you base that fine conclusion? Not on
the evidence, certainly. On your intuition perhaps? I
remember you were always keen on that during your brief
sojourn at Palace Security."

He smiles mockingly.

"And now you're in a tavern in Twelve Seas, scrabbling
round for a few gurans to pay the rent. Yes, a man can go
a long way with intuition like that."

"Does the state have any direct evidence that Lodius
had carasin on him at the meeting?"

"He is the only importer of the substance into the city."

"Did you check out the other people at the meeting?
Did you get a Sorcerer to take a look at them? A Sorcerer
might have been able to detect traces of poison if it was
brought there by someone else."

"Quite unnecessary," says Rittius. "There is clear proof
of the Senator's guilt."

"Have you checked out who else might benefit from
Galwinius's death?"

"There are no other strong suspects."

"You really haven't investigated a hell of a lot, have you?" Rittius leans forward.

"Have you? Have you looked into the matter of the forged will?"

"I'm working on it."

"Then unless you're even more incompetent than I remember, you'll know by now that Senator Lodius had indeed defrauded Prefect Galwinius of a great sum of money. The Prefect was taking the matter to court and would have won the case. The only thing that could have stopped the prosecution and the subsequent disgrace of Lodius was the death of Galwinius."

This is true. Under Turanian law, only the injured party can sue in the matter of a forged will. With Galwinius out the way, Lodius is in the clear.

"What stronger motive could you wish for?"

"A strong motive is not evidence."

"Nothing is evidence to an Investigator like you unless he wishes it to be."

I'm swallowing Rittius's insults. I'm not enjoying it.

"I don't see why you're so keen on the prosecution, Rittius. After all, you're a supporter of Lodius's party."

"I have a job to do for this city," says Rittius. "Personal considerations don't enter into it. Particularly when the nation is in danger."

It's puzzling. I wasn't expecting Rittius to have fallen so completely in line with the Consul on this one. Rittius has been Deputy Consul in his time, and as head of Palace Security he's still a very important politician in Turai. Up till now he's been a firm supporter of the Populares. I can't believe he's decided to desert his political master merely because he thinks he's guilty of murder. What does Rittius care if a man is guilty of murder? Absolutely nothing, to my certain knowledge. It's not as if he's an honest man, or anything like it.

I question him some more but I'm not getting anything. Nothing useful anyway. I plug away at the notion of who else might have had a motive for killing Prefect Galwinius.

"The Society of Friends were annoyed when he closed down their establishments."

"We have good intelligence concerning that group. They didn't do it."

"Government intelligence on organised crime isn't usually that good. Mainly because the criminals bribe the government. And if the Society of Friends aren't behind it, the Prefect had other enemies. The Association of Gentlewomen, for instance."

Rittius laughs.

"You can't be serious. That collection of harlots likes to make a lot of noise but they're not murderers."

I suppose not. Though I wonder if Rittius is fully aware of just how many of Turai's most powerful women support the association. Lisutaris does, for sure, and Melus the Fair. All the way through society, from the richest matron to the poorest barmaid—Makri, for instance—the Association of Gentlewomen have a lot of tacit support. I'm sure that Hanama has had some involvement with the group, and with an assassin like her on your side, any murder would be theoretically possible. But I don't really believe it myself. Killing Galwinius wouldn't have advanced their cause. The Prefect's death hasn't set Herminis free.

Unlike the forging of a will, which is a civil matter between the parties involved, murder is prosecuted by the state. Galwinius's successor as Prefect will take over the case. Unless the Association has somehow arranged things so that the next Prefect might pardon her? Not completely impossible, given Lisutaris's power and influence. I file it away for future consideration.

"What about the war? Have the Civil Guards considered that angle? The Prefect of Thamlin handles a lot of sensitive information. Maybe he got news that someone was charging the state treasury too much for supplying weapons."

"This is all pointless speculation."

"A man's life is worth a little speculation."

Rittius draws his toga around him and rises to his feet. "Thraxas. I'll go this far. Senator Lodius deserves a fair trial. The evidence has to be investigated. It's a hopeless task but he has the right to a defence. Maybe you're the man for the job. You can get things done when you want. Good luck with the investigation. But we both know it's hopeless."

And with that Rittius walks out of the room. I stare at the floor for a while. Then I stare at my boots. They're in a bad state. I could do with a new pair. I'll have to attend to it before the Orcs attack. I stare at the wall. Some nice artwork here, a good Elvish tapestry. I head south slowly, drawing my magic warm cloak around me to protect me from the chilling wind. After a while I stop and stare at a wall. It's a blank wall. Nothing of interest at all. Two children, well wrapped up against the cold, hurry by in the company of a governess. They're shouting happily to each other. Unaware of the imminent attack, maybe, or too young to care. I stare at the wall for a while more. There's something seriously wrong here. Rittius came close to paying me a compliment. He said I might be the man for the job. I'm familiar with his mocking humour. I don't think he was trying to be humorous. I walk on, my eyes on the ground. If Rittius is paying me a compliment, there's definitely something wrong. I just don't know what.

I walk a long way down Moon and Stars Boulevard, over the river and into Pashish. When I reach St. Rominius's Lane I take it as the shortest route to the Avenging Axe. Last summer I met a unicorn in this alley. I ran after it but it disappeared. It was a strange summer. When I turn the corner three men with swords step out in front of me. They raise their weapons.

I'm still carrying my sleep spell; I never go on a case without it. I intone the arcane words and they fall down in a heap. Suckers. They should have known better. There's a noise behind me. I spin round. Four men with swords are approaching fast. Two more appear in front of me, stepping over the unconscious bodies of their comrades. I guess they did know better. Sent in a couple of decoys to draw out my magic. Now it's out of my mind, I can't use it again till I re-learn it. It's the only spell I was carrying. These days I find carrying any more too much of a mental strain. I put my back to the wall. The six men approach in a semicircle, blades in hand. Things are starting to look bleak.

My sword is in my right hand and my dagger in my left. Street toughs in Turai generally aren't experts with their weapons. Even so, faced by six men with nowhere to retreat I'm unlikely to survive. Someone is going to get their sword through my guard.

"One step closer and I'll roast you with a spell," I say.

My assailants' eyes flicker towards their two comrades lying on the frozen dirt. They're wondering if I could really do it. One of them—large, red-haired, seems to be their leader—sneers at me.

"We heard you only carry one spell these days, Investigator."

With that he urges his men forward and I'm immediately engulfed in a furious battle for survival. I kill the man on my right with a well-placed thrust to the throat and fend off both blades that flicker towards me from my left. The man directly ahead of me lunges in but I sidestep sharply and his blade sinks into the soft plaster of the old alleyway wall. Before he can retrieve it I slash at his arm and he goes down howling. I'm working my defence furiously, keeping off four blades. In my younger days I was a champion sword fighter and since then I've had a lot of experience. Enough experience to know that these men are not rank amateurs. I can't defeat them all. I slash at the groin of one opponent, missing but forcing him back. He nudges into his companion and in the tiny fraction of a second he's distracted I stick my sword in his chest. He's wearing a thick leather breastplate and it doesn't penetrate. I wrench my sword free to parry the next blade that comes at me, simultaneously parrying another sword with my dagger. In doing so I leave my left shoulder exposed and suffer a painful cut. Blood seeps down my tunic. I can't keep this up. I'll tire long before they do. Worse, the two victims of my sleep spell are starting to come round.

Though I've sent three of my attackers to the ground I'm still faced with five men.

Suddenly there's a roar like an angry dragon from further down the alley. I recognise that roar. Once you've heard Viriggax going into battle, you don't forget the sound. My five assailants find themselves attacked from behind by one of the largest axes in the western world. One of them collapses, his head nearly hewn from his body, and another falls to the axe almost immediately after. I take advantage of their confusion to ram my dagger into the back of yet another and he collapses at my feet. The remaining assailants, including the man with red hair, finding the odds not so much to their liking, run for their lives. They disappear down Saint Rominius's Lane at a rate I could never match, even if I wasn't bleeding and gasping for breath.

Viriggax watches them go, then glances down at the bodies on the ground.

"Good to see you haven't forgotten how to fight, Thraxas," he roars. He peers at my wound. "A bit of a scratch. Nothing to worry about. Time to celebrate victory!"

Viriggax thumps me heartily on the back and we walk down to Quintessence Street. I don't thank him for his help. If I did I know he'd be insulted, almost as if I'd implied there was some possibility of him not coming to my aid. When Viriggax comes upon a comrade in trouble, he doesn't need to be asked for help and he doesn't expect to be thanked.

At the Avenging Axe Tanrose fusses over my wound. Not wishing to appear weak in front of the mercenaries I tell her it's nothing, but I'm not displeased when she sends for Chiaraxi, the local healer. Chiaraxi dresses the wound and tell me I'll live, unless I'm foolish enough to make a habit of taking on eight opponents at once.

I shrug, making light of the affair.

"I was cursing Viriggax for butting in and spoiling things," I say, lifting a jar of ale to my lips. "If he'd had any sense he'd have stayed out of it. It's not like eight attackers were going to bother me."

Viriggax laughs.

"Only eight? I thought there were more, else I'd have left you to it!"

CHAPTER THIRTEEN

A few beers later it's time to head up to my office. The fight took it out of me and I could do with some sleep. Dandelion is collecting tankards from the tables.

"I heard some people in your office," she says.

Viriggax glances over.

"Are you expecting anyone?"

I shake my head.

Viriggax rises to his feet and motions to a few of his men. I don't protest. After being assaulted by eight armed thugs I don't mind an escort. If anyone is lying in wait for me they're in for an unpleasant shock.

"I thought you might have gone soft in the city, Thraxas. But I see you still get in plenty of trouble!"

I draw my sword as I put my ear to my office door. Inside I can hear faint noises. Dandelion was right. Uninvited visitors. I kick the door open and charge into the room, sword raised. Viriggax and his men follow with their axes aloft, ready to meet any danger. In my time as an Investigator I've confronted assassins, dragons and the worst scum the streets have to offer, so I'm prepared for anything. Even so, I have to admit I'm surprised to find that my office is full of women, who've tidied the place up and put a nice rug on the floor. There are flowers on the windowsill and sweet-smelling incense hangs in the air. A pot of deat, a herbal drink, is brewing gently in front of the fire.

"Thraxas," says Makri, rising from the couch. "What are you doing here? You're meant to be investigating."

I'm speechless. I look round at the twelve or so women gathered here. The powerful Sorcerers Lisutaris, Mistress of the Sky, and Melus the Fair sit next to Ginixa, manager of the local public baths, and Morixa, the young baker. Two women in the robes of the senatorial class, one grey-haired and the other much younger, are perched on the arms of a chair. Next to them are a few other market workers and another woman who I think I've seen driving a wagon down by the docks. Sitting in the far corner is Hanama, Assassin.

I regain my voice.

"What the hell is going on here?"

"We're having a meeting," says Makri.

I find myself blinking in bewilderment.

"A meeting?"

Viriggax lowers his axe and gives me an odd look.

"You have women's meetings in your room?"

"No!"

"I'm sorry about this," says Makri, to her companions. "I thought we wouldn't be disturbed."

"It's all right," replies Lisutaris. "I'm sure Thraxas won't mind leaving us in peace for a little longer."

I glare at the head of the Sorcerers Guild.

"Is that so? Well, I'm not sure about that at all. Since when did my office become a meeting place for . . . for . . ." I struggle to find the word. "For women," I conclude, lamely. "And what are you doing here anyway?"

"Reading group."

"Reading group? Are you telling me that Melus the Fair doesn't know how to read?"

"We were discussing ways of broadening the programme," says Melus. "Many women around the Stadium Superbius wish to join."

"Then go to the stadium and recruit them," I counter.

"We did," says Lisutaris. "But you interrupted us in Samilius's carriage."

"I still don't see why you're all gathering in Twelve Seas. What is it about my office that's so attractive?"

"I invited them to my room," explains Makri. "But it was too small."

"You didn't think of that earlier?"

"Could these people leave and let us go about our business?" says the wagon driver.

Throughout all this I'm distracted by the amused looks on the faces of Viriggax's mercenaries, who, I can tell, are rapidly revising their opinion of Thraxas, legendary warrior. Trying to prevent my status from plummeting further, I demand that everyone leaves.

"Really, Thraxas," drawls Lisutaris, her voice suggesting that she's well up on her intake of thazis. "Didn't you invade my house recently? Uninvited, as I recall. And don't you frequent the Stadium, as protected by my good friend Melus?"

"You eat at my bakery every day," says Morixa.

"And he sometimes visits Ginixa's public baths," adds Makri, helpfully. "Maybe not that often."

"So really, you can lend us your office for a little while longer."

"But it's my office! It's not a meeting place for—" I break off before finishing the sentence, too ashamed to pronounce the words "Association of Gentlewomen" in front of Viriggax.

"This wouldn't have happened if Makri had a bigger room," points out Lisutaris.

"Don't you think she should have a larger living space?" says Ginixa.

"Well, possibly, but—that's not the point! The point is—"

"I have to work long shifts every day serving beer in a chainmail bikini and then study at college in my spare time," says Makri, pathetically. Everyone looks sympathetically at her before turning their gazes accusingly on me.

"You make her wear a chainmail bikini?" says one of the Senator's wives, sounding quite outraged.

"She doesn't have to wear anything!"

There's a shocked intake of breath from the assembled harridans.

"You would prefer her to be naked?" asks Melus, incredulously.

"That's not what I meant—"

"Things are worse than we feared," says the Senator's

wife. "Even from a man like this I did not expect to hear such a thing."

Viriggax, probably imagining he's making a quiet comment to his comrades, loudly informs the entire room that he does recall that "the old dog Thraxas was always keen on the dancing girls."

"Paid a lot of money to that red-haired wench down in Juval. I remember the way she used to take off—"

I interrupt him hastily.

"Could we stick to the subject? My office has been invaded by Sorcerers, Assassins, and assorted women from hell and I'd like it back. Makri, get rid of these people. And also the rug. Why is there a new rug?"

"I just made the place look a bit better."

"You used my flowers," says a large young mercenary, Toraggax, Viriggax's nephew.

"They lend a nice splash of colour," says Makri.

Toraggax looks pleased.

"I could bring more."

"Everybody get out of my office!" I roar.

"My poor Makri," says Lisutaris, and pats her on the arm. "I never fully appreciated how unpleasant your life here must be."

Before I can fire off an angry retort there's a knock on my outside door. I march over and haul it open, expecting it to be some latecomer to the meeting who I fully intend to send away with a stinging reminder that this is a private place of work, not a gathering point for the city's female malcontents. Unfortunately I find Captain Rallee on the doorstep.

"I need to talk to—" he begins, then halts as he catches sight of the assortment of women in my office.

"What's going on here?"

I'm stuck for a good reply. The Captain steps past me into my office.

"Association of Gentlewomen? Here?"

Captain Rallee sounds very suspicious. The association is a legal body but not one that's popular with the city authorities. He turns towards Lisutaris.

"What's this about?"

"It does not concern you, Captain Rallee."

"This is my beat. Everything that goes on here concerns me."

"No," repeats Lisutaris. "It does not concern you."

Lisutaris is using a spell. It's probably not noticeable to anyone else except Melus the Fair, but with my sorcerous background I can sense it. Captain Rallee appears momentarily confused.

"You're right. It doesn't concern me."

"And you will forget all about it," says Lisutaris.

"I'll forget all about it," repeats the Captain.

He withdraws, closing the door behind him.

"Well that's fantastic," I growl. "Now you've used sorcery on a Captain of the Civil Guards right here in my office. That's illegal. If the authorities hear about this they'll be down on me like a bad spell."

"But they won't get to hear of it," says Lisutaris.

"Don't try using a spell on me."

"I wouldn't dream of it," says Lisutaris. "After all, we are using your office. But we would appreciate it if you would keep this quiet, and leave us alone for a little while longer."

"That sounds like a good idea," says Viriggax, in an unusually soft voice. He leads his men out of the room.

"Did you use a spell on them?" I demand. "You can't just come into my office and start throwing spells around."

"Thraxas," says Makri. "Could you just stop asking questions and get the hell out of here? I've saved your damned life enough times that you can do me one small favour."

"One small favour? I can't move in this city without trampling over you and your friends. How many times is this going to happen?"

"Even the northern mercenaries treat her better," says the wagon driver to Hanama. "They brought her flowers."

"He has a very violent temper," replies Hanama. "Any act of kindness would be quite beyond him."

I find myself again confronted by twelve sets of accusing eyes. Suddenly feeling very isolated, I back towards the inner door.

"Fine. But you haven't heard the last of this. And stay away from my klee."

"We already drank it," says Makri, who never knows when it's a good time not to tell the truth.

"We'll buy you another bottle," adds Melus the Fair.

An angry rejoinder springs readily to mind. But somehow, with so many women staring at me, my spirit seems to quail. There's something unnerving about it. Maybe it's the new rug. It's very disconcerting. I withdraw with what dignity I can muster and head downstairs for the bar.

Viriggax and his men are drinking heartily in the corner. They have no memory of the incident. Lisutaris has erased it. I march angrily to the bar, glare at Dandelion and in my roughest voice demand a beer. Dandelion, fool

that she is, isn't aware that I'm angry and hands it over
with a smile. Realising there's no point in trying to annoy
her, I move along the bar to where Tanrose is ladling out
the stew.

"Tanrose, do I look like a man with progressive political
views?"

"No," replies Tanrose. "You don't."

"Not the sort of man to encourage new ways of thinking in western society?"

"Definitely not."

"I didn't think so. So why does Makri think it's okay to
bring her foul Association of Gentlewomen friends into
my office? Don't they have houses of their own?"

"It's always awkward for them to find a meeting place,"
says Tanrose. "The Senators don't like it, Morixa's staff at
the bakery get in the way, that sort of thing."

"You seem to know a lot about it."

Tanrose shrugs.

"I expect Makri's room was just the most convenient
place they could find in a hurry."

"They're not in Makri's room. They're in my office."

"Well, Makri's room is very small," points out Tanrose.
"I suppose they needed more space."

I seem to have been in this conversation before.
Realising that the city is descending into pre-war madness
and there's probably nothing I can do about it except go
down fighting, I take my beer to a table in front of the fire
and look forward to the arrival of the Orcs. At least a man
knows where he is when the dragons are swooping from
the skies.

Outside the temperature is falling. Soon the whole city

will be as cold as the Ice Queen's grave. At least the grim weather will suppress the panic that's been simmering since news of the invasion broke. Come the first day of spring, there will be a long trail of fainthearted citizens leaving the city by the Western Gate, but in the meantime we're all stuck here and have to make the best of it. Making the best of it won't be easy, because there are bound to be shortages. Supplies are always scarce in winter and this year it will be far harder because the population, fearing the worst from the war, have bought up everything that can be bought and the warehouses are empty. Stockpiling supplies is standard practice in war, no matter how the authorities try to prevent it.

Further military drill has been scheduled but I'm not certain how much of it will take place, given the bad weather. We'll have to try. At least the King had the foresight to hire a good number of mercenaries, most of them reliable troops like Viriggax. They won't go down without a fight. And then there're our Sorcerers, something with which Turai has always been well supplied. It's unfortunate that we've lost a few powerful members of the Guild in recent years—Tas of the Eastern Lightning would have been a good man to have on the battlefield, but he handed in his toga a couple of years ago—but we still have more than our share.

Weighing things up, I'd say it's going to be a close thing. Depends on what sort of army Prince Amrag brings over. Our Sorcerers should be able to give us plenty of advance warning about its size, but until we confront it we won't know how well disciplined it is. Equally, it depends on how our allies respond. Things still look reasonably good on this front. The Human armies are gathering and the Elves will be ready to sail with the first calm weather.

I wonder what Queen Direeva, ruler of the Southern Hills, will do. Probably remain tucked up safely in her kingdom. She's not a friend of the Orcs, but the Southern Hills is close to the Orcish Lands and she won't want to become embroiled in the war if she can avoid it. Who knows what's going to happen? We've beaten the Orcs before. I might yet survive into my forty-fourth year.

Which brings me back to my investigation. If I do survive the war I'm gong to be plenty annoyed if Lodius is hanged for a murder he didn't commit. I stare into the fire and mull over the case, trying to find some angle I haven't yet considered. I was there when the murder happened. I'm a trained observer, or meant to be. Have I missed anything? I reconstruct events in my mind, as I've done many times over the past weeks. Try as I might, nothing new springs to mind. If there was a vital clue, it passed me by. All I can remember is the excellence of the pastries on offer. Worth attending the meeting for. A vague thought of something unconnected to pastries floats by. I can't identify it. Why was Galwinius murdered right then? Why not later, when there were fewer people around? Surely that would have been safer. Those pastries were really excellent. Although, as I recall, one of them was slightly undercooked. There's something else I should be remembering. I try and clear my mind of all thoughts of pastries. There was a scroll. Is that right? I strain to remember. Galwinius had a scroll. And after the murder was committed I didn't see any scroll. Might that be significant? Maybe he just fell on top of it, though I don't think so. Possibly it just disappeared among the crowd in the confusion. I make a mental note to see if anyone can tell me anything about the scroll.

I get to wondering about the Society of Friends. As always, when that organisation is involved in some affair I'm investigating, I'm hampered by a lack of contacts. The Society works in the north of the city and that's not my territory. I can sometimes pick up information about them in Kushni, but I've no informant who can really be relied on. I could do with learning a little more about their recent activities. Captain Rallee might have heard something. I should visit the Captain, find out what he wanted from me before Lisutaris send him away confused and forgetful.

My magic warm cloak is in my room. I don't want to go upstairs while all those women are still there. Cursing them for making me venture out into the grim winter evening without the benefit of my cloak, I head out into Quintessence Street. The first people I bump into are Palax and Kaby, a young pair of buskers who earn their living by singing and performing acrobatics on street corners. Generally domiciled in a caravan behind the Avenging Axe, they've been out of the city for a while, plying their trade in foreign parts. They've now returned to spend the winter in Turai. A poor choice, given what's coming.

I used to be suspicious of the young couple, primarily because of their unheard-of sartorial outrages—Palax has parts of his hair dyed green, and Kaby has piercings through her lips and eyebrow, things which would cause any normal citizen to be stoned in the streets and maybe thrown from the city walls, but as travelling musicians, they seem to get away with it. These days I'm used to them, and greet them politely enough.

"Just made it back in time. The roads are almost impassable. We thought we were going to get stuck."

"You might wish you had, if you're still here in the spring."

I notice Kaby is carrying a bundle wrapped in paper.

"What's that?"

"Flowers," says Kaby.

"We brought them for Makri," says Palax.

"We know how much she likes them."

I bid them a stiff goodbye and depart along the frozen stretch of Quintessence Street. I'm really sick of this city. A man can't live an honest life here any more. The whole place is degenerate. If the Orcs burn the place down they'll be doing us all a favour.

There are few people about on Quintessence Street. I realise I'm not carrying my sleep spell or any other form of sorcerous protection. I'd have to look at the written spell in my grimoire to learn it again. Which of course would mean going to my office. Another reason to curse Makri and her friends. Only a few hours ago I was attacked in the street. For all I know, another band of assailants could be on their way at this moment. I wonder who they were and who sent them. If anyone in the city is feeling nervous because of my current investigation, they must imagine I've made a lot more progress than I actually have.

A voice from a doorway calls out my name. A ragged figure, shivering in the cold. It's Kerk. An informer of mine, or used to be. These days he's so deep in his dwa addiction he's not much use for anything, except begging.

"I've got something for you," he says, eagerly.

"What?"

Kerk holds out his hand for money.

"It's a long time since you gave me any useful information."

Kerk is in a bad way. He's little more than skin and bones. Doesn't look like he's eaten for weeks. Whatever small amounts of money he can raise are spent on dwa. From the look of him I'd say he was unlikely to make it through the winter. I take out a few coins and hand them over, more from memory of service he's given me in the past than any expectation that he might know anything useful.

"So what have you got?"

"You're investigating Galwinius, right?"

"Right."

"The same day that Galwinius was murdered, the Guards found another body in Thamlin. Oraxin. He was a dwa dealer. Small time."

"So?"

"Oraxin did some work for Galwinius."

"What sort of work?"

"Informing."

According to Kerk, Oraxin enhanced his income by taking any useful information he came across to Prefect Galwinius. As a dealer in dwa, Oraxin might occasionally have learned something that would interest the Prefect.

"How did he die?"

"Stab wounds. They haven't arrested anyone."

I give Kerk another coin and walk off. Might be useful. An informant working for Galwinius, murdered on the same day. It could be connected. More likely Oraxin was murdered over dwa, a common fate for a small-time dealer.

At the Guards station the Captain is as pleased to see me as ever, which is to say, not at all. We go back a long way, the Captain and I. We fought together. And we worked together for a while, when I was employed by Palace Security and the Captain had a better job up town. Since I left the Palace and set up on my own, the Captain hasn't been so friendly. The Guards don't have a lot of time for private Investigators. And since the Captain was manoeuvred out of his comfy job and sent to pound the streets in Twelve Seas, he's not exactly been friendly with anyone. I sympathise with Rallee, more or less. He's an honest man in a city where it doesn't pay to be honest.

He's a large man, long fair hair tied back, still handsome in his black uniform, better preserved than me.

"How's life in the Guards?"

"Better than rowing a slave galley," growls the Captain. "What do you want?"

"I had a hunch you might want to see me."

Captain Rallee looks confused. Lisutaris's spell of bafflement has wiped a small part of his memory. For a day or two, he'll have a feeling that something happened, something he can't quite remember. After that he'll forget all about it. Lisutaris is a powerful woman, no doubt about it.

"I did want to see you, now you mention it. About a pile of bodies in Saint Rominius's Lane. Not far from the Avenging Axe. You know anything about it?"

"Nothing at all. Probably some dwa-related violence."

It might have been wiser to tell the Captain about the

attack, but it just comes naturally to deny everything to the Guards. Unusually, the Captain lets it pass without probing further.

"Dwa-related violence? Maybe. Wasn't anyone we recognised from the trade, though. Not that I care much right now. If you've got some gang on your tail you can sort it out yourself. I'm busy with more important things."

"Like what?"

"Like espionage. We got word there's some spying going on in the city. All guards to be on the lookout for strangers, unexplained events, that sort of thing. I just wanted to let you know. You're still a Tribune for a few more weeks—God help the city—so I had to notify you. But if you come across anything strange, make sure you report it to me."

I raise an eyebrow.

"Strange things happen to me all the time, Captain. But I generally don't go running to the Civil Guards."

"Forget the attitude," snaps the Captain. "This is war, not one of your petty cases. If you get wind of anything strange going on, you tell me about it. Or Prefect Drinius, if you prefer. Though I doubt he'll be that keen on meeting you, seeing as you're trying to protect the man who murdered his fellow Prefect."

"Which brings me nicely to the reason for my visit, Captain. I can't get an angle on the case."

"And?"

"And I was wondering what you might have heard."

The Captain stares at me for a long time.

"I am talking to Thraxas the Investigator, right?"

"I believe so."

"Would that be the same Thraxas who sent me to sleep with a spell last summer?" he demands.

"I was engaged in vital government work, Captain. You know they exonerated me."

"I know Lisutaris, Mistress of the Sky, got the charges dropped," says the Captain. "I didn't like it then and I don't like it now. I gave up helping you a long time ago, Thraxas. Take a walk."

CHAPTER FOURTEEN

My office desk is an old piece of furniture, stained almost black with beer, smoke and the sweat of vain endeavour. It's large and ugly. Not easy on the eye. Something that could also be said about me. I'm sitting in front of said desk staring at a list of names. Names of people I've asked about the scroll Galwinius was carrying when he died. Twenty people or so, mostly Senators and government officials. Tracking them down and questioning them hasn't been easy. Nor has it been productive. Most of them don't even remember that Galwinius was carrying anything. Or so they claim. Even those Senators who were previously supporters of Lodius seem to be uncooperative. Rittius isn't the only one deserting his leader. It is a good time for Consul Kalius to press his attack against Senator Lodius. With the war approaching, no one wants to be seen as disloyal.

Yesterday I made a report to Lodius's wife. She had the

good grace to thank me for all the work I've done on her husband's behalf. I had the honesty to tell her it's all been for nothing, so far. Before I left I tried to offer some encouragement and she pretended to be encouraged. As for Lodius himself, he refuses to see me. I should walk away from the case. There's no disgrace in deserting a client who doesn't want you working for him. I might have quit if his wife hadn't sent a servant to the kitchen to bring me a tray of food. Damn the woman and her good manners.

I tried to consult Astrath Triple Moon again but the Sorcerer isn't at home. He's been recalled to the Sorcerers Guild for the duration of the war. Astrath is consequently as happy as an Elf in a tree. I made enquiries about Oraxin. There's nothing to indicate that his death was connected with the fate of Galwinius. He did work as an informer for the Prefect and he'd sold information about the dwa trade to the Prefect's office. No one was much surprised when they learned that he'd been murdered. The Society of Friends are very active in the dwa trade and not keen on informers. Oraxin didn't leave any friends or family grieving for him. Just a bare room, a dwa pipe and a landlord looking for his rent. Standard fate of the small-time dwa dealer.

Tomorrow morning I'm due to visit Domasius, a lawyer I've hired to give a judgement on the matter of the forged will. I'm hoping that his expert knowledge might give me a new lead. If that fails, I don't know what else I'll do.

Makri walks uninvited into my office. I eye her with annoyance. It's amazing quite how offensive this woman is. She paints her toenails gold like a Simnian whore. That alone should be enough to separate her from all decent society. Add in the pierced nose, the outlandishly long thick hair, the Orcish blood and the men's clothes and we're talking about a person who shouldn't be allowed to pollute a Human city. Consul Kalius is far too lax in the matter of permitting aliens to live in Turai. Time was we didn't let people like Makri in.

"Still upset about the meeting?" she says, brightly.

"Upset? About the meeting of women in my office which reduced me in the eyes of Viriggax's mercenaries to the status of nursemaid?"

"Only for a little while," points out Makri. "Lisutaris wiped their memories,"

"Well that makes everything all right. Now, if you'll excuse me, I'm busy doing men's work. Go away and serve beer."

"I have news," says Makri, eagerly.

I turn on my coldest stare.

"Unless that news involves you leaving the city on the next horse, I'm not interested."

"But I want to tell you," says Makri, sounding agitated.

"Tell it to your Association of Gentlewomen buddies. Anywhere you like as long as it's not in my office."

"You're not being fair. So I used your office without asking. What's so bad about that? It's tidier than it's ever been."

"I like it untidy."

"We brought you a new rug."

"I hate the rug. You see, Makri, it's the problem we always come up against. You've no idea of how to behave in civilised society."

"You're so obsessed with this civilisation thing," protests

Makri. "So what if I took over your damned office without asking? When I grew up in the gladiator slave pits, we didn't have appointment books. Anyway, did I have to make an appointment when I was saving your life from Horm the Dead? I didn't need an appointment when I was rescuing you—"

I hold up my hand.

"Enough. Whatever services you may have rendered in the past have been duly noted. But from now on, Thraxas Investigations can manage very well without you."

Makri stamps her foot in frustration, something I don't remember her ever doing before.

"I've got a job for the war!" she says. "I'm going to be in Lisutaris's bodyguard. I get to protect her from the Orcs!"

"Fascinating. In between attacks you'll be able to discuss the advancement of women's status in Turai. Now depart."

Makri looks extremely frustrated. She doesn't really know how to deal with sustained hostility, apart from by using violence. I make ready to defend myself, just in case. After a few seconds she turns sharply on her heel and marches out, slamming the door. I get back to my list. There must be someone else I should talk to.

Outside it's cold but the snow has stopped falling. I'm scheduled for phalanx practice later in the day. Another six hours stumbling around with a bunch of novices. The Turanian phalanx advances with a row of thirty-foot spears pointing forwards. It takes a lot of discipline to maintain a concentrated front. So far phalanx number seven has shown a marked lack of discipline. I give up on the list and go downstairs for a beer.

"Setting yourself up for practice?" asks Gurd, handing one over.

Gurd is also undergoing phalanx training, something he's not too happy about. As a resident alien in Turai he's obliged to join the army in times of crisis, which is fine with him, but he wasn't anticipating the chaos he'd be stepping into with his own company of novices. Though Gurd is more used to fighting in the less rigid formation of a mercenary company, he's been involved in his share of phalanx work in the past and he knows how it's done. Like me, he's appalled by the poor state of the troops among whom he now finds himself.

"They can't advance, they can't retreat and they can't go sideways. If my phalanx is called on to move more than eight feet in any direction, we're all done for."

"Me too. If the young guy behind me drops his spear on my shoulder one more time I swear I'm going to stick it down his throat."

"You remember the phalanx we were in down on the fringes of the Simian Desert?" asks Gurd. "Now that was a phalanx. Charged over hills and valleys without once breaking formation."

I nod. We did. The Unbreakables, they used to call us. Finest phalanx in the desert. Chased off an army three times our size with our superior manoeuvring.

"We could do with the Unbreakables right now," muses Gurd. "How well organised do you think the Orcs are going to be?"

"Probably not that well organised. Prince Amrag hasn't been war leader for long. He hasn't had time to drill them into shape. Probably they'll be a huge mass of Orcs without any formation, and a few phalanxes of trained troops. That's what they're usually like."

"Gives us an advantage then, if we can get our formations in order. The city should have been doing it long ago."

Gurd mentions that Makri is at present as mad as a mad dragon.

"What have you been doing to her?"

I explain the matter of the latest meeting which she held in my office. Gurd looks shocked.

"What do these women want to hold meetings for?"

"Because they're crazy. Like Hanama. She's an Assassin, for God's sake. Heavily rumoured to have killed the deputy head of the Honourable Association of Merchants only last month after his unfortunate dispute with the head of his Guild. Hardly the sort of woman you'd associate with progressive politics, yet there she is, drinking wine with Lisutaris and plotting the overthrow of society."

Gurd looks worried.

"Are they plotting the overthrow of society?"

"Who knows? Makri says its a reading group, but she's lying. Anything's possible."

"At least Tanrose doesn't have anything to do with them," says Gurd.

"Oh no? She lent them a rug."

"She lent them a rug? What for?"

"To make my office look nicer."

Gurd winces. It's all more serious than he realised.

"I'll talk to Makri," he says. "I can't have this sort of thing going on."

Gurd asks if I've discovered who was behind the attack on me in Saint Rominius's Lane.

"No idea. Haven't had time to look into it yet."

It shows what a sorry state I'm in. With the Lodius investigation and my military practice I haven't even had time to investigate a lethal assault on my own person.

"Maybe you're getting close to the culprit?"

"If I am, it's news to me."

Makri hurries by with a tray in her hand. The tray has six large flagons of ale on it and Makri carries it through the crowd without spilling a drop. Another of her talents. She takes it to Viriggax's table. Viriggax and his men roar with pleasure when Makri arrives, partly at the sight of the beer and partly at the sight of Makri. They shout out some crude comments about her figure and Makri insults them back, but good-humouredly. I notice that Toraggax doesn't join in with the banter but just thanks her politely for his beer. As if being good-mannered will have any impression on the mad warrior woman. The young mercenary is a fool. Makri picks up her tip, crams it into the fat purse she has slung around her neck and moves on to the next table. Outside, Quintessence Street is caked with ice, but inside the Avenging Axe it's hot from the fire and the press of bodies. Perspiration runs down Makri's neck. I find myself dabbing my brow with my sleeve.

"Business is good."

Gurd nods.

"I'll have a fair bit saved after this winter is over—"

He breaks off, looking at me in a now familiar manner. For once in my life I find myself frustrated with Gurd. How indecisive can a man who once charged a dragon be?

"Ask her to marry you, for God's sake. Or don't ask her. Just pick one."

"Which one?" says Gurd.

"How would I know? How much more can I do to demonstrate my complete lack of competence in this field?"

"I just need your opinion."

"I'm begging you not to ask me."

"I'm asking your advice as an old friend," says Gurd, and looks slightly hurt.

I shake my head.

"Then ask Tanrose to marry you. After all, we're quite likely to be dead before spring is over."

Gurd nods.

"That's true."

"So even if things go badly, it probably won't last too long. I mean, marriage is a big step, Gurd, but when we're all going to be slaughtered by the Orcs, it's not the end of the world. If I was a poetic man, I might have something to say about going off into the next life together."

Gurd slams his mighty palm on the table top.

"Yes!" he exclaims. "That is good! Off to the next life together!"

The image seems to have touched his Barbarian heart. He rises to his feet, drains the dregs of his ale, and marches off, strong, erect and barbaric, his grey ponytail swinging jauntily behind him. I drain my own flagon and head off to my office. Any more talk of romance and I'm liable to remember that my wife left me for a Sorcerer's apprentice many years ago. Mostly I try not to remember that.

As a consequence of fleeing the tavern some time

before I'd intended, I arrive early for phalanx practice and stand around on the cold field outside the city gates waiting for the others to arrive. I'm the first regular trooper there, and when Senator Marius sees me he congratulates me on my enthusiasm.

"Maybe you're not such a waste of time after all."

Senator Marius asks me how this phalanx compares to the others I've fought in.

"Badly."

He nods.

"I know. You'd think some of these young men had never held a long spear before. You're not a great soldier, Thraxas, and you're never going to be. But compared to the rest of them, you're not such a disaster. I'm promoting you to corporal."

I nod. It makes sense.

"Maybe we can get them into shape before the Orcs come," says the Senator.

"Maybe."

Neither of us sounds too convinced. By now the other recruits are arriving and the Senator moves off to confer with General Pomius on a hillock nearby.

So now I'm a corporal. Not that important a position. There are ten corporals in the five-hundred-man phalanx, subordinate to the five centurions, and our commander. But it's a position of some responsibility. It carries enough weight to make anyone regret it if they stick their spear in me again.

As we're forming up, I notice Praetor Capatius's phalanx moving off in front of us. The Praetor is one of Turai's richest men. He owns his own bank and plenty more besides. One of my recent cases brought me up against him and for a while I thought it was him that had levelled the charge of cowardice against me. Now I'm not sure. Professor Toarius, the head of Makri's college, also had it in for me, and the Professor is very well connected in aristocratic circles. It could have been him.

Wherever it originated, the person who actually brought the charge to court was Vedinax, a large and very thuggish individual in the employ of Capatius. I can see him striding along at the front of Capatius's phalanx. We were mercenaries together. He's a bad man in many ways, but a good soldier, which is going to be more important in the months to come.

Being a corporal doesn't make the phalanx practice any easier. We stumble around, shivering in the wind. When Senator Marius gives a command, half the men obey it while the others get it wrong. Strong abuse flows from the Senator to his centurions and from them to the corporals. I pass the abuse on to the men under me, not as vehemently as I might. I was never really officer material. There are some men around me so unsuited to being in the army that it seems almost a crime to abuse them. One man, thirty or so, small and skinny, only moved to Turai the year before last to take up a position at the Imperial Library. Now he finds himself with a thirty-foot spear in his hand and no real idea what to do with it. I try and point him in the right direction, genially at first, then more harshly as my patience wears thin. He's going to be beside me when the Orcs attack. I've some sympathy for him but I don't want to lose my life because of his incompetence.

My unit isn't the only one suffering from the unsuitability

of some of its members. In a nearby unit I actually see the head of the Leatherworkers Guild attempting to march in formation, and the head of the Leatherworkers Guild is famous for being the fattest man in Turai, with a girth so enormous that my not inconsiderable bulk pales in comparison. I'm surprised he can walk, let alone carry a spear. God knows what will happen if he's required to break into a run. To give him his due, at least he's here. As head of the guild, he could probably have pulled some strings to avoid military service. The same could be said for Samanatius, another person I am astonished to see wielding a spear. Samanatius is Turai's most prominent philosopher. A fraud, as far as I can see, though Makri holds him in high regard. Fraud or not, he could legitimately have avoided service due to his advanced age, yet here he is, marching along with a group of young men from the philosophers' academy he runs. I'd always assumed he would be some sort of pacifist, but Makri once informed me that he regards the military defence of the state against outside aggression as the duty of all citizens. It made me like him a little better.

At the end of practice I'm as cold as a frozen pixie and confidently looking forward to death the first time we're called into action. Senator Marius speaks to his centurions and corporals as the men drift away.

"Don't worry," he says, surprisingly cheerfully. "I've lashed worse men than these into shape."

"There are worse men than these?" I mutter.

We watch as a phalanx of professional soldiers from the King's guard marches past in splendid formation. We saw them practising earlier, and the difference between their performance and ours could hardly have been greater. They won't break at the first assault, or come apart when they're charging the enemy.

There's a marked lack of cheerful war stories among the corporals. Bad memories are coming to the fore.

"We were saved by the Elves last time," says one, a sail-maker from Twelve Seas. "If they'd arrived one day later Turai would have fallen. Rezaz the Butcher would have marched in and we'd all be long dead."

No one cares to dispute this. It's true. In reality, if the Elves had arrived one hour later, Turai would have fallen. The east wall was already starting to crumble when the Elvish armies arrived on the battlefield.

I'm hungry. I look around for Consul Kalius's tent, hoping to snag a pastry from his chef, but the Consul isn't on the field this day, and I trudge from the practice fields hungrily, in a poor mood. At the Eastern Gate I come face to face with Vedinax. He's a head taller than me, muscled like an ox, with a long sword slung over his back. I walk up to him and stand close.

"Take a good look round," I growl.

"Why?"

"You won't be seeing it for much longer. If the Orcs don't kill you I will."

Vedinax sneers down at me. He's not scared of any sorcery I might be able to muster against him. He wears a spell protection charm around his neck. They're expensive items, rare in the city, but obviously his boss Capatius provides for him well.

"No chance of that, fat man."

"We both know I didn't flee from the Battle of Sanasa."

"I seem to remember you did," says Vedinax.

I decide to kill him now. It was a bad idea to fight the case in court. I draw my sword. Vedinax draws his. Suddenly four men in uniform stride between us. Praetor Capatius has arrived with his guard. I sheathe my sword.

"I'll kill you later," I say. Vedinax isn't intimidated. He once took the award for valour for being first over the enemy walls at a siege. I don't care if he's intimidated or not. I'll still kill him one day.

CHAPTER FIFTEEN

Domasius isn't a bad lawyer. A little too fond of wine. Maybe not immune from taking a bribe in one of the minor cases he conducts in the courts. But he's sharp as an Elf's ear at sifting through evidence. I'd consult him more often, but even at the cheap end of the market, lawyers' fees are expensive. Domasius lives between Jade Temple Fields and Thamlin. Probably he'd like to make the move into Thamlin proper, but unless he gets appointed to some high-profile cases that's not going to happen, and at his age, nearly fifty, it's unlikely to. His office is a little seedy, with a lot of scrolls and documents waiting to be filed away, and a faint aroma of thazis hanging over everything.

I turn up for my consultation around midday and find him buried in *The Renowned and Truthful Record of All the World's Events*, the daily news-sheet which focuses on the grimier side of life in Turai. Of which there's a lot to focus on. He shakes his head, pointing to the lead story, which concerns a merchant who's just been convicted of insurance fraud, claiming money for a lost cargo of wheat which never actually existed.

"He should have hired me," says Domasius. "I'd have got him off."

"He was guilty."

Domasius shrugs.

"How many guilty clients have you worked for?" he asks.

"One or two."

Domasius adjusts his toga—not sparkling white—and pours me a goblet of wine. His grey hair is cut short, as is the fashion with the senatorial class, but it's a little ragged, and his beard could do with a trim. It's obvious that Domasius is never really going to move up in the world. It strikes me that it must be equally obvious to my clients that I'm not going anywhere either.

"How did you make out with the documents?"

Domasius shuffles around on his desk, pulling out a few pieces of paper and glancing at them.

"You want it in technical language?"

"Simple will do."

"Senator Lodius is guilty as hell. He organised the forgery of that will and he didn't even do it that well. Prefect Galwinius was going to nail him in court."

I finish my wine and climb to my feet.

"Don't you want a fuller report?"

"That'll do for now. You can send the report to my office with your bill."

I head for the door.

"Make sure you pay the bill before the Orcs attack,"

calls Domasius after me. He's not the only person in town worried about settling their accounts before Prince Amrag arrives.

Senator Lodius is still under house arrest. The guards outside his gates let me through, used to me by now. I wait a long time at the front door while a servant goes to fetch Lodius's wife. The door is painted white. Every front door in Turai is, even mine. It's the lucky colour for front doors.

Ivaris is a little apprehensive when she arrives in the hallway. I didn't send a message warning her of my arrival, which means she hasn't had the opportunity to get her husband out of the way.

"That's fine. I don't want him out the way, I want to see him."

She looks apologetic.

"I'm afraid he still refuses to see you."

I look apologetic back.

"Doesn't matter. I need to see him."

Her mouth sets in a firm little line.

"I'm afraid you can't. It's been very awkward for me, keeping you engaged. It's caused us great stress. I've done it because I believe you can help, but there are limits. You really cannot see my husband."

"Ivaris, I'm sorry. I know this is awkward. And I don't like being awkward towards a lady who invited me into her private prayer chapel and makes sure I get food when I visit. But I'm here to see Lodius and that's what I'm going to do."

She stands right in front of me.

"If you think I won't bat you out the way, you're mistaken," I tell her.

"You certainly would not bat me out of the way."

"I certainly would. When you hire Thraxas you get the full package. Hitting people included in the price. So take me to your husband before I search the house for him, and tell those servants behind you not to bother trying to stop me, they'll only get hurt."

I move past her, not exactly batting her out the way but not letting her stop me either. A servant does try to prevent my advance but I brush him aside and carry on to the private rooms in the centre of the house. Hearing the commotion, Senator Lodius makes a swift appearance.

"He forced his way past me," says his wife, bringing up the rear, and sounding betrayed.

The Senator casts an evil glance in her direction before turning his glare on me.

"Save the stare, I need to talk to you. Here will do, or somewhere private if you'd rather the servants didn't hear."

"This way," says Senator Lodius, and leads me further back into an office.

"Is there any reason why I should not call for the Civil Guard to throw you out?"

"No reason at all. But the way your popularity has waned recently, I'm not sure they'd be all that quick in coming to your rescue. I have questions."

"I have already made it abundantly clear that I do not wish to talk to you. You do not represent me."

"I do. Or maybe I represent your wife. Either way I'm working on your case. And I just learned from a lawyer that you're guilty in the matter of forging a will."

"I beg your pardon?"

"Comosius's will. You forged it, or rather, you had it forged for you. Galwinius was right, you were trying to defraud him of an inheritance. He had witnesses and documents. He was going to skewer you in court."

I'm expecting a lot of arguments and denials. I'm expecting wrong.

"You are quite right. I did cause the will to be forged."

"You admit it?"

"Yes."

"Why did you do it?"

"I needed the money. My political campaigning is prohibitively expensive. The Populares do not have the resources of the King's treasury behind us."

"So you just thought you'd help yourself to someone else's fortune?"

"You could put it like that. As Galwinius was a miserable parasite who built his fortune largely by robbing the poor, I thought it was not an unreasonable thing to do."

Senator Lodius is looking me right in the eye. I wouldn't say he was crushed with guilt. I wouldn't say he was bothered at all. Cold as an Orc's heart, like all ambitious politicians.

"Are you still denying you murdered Galwinius?"

"I am."

"Even though he was about to prosecute you for a crime you had committed and would be found guilty of?"

"It was not certain that I would be found guilty."

"It was likely."

The Senator shrugs. He's calm in a crisis, I'll give him that.

"Is this why you didn't want me on the case? Because I'd find out about the will?"

"No. Any Investigator would have found out. I didn't want you working for me because you're not a suitable man to be associated with my family."

"I'm not the one who's been forging wills around here."

"No, you're the one who lives in a cheap tavern in Twelve Seas in conditions of squalor. I have been in your office, if you remember."

"I remember all right. You blackmailed me."

I feel a strong need for a beer.

"Any chance of some traditional hospitality?"

"No."

"I figured it was worth a shot. You realise you're going to hang for Prefect Galwinius's murder?"

"Perhaps."

"No perhaps about it. The fraud case ended with Galwinius's death but they're going to pin the murder on you for sure. And they're not going to let you retreat into exile. Are you planning to flee the city before the case comes to court?"

"My affairs are no business of yours, Investigator. I insist that you leave now."

I try to think of something good to say. Nothing occurs to me. So I take the Senator's advice and walk out of the office and along the corridor towards the front door. Senator Lodius's wife is waiting for me. She looks at me with hurt in her eyes.

"Do not come back here," she says. "And please regard your work as finished. I will no longer employ you."

I leave the house without saying goodbye. The guards at the front gate look at me blankly as I pass, stamping their feet to keep out the cold. Now I've been ejected by both the Senator and his wife. I hang around, wondering what to do. I could give up on the case. I should give up on the case. No one wants me to investigate it. As of now, no one's paying me. It's stupid to carry on, But I want to know who killed Galwinius. All my life, I've been more curious than is good for me.

I decide to visit Lisutaris. Probably she'll be either too busy or else unwilling to see me. Still angry over the harsh words I spoke to her in the Avenging Axe, no doubt. Damn these women, and in particular, damn these women Sorcerers. Realising that knocking on Lisutaris's door unfortified by alcohol is asking too much of a man, I look round for a tavern. Taverns are in short supply in Thamlin and I have to make a diversion to find one. Inside I feel out of place among the Senators' servants, so I make haste in downing a few ales and take a bottle of klee with me for the journey. I knock it back quickly as I walk, and it lifts my spirits somewhat. By the time I'm strolling into Truth is Beauty Lane I've mellowed a good deal and am feeling more benevolent towards Lisutaris. Not such a bad sort really. Fought bravely in the war, and paid me well when I helped her in the election.

I'm shown to a reception room by a surly servant. These days I'm really unpopular with the servants. I'm uncertain what I'm going to say to Lisutaris but I'll have to try to persuade her to use her powers to help me somehow. Maybe she can trace the elusive scroll. It's pretty much my last hope, so I'm even prepared to go so far as to offer an apology for my angry words at the Avenging Axe. I take another healthy slug of klee. I notice I've drunk more than half the bottle of the powerful spirit, which is fine for a man of my capacity. For others, less experienced, it might cause problems.

After ten minutes or so another servant leads me to Lisutaris's favourite room, overlooking the garden, now covered with snow. The garden contains private fish-ponds, as is customary among the very wealthy. If you're rich enough you can serve fish to your guests from your own stock. It always impresses the guests. Lisutaris regards me with displeasure.

"Lisutaris, I need your help," I begin quickly. "I'm sorry I spoke harshly to you at the Avenging Axe the other night. No need for it. Though it was understandable, I suppose. It was quite a shock to find my office full of strange women. Anyone would have been surprised. You can't really blame a man for reacting badly. I mean, it's not like the Association of Gentlewomen are favourites of mine. A bunch of troublemakers, you might even say. From a certain point of view, that is. Your view, equally valid of course, may differ. So though I'd say I'm really the victim here I'm prepared to let bygones be bygones."

Lisutaris is looking confused.

"What is this?" she demands.

"I'm apologising."

"It doesn't sound like it."

"Well, how much apologising does a man have to do when he finds his office filled up with a bunch of harpies intent on persecuting the hard-working men of Turai? Goddammit, who told you you could cram my office full of murderous Assassins, half-witted barmaids and parasitic Senators' wives? What the hell have Senators' wives got to complain about anyway? They're all raking in a lot more money than me and no doubt cavorting with professional athletes while their husbands are busy at the Senate. I tell you, it's this sort of behaviour that's dragged this city into the dust. When I was a young man the Consul would've exiled the lot of you."

I take another drink from my bottle of klee. Lisutaris raises one eyebrow.

"Is this still part of the apology?"

"So you expect me to apologise? Is that why you dragged me here? I'm not the one who should be apologising. What have you got to say for yourself, that's what I want to know."

"Are you drunk?"

"Possibly. No doubt when the Association of Gentlewomen takes over the city your first action will be to close down the taverns. Admit it, you're nothing but a bunch of hypocrites. Continually criticising me—"

"We've never mentioned you," interrupts Lisutaris.

I wave her quiet.

"Continually criticising me for a modest intake of ale when the whole world knows the Association of Gentlewomen is no more than a front for some of the wildest, most degenerate drinking ever seen in the city. Since Makri fell in with you she's rarely been sober. And what about your abuse of thazis? I don't see any mention of that at your meetings. No, just prolonged criticism of Investigators, honest landlords and the hard-working masses. You're all so bitter you can't stand to see a man enjoying a quiet tankard of ale. And who was it helped you get elected as head of the Sorcerers Guild anyway? I'll tell you who, it was me. Just like it was me who saved your sorry hide when you lost the green jewel last summer. That wouldn't have looked so good if the Consul had got to know about it. I chased all over the city looking for that gem, and how do you repay me? By barging into my offices uninvited and fouling up the place with incense and a new rug. I tell you—"

I break off. I might be mistaken, but it seems to me that there's a tear rolling from the corner of Lisutaris's eye. Immediately I'm uncomfortable. I hate it when anyone cries, always have. I never know what to say. Have I been too harsh? I remember that I'd planned to apologise to Lisutaris, not lambaste her. It's odd that she'd start crying. She's not the sort of woman to crumple in the face of a little mild criticism.

"Eh . . . I'm sorry . . . maybe I spoke a little harshly. Didn't mean to make you cry."

Lisutaris rises to her feet.

"Thraxas, you imbecile. Nothing you could say would make me shed a tear. You insufferable buffoon, how dare you force your way into my house and criticise me!"

"So who's upset about uninvited guests now? You think it's okay to barge into my office—"

"Will you be quiet about that!" roars the Mistress of the Sky.

"Oh fine, it's okay for you to complain, but not—"

Lisutaris clenches her fists.

"If you continue with this I will blast you all the way to Simnia!" she yells. "I'm not concerned about your office, your rug, or even your abominable drunkenness. Today I was sacked from the War Council! Me! Lisutaris, head of the Sorcerers Guild!"

I find myself sobering up surprisingly quickly.

"What? They can't sack you. It's impossible."

"They can. Prince Dees-Akan moved to suspend me. By his reckoning I am no longer a trustworthy adviser."

Lisutaris slumps back into her chair. Another tear forms in her eye. I'm not surprised. The shame and disgrace of being thrown of the War Council would be hard for any-one to bear. When you're the head of the Sorcerers Guild, it's unthinkable. As the tear rolls down Lisutaris's cheek I find myself feeling both sober and desperate.

"Do you want me to call for a servant?"

The Sorceress shakes her head. I really want someone to come and console her, because God knows, I can't do it.

"How about your secretary? You know, the crazy niece?"

"She's gone," says Lisutaris. Her lip trembles. I curse under my breath. I've seen this woman lop an Orc's head off with a broken sword. Why does she have to pick this moment to start crying? When I'm the only one in the room? She should know it will have a very bad effect on me.

"Tell me what happened," I say, desperately.

"I gave them a warning. They disregarded it. Rittius and Ovinian the True mocked me. Prince Dees-Akan was of the opinion that my warnings were the result of too much thazis and informed me I was no longer welcome at the War Council."

Any second now she's going to weep. I'm twitching with agitation.

"It's the most outrageous thing I've ever heard," I blurt

out. "You're the greatest Sorcerer in Turai. You're the greatest Sorcerer in the Human lands. Everyone knows that. That's why they elected you head of the Guild."

"I thought that was because you and Cicerius cheated for me."

"Our cheating had nothing to do with it. You were elected because you're the best Sorcerer, period. You're worth more to this city than ten princes. What's that man ever done for Turai? You were bringing down dragons and defending the walls when he was still hanging on to his tutor's toga. He's never even seen action. Half the War Council's never seen action. Every person who fought in the war remembers what you did. People all over the world remember it. The Elves remember it. They made a song about it."

"No they didn't," says Lisutaris.

"They're composing it at this moment. There were some odes about trees to get finished first. You know, the tree odes can take a long time."

Lisutaris manages to smile, and wipes the tears from her eyes.

"Well, thanks for the thought. But you did have to cheat to get me elected. Half of Turai was in on the conspiracy."

"And a magnificent job we did too! I swear some of those foreign delegates are still rolling around drunk in brothels in Kushni. But really, you are the best Sorcerer, everybody knows it."

Lisutaris ponders this. The risk of weeping seems to be receding. She looks at me, raising one eyebrow again.

"I've never heard you give out compliments before, Thraxas."

"You haven't? I'm generally ready to give credit where it's due."

"You mean you're so terrified of seeing me cry you're prepared to go to any lengths to prevent it."

"That as well. Are you feeling better now? Because I'm all out of reassurance. Do you think a fine bottle of wine from your excellent cellars might help things?"

The Sorcerer almost smiles, but at the memory of the War Council her brow wrinkles again. She waves her hand and the thazis pipe by her chair lifts gently into the air. She studies it for a few moments.

"The Prince is right," she says. "I do smoke too much thazis."

I'm startled. Lisutaris is an unusually heavy thazis user, it's true, but I never expected to hear her voice any concern over it.

"I couldn't give the substance up even if I wished. It's a flaw in my character."

"Everyone has a flaw. How is a person meant to live in this city without developing a few flaws? People have hinted I drink too much. To hell with them, I say. About your wine cellars . . . ?"

Lisutaris laughs. She lights her pipe and pulls on a bell rope for a servant. I ask her about the warning she gave to the War Council.

"I told them I believed it was possible that Prince Amrag had already sent an army to Yal, kingdom of Horm the Dead. Yal is not so far from Turai. I suspect that they may attack before the winter is out."

"I can see why they found that hard to believe. But surely the other Sorcerers on the Council could check?"

"That's the problem," admits Lisutaris. "No other Sorcerer can detect any trace of an Orcish army in Yal. And neither can I, now. But for a second, as I scanned the east with the green jewel, I was sure that I saw them. Now, there's no trace."

"So when Old Hasius and his friends tried to check they found no sign of them?"

Lisutaris nods, and draws deeply on her water pipe.

"Prince Dees-Akan openly stated that I was suffering from hallucinations brought on by thazis. Maybe he's right."

"Is he?"

Lisutaris looks doubtful.

"I think I saw them. It's difficult. The Orcish Sorcerers Guild is so strong these days. They've learned how to countermand most of our far-seeing spells. Even using the green jewel is no longer easy. I can sense some sort of spell working against it."

The green jewel is something of a state secret in Turai, a magical artifact for far-seeing which cannot be blocked by enemy Sorcerers. Or couldn't, up till now. Lisutaris stares into space, as if scanning the ether for sorcery.

"I don't think the green jewel is being directly interfered with. But there's something wrong. Something so intangible that no other Sorcerer can detect it. So vague that most times I can't either. Just something that's interfering with my seeing spells."

"New blocking spells?"

She shakes her head.

"No. We can always detect Orcish blocking spells, even if we can't work around them. This doesn't feel like a blocking spell. It doesn't feel like anything. I just have the feeling that something is interfering with my far-seeing magic. But there's nothing I can demonstrate. And there's no way the Orcs should be able to interfere with my sorcery from so far away."

"Might they have moved some Sorcerers closer to Turai?"

Lisutaris has considered this but feels certain she'd be able to detect them if that had happened.

"But there's something wrong, even if I can't explain it. Unfortunately no other Sorcerer feels anything at all. Nor has any seen an Orcish army in Yal."

This all sounds like very grim tidings. It seems strange to me that the War Council should give her warning so little credence.

"I have opponents on the Council. The Prince has never liked me. And as for Rittius, he's been against me since the first meeting."

"Rittius is a dog," I say, with feeling.

"He is. But he's head of Palace Security. He carries a lot of weight, particularly now he's been persuaded to abandon Senator Lodius."

"Which brings me to my reason for visiting."

"I thought you came here to apologise?"

"I did. Also I need help."

I give Lisutaris a brief description of my lack of progress on the Lodius case. She wonders why I'm still involved. It's hard to give a satisfactory answer.

"I don't like to see a murderer go unpunished. Or maybe I'm just stubborn."

"I have already looked at the circumstances surrounding

the death, at the request of the Abode of Justice," points out Lisutaris. "We could not tell when the poison was administered."

"Are you sure you looked properly?"

"Is that as much of an insult as I take it to be?"

"No insult intended. You've been busy with the war preparations. And you weren't that fond of Galwinius."

"I'd say that was an insult."

"Merely a statement of fact," I say. "After all, he refused to allow Herminis to go into exile. One of the main complaints of the Association of Gentlewomen, I understand."

"Why don't you just ask if we killed him?"

"Did you?"

"No. Though we're not shedding many tears about it."

"His family is. Strange thing about this city, Lisutaris. No one seems to mind when a man is murdered if the man was an opponent. Myself, I never see things that way."

"Spare me the lecture," says Lisutaris, and draws on her thazis pipe.

"Galwinius was carrying a scroll before he fell. I want to know what happened to it."

Lisutaris rises from her chair, takes a gold saucer from a table nearby, and pours a little black liquid into it. It's kuriya, a tool for looking into the past. This is an art over which I have some control, but nothing compared to the power of Lisutaris. She waves her hand. For performing any sort of spell, no matter how difficult, the Mistress of the Sky never seems to need any preparation. All she does is wave her hand and it starts to work. A picture forms in the pool. I watch as Galwinius takes the food from Lodius.

He is carrying a scroll. He falls to the ground. Lisutaris twitches her fingers and the picture alters, focusing on the floor where he falls. The scroll is partially obscured by his body. A hand reaches for it, scoops it up and tuck it inside his toga. It's Bevarius, assistant to Consul Kalius.

The picture fades. The pool goes dark.

"Bevarius?"

I'm perturbed. I don't know what to think.

"I wasn't expecting any sort of involvement from the Consul's office. Maybe it doesn't mean anything. I still don't know what was on that scroll."

I thank Lisutaris for her help. I remember that Makri is going to be part of Lisutaris's bodyguard. She has served as Lisutaris's bodyguard before, though not in such dangerous circumstances. The Sorceress is pleased. "Casting spells in the middle of a battle, it's hard to keep a lookout for your own safety. I've got a company of good men to protect me and Makri can probably fight better than any of them."

"Probably. Though she's never been on a battlefield."

"She can look after herself."

"I know. But she'll probably die anyway."

"We'll all probably die," says Lisutaris, and sounds quite serious about it. Obviously my own assessment of our prospects is not unduly pessimistic.

CHAPTER SIXTEEN

I send a message to Domasius, asking him to make some enquiries regarding Bevarius, Kalius and Galwinius. The Messengers Guild never stops working, even in the worst of conditions. Their young carriers are dedicated to their work. God knows why.

By now my magic warm cloak is cooling off. On the long walk down Moon and Stars Boulevard I start to feel the cold creeping in. I hurry on, cursing as my heels slip on the ice. There are a lot of people still about on the main thoroughfare and they're the gloomiest collection of faces I've seen for some time. In times of crisis the city naturally looks towards the royal family, but the royal family is not such a shining example these days. The King is still respected, but he's old, and rarely appears in public. He's been ruling through his ministers for a long time now and is no longer quite the figurehead he used to be. His elder son, Prince Frisen-Akan, is such a degenerate lush that not even the most hardened royalist can pretend he's an inspiration. The younger son, Prince Dees-Akan, head of the War Council, is a much more competent sort of character, but somehow not the sort of prince the public has ever really warmed to. Too abrasive perhaps. Lacking the common touch. Young Princess Du-Akai is very popular and quite glamorous, but at a time like this the population is looking more for a military leader than a beautiful princess.

I wonder about Bevarius. He picked up the scroll. Why? Was he just clearing the way for the doctor? Or was there something written on it he wanted kept private? What happened to the scroll afterwards? I'll have to question the Consul's assistant again. By this time I've reached the entrance to Saint Rominius's Lane, scene of the recent attack on my person. I could take the long way home and avoid the lane. But I'm cold. It's probably safe enough. I head into the narrow passageway. After turning the first corner I find myself confronted by three men with swords.

"Here we go again."

I intone my sleep spell and they crumple gently into the snow. I take a few steps then halt at the sound of footsteps behind me. When I turn round I find the man with red hair standing there with a mocking smile on his face. Behind him are four armed companions.

"You're pretty dumb for an Investigator, falling for the same trick twice. Now you've gone and used up your magic again."

He motions his men to advance. I speak another spell and they all fall unconscious to the ground.

"Not that dumb," I say.

Before leaving Lisutaris's villa I'd asked her if she could give me something to temporarily boost my spell-casting powers, and she duly obliged. I've got enough power to put any number of assailants to sleep, and it'll last for a few hours yet. I hoist the red-haired man over my shoulder and set off for the Avenging Axe. He's no lightweight and by the time I reach the outside steps I'm panting for breath. I haul my captive up the stairs and into my office. By the time I've dumped him in a chair and thrown a coil of rope around him to hold him there, he's starting to revive. I search his pockets, finding nothing but a draw-string purse with a few half-gurans inside. A name is embroidered on the purse: "Kerinox."

He opens his eyes to finds the point of my sword only a few inches from his face.

"Who sent you to kill me, Kerinox?" I demand, hoping to catch him before he has time to focus his thoughts. Unfortunately he's either too smart or too dumb to remain unfocused for long. He shakes his head to clear it, swears loudly at me and then tells me to go to hell. I bat him across the face. He swears at me again.

"Who sent you?"

"As soon as I'm out of this chair I'll kill you, fat man."

I hit him across the face again and he falls silent. Silent, but not cowed.

"You want me to use a truth spell on you?"

My prisoner laughs.

"Everyone knows you don't have that sort of power. All you can do is send a person to sleep, fat man."

It's getting on my nerves, the way he keeps calling me fat man. I stare at him, unsure of my next move. Being a private Investigator isn't like working for the Civil Guards or Palace Security. You can't just brutalize people, it's against the law. Not that I'm too worried about the law, as this man has twice tried to kill me. But if I hurt him too badly and he goes complaining about it to the authorities, I could find myself in trouble. I press my sword right up against his throat. He looks at me coolly.

"It won't take my friends long to work out where I am. This time we will kill you."

He's right, at least about the part where his friends find him. When they wake up and get to wondering where their leader is, they might well decide to take a look in the Avenging Axe. Or they might just decide to go home, depending on how well they're being paid. While I'm wondering what to do, I hear a door closing softly further along the corridor. I stick my head out the door. Makri walks past with her nose in the air.

"Makri—"

"Don't talk to me, oaf," she says.

I get in front of her.

"I need your help."

"That's unfortunate. I rarely help people who abuse me and throw me out of their office."

"Did I do that?"

"Yes."

"I expect I was being drunk and unreasonable. You know how I get. Incidentally, I've just been in Lisutaris's villa, complimenting her on choosing you as a bodyguard."

"Oh yes?"

"Yes. We both agreed you were the ideal woman for the job."

"Forget it, Thraxas. You can't win me over with flattery."

"I understand the Consul himself has expressed satisfaction."

"Really? Did he say that?"

Makri looks pleased. Then she frowns.

"I'm still annoyed at you."

Time was, Makri was easy prey for a cheap compliment. Now, it doesn't work so well. Civilisation has corrupted her. Fortunately she does remain sorely in need of money. Classes at the Guild College don't come cheap.

"I'll pay you five gurans."

"Ten."

"Seven and a half."

"Okay. What do you want me to do?"

I quickly fill her in on the situation. Makri nods.

"So you want me to scare this Kerinox till he starts answering?"

I shake my head.

"No good. He doesn't scare easily and he's expecting to be rescued. Subtlety is required. Back at Palace Security we had a technique for questioning recalcitrant prisoners. Used to call it Good Civil Guard Bad Civil Guard. Or Good Guard Bad Guard for short."

"What?"

"It's easy. We go in there together. I threaten him, rough him up a little and then you start in with the sympathy. Tell him you know he's suffering and how I'm such an unreasonable guy, and in no time he's telling you everything."

"Why would he do that?" asks Makri, puzzled.

"I don't exactly know. But it seemed to work back in

Palace Security. Something to do with the inner working of the mind. You know, brutal captor followed by kindly sympathy."

Makri looks thoughtful for a moment or two. I'm expecting her to waste time with a lot more questions, but instead she nods.

"Yes, I think I see what you're getting at. Something similar happens in the great Elvish Epic *The Tale of the Two Oaks and the Warring Princes.* There's a moment when one prince has been thrown in a dungeon—"

I hold up my hand.

"Could we discuss Elvish poetry another time? We have a suspect to question."

"All right. But are you sure I should be the good guard? Shouldn't I be the bad one?"

"No, you're much more suitable for lending a sympathetic ear."

"No I'm not," protests Makri. "Last night I punched out a mercenary when he was telling me about his lover back in the north. He seemed to get confused about where his lover was and started groping my thigh."

"Well, provided Kerinox doesn't start fondling you, I think you can manage to be sympathetic. Or pretend to be. Don't curse him in Orcish."

Makri agrees to give it a try and we march back into the office. I start in on the red-haired man right away, slapping him a few times, threatening him with my sword and dagger and generally giving him a hard time. And while he shows no more signs of being ready to talk than he did before, he's certainly becoming uncomfortable under the harsh treatment. I keep it up for a while. Makri sits quietly at my desk, watching. When I judge that I might have made him uncomfortable enough, I pull a face as if disgusted with the whole thing, and back off.

"You better talk soon or I'll kill you right here," I threaten, before withdrawing. Makri rises to her feet.

"Remember, be sympathetic," I whisper. I take a seat at the desk and Makri stands in front of the prisoner.

"Is it uncomfortable for you sitting there, Kerinox?" says Makri, managing to sound quite pleasant. "Should I loosen your bonds?"

"Get away from me," snarls the man in the chair.

"Would you like a drink of water?"

"Go to hell."

Makri looks confused.

"Wouldn't you like to tell me your problems?" she ventures.

"Shut up, bitch," growls our captive.

"Why don't you just answer the damned questions!" roars Makri, and hits him so hard that the chair goes over on to the ground.

I look at the body now unconscious on the floor.

"Well that was splendid, Makri. Now you've killed him. What happened to the sympathy?"

"I got annoyed when he insulted me."

Makri purses her lips.

"You should have let me be the bad guard. I'm much more suited to it."

We haul the chair upright. Kerinox sags, unconscious in his bonds. He moans. At least he isn't dead. I spread my arms wide and turn to Makri.

"Now I don't know what to do."

"How about if you try being the good guard?" she suggests.

"It's too late for that. I've already hit him. Couldn't you have controlled your temper for once?"

Makri brushes this aside.

"Hey, I did my best. The problem as I see it is that you have no real leverage. He knows you're not going to kill him. All he has to do is wait and you have to let him go eventually. The whole thing has been a tactical blunder on your part. You should have thought about it more before you started."

"When it started I was knee deep in snow with four guys attacking me. I didn't have a lot of time to think."

"Well, the plan you came up with was a bust," says Makri. "Too elaborate."

"It might have worked if you hadn't slugged him at the first opportunity. You were meant to be good guard, not violent aggressive guard."

"I can't be blamed for this debacle," objects Makri. "I was miscast right from the start."

By now my captive is beginning to show signs of life.

"You're just not threatening enough," says Makri.

"What? I'm plenty threatening."

"You're not. Remember how I scared that guy up in Kushni when we needed to find the green jewel? Now that was threatening. Wait here."

With that Makri disappears from the room, appearing back in moments with her black Orcish sword. It's an ugly weapon, dark and razor sharp. Rather than reflecting light, it seems to suck it in.

"I'll show you threatening," mutters Makri. She strides

over to the red-haired man, places her sword near to his throat and yanks his head back.

"You see this? This sword was forged by demons in an Orcish furnace beneath the cursed mountain of Zarax. When it cuts into you it'll drink your soul and send you down to Orcish hell, where you'll spend the rest of eternity as the only tortured Human in an inferno of damned Orcs. And you see these?"

Makri pulls back her hair, displaying her pointed ears. "These mean I know how to use it. And today I'm feeling very bad towards all Humans. So you give me the information before I count to five or get ready to meet the legions of the Orcish damned."

Makri starts counting, and she doesn't linger over it. By now the unfortunate Kerinox is looking genuinely frightened and I think he might be about to talk when Makri suddenly slices at him. He screams. I'm expecting to see his head fly off his body but Makri miraculously stops the blade just as it touches his throat.

"You were saying?"

The red-haired man looks at me imploringly.

"Get this demon away from me. I'll tell you who sent me."

I feel rather sorry for him. I wouldn't like to be tied in a chair with Makri waving that sword around my head either. Makri retreats to my desk and sits calmly smoking my thazis while I question him.

He tells me that he was sent to kill me by Bevarius. The Consul's assistant. The man who picked up the scroll.

"Do you often kill people for money?"

Kerinox shrugs.

"Now and then."

I don't learn much more, and in truth I'm sick of the whole thing. Once I've learned that it was Bevarius who hired men to attack me I don't need to know much more. Not from Kerinox anyway.

"If you come anywhere near the Avenging Axe again Makri will kill you with the Orcish sword. I've seen men die from it. They never seem to go easily."

I untie him. He's bruised, and bleeding from a cut under his left eye. I shouldn't feel any sympathy. He's twice tried to kill me. For some reason I feel some sympathy. He departs without another word. Throughout this, Makri has been sitting quietly at my desk, smoking thazis. I hand over seven and a half gurans and thank her for her help. She accepts my thanks as graciously as she normally does, which is not that graciously.

"You've been really bad-tempered recently. Even by your standards."

I shrug, and light a thazis stick for myself.

"Difficult case. Men trying to kill me. Snow on the ground. War looming. Never makes for a happy life."

"I suppose not," says Makri. "Though I don't see why you have to start complaining every time someone sends me flowers. It's not my fault everyone is sending me flowers. Do you have any idea why everyone is sending me flowers?"

"It baffles me. I see you have a new admirer."

"Toraggax?" says Makri. "I quite like him."

"You do? I wouldn't have thought he was your type."

Makri has never expressed any interest in any mercenary before. Or any Human, that I can remember.

"He's quite intelligent," she says. "And polite."

She stubs out her thazis stick.

"I was talking to a professor at the academy. A friend of Samanatius. He studies plants. I asked him about carasin. You said Galwinius was poisoned with carasin and Senator Lodius is the only person who imports it into Turai."

"True."

"Well there's a whole family of plants that act in the same way," says Makri.

"What do you mean, family? Plants don't have families."

"Yes they do. Sort of. The professor classifies them into different species. Like they're related to each other."

"It's the first I've heard about it. So what?"

"So there are three other plants like the carasin bush that can be used to make poison. The effect is very similar. Similar enough to fool almost anyone. They're not well known because they have no commercial use. But the professor said that a person who knew about them could make a poison that the authorities would identify as carasin because its action was just the same."

Makri smiles.

"Interesting?"

"Very interesting. Where do these plants grow?"

"One of them grows in the hills just north of the city. So while you've been wondering who else could possibly have brought carasin into Turai, it probably wasn't carasin at all. Just some plant from the hills that anyone with a bit of knowledge could have collected."

Makri is pleased with herself, which I suppose she has a right to be. I wonder who might have such specialised knowledge of poisonous plants. The Assassins, I suppose.

Or maybe just someone from a law enforcement agency who came across the rare poison in the line of his work.

Night is falling. I ask Makri if she's working downstairs but she shakes her head.

"Studying?"

"No. I'm going out."

"Out? Where?"

"Just out," says Makri and looks furtive.

"Is this connected with these mysterious meetings?"

"There are no mysterious meetings. It's my reading group."

It's none of my business. I let it drop.

"It's cold as the Ice Queen's grave outside," says Makri.

"So?"

"So lend me the magic warm cloak."

"I need it."

Makri complains loudly about the ingratitude of an Investigator who'd never get a single thing done if it wasn't for the aid of a far more intelligent companion who time after time lends him her valuable assistance. I scowl at her and hand over the cloak.

"Make sure I get it back in the morning. I didn't spend all that time as a Sorcerer's apprentice just so my far more intelligent companion could walk around in my magic warm cloak."

Makri drapes the cloak around her, takes another thazis stick without asking, and departs. A messenger arrives at my door. He's carrying a reply from Domasius.

"Prefect Galwinius's estate split between wife and Consul Kalius," says the message.

It's not such an unusual arrangement among the senatorial

classes. Galwinius is a cousin of Kalius. Keeping the fortune in the family is important. His will leaves half of his money to his wife and the other half to the Consul. Nothing strange about that. Nothing strange except I've been investigating Galwinius's death and now the Consul's assistant has been trying to kill me. And the Consul's assistant picked up some scroll that Galwinius was carrying right before he was murdered. And Bevarius and Kalius were in the room when Galwinius died. And the food came from the Consul's kitchen. And now Kalius is a great deal richer than he used to be. I look at the second part of Domasius's message.

"Consul Kalius greatly in debt," it reads. "Lost money speculating on corn imports and has been borrowing all round town."

It's something to think about. I'm tired. I'll think about it tomorrow. I finish my thazis stick and go through to my bedroom, which is small, cold, and generally cheerless. I speak a word of power and my illuminated staff bursts into life. It's an excellent illuminated staff, a much finer item than a man with such a poor command of sorcery as myself has any right to own. I won it from an Elf lord, at Niarit. The golden light makes my room look rather less grim. I speak another word of power to tone down the light to a soft, warm radiance. On a whim, I leave it lit while I go to sleep, something I haven't done for a long time.

CHAPTER SEVENTEEN

I'm woken in the middle of the night by someone shaking my arm. I'm already reaching for my sword as I haul myself upright.

"Thraxas, it's me!"

It's Makri, looking agitated. The magic warm cloak is ripped and there are grazes on her shoulders and forehead.

"What's happening?"

"Listen and don't interrupt. Tonight we went to rescue Herminis. That's what the Association meetings were about. Planning the rescue. But it went wrong."

"Of course."

"Why of course?"

"Because your useless Association couldn't organise a sword fight in an armoury."

"I asked you not to interrupt," says Makri, sharply. "Herminis was being transferred from prison to the execution site and we knew when this was happening because the woman who cooks at the prison is a member of the Association. So Lisutaris and Tirini Snake Smiter—"

"Tirini?"

"Yes."

Tirini Snake Smiter is a powerful Sorcerer but not one ever known to do anything except wear expensive outfits and host fabulous parties.

"Tirini and Lisutaris worked magic to make all the guards forget what they were doing while me and Hanama intercepted the wagon and drove off with Herminis."

"This all sounds crazy. The Guards will be down on you like a bad spell."

"No they won't. Lisutaris worked out how and when to do it so the Guards' Sorcerers would never be able to find out what happened. She is head of the Sorcerers Guild, after all. Stop interrupting. Everything was going fine and we drove the wagon down to Kushni without anyone spotting us because it's snowing heavily, and then we went to the secret villa, which is a large house just on the edge of Kushni owned by the Palace and which has a secret room lined with Red Elvish Cloth."

"What?"

"Red Elvish Cloth. It prevents all sorcery from penetrating."

"I know what it does. I just didn't know there was a secret room full of the stuff in Kushni."

"Built by a former king for liaisons with his mistress, apparently. It's a secret. That's why it's called the secret villa."

"How did you know about this place?" I ask.

"Tirini had an affair with Prince Dees-Akan last year.

They used to meet there. Tirini made a copy of the keys, also in secret."

"I get the picture. Go on. No, wait. Is this story going to end with you telling me that Herminis is currently next door in my office?"

"Of course not. How stupid do you think we are? We were going to hide her in the secret villa and then smuggle her out of the city afterwards. So we got to the villa and Tirini met us there and everything would've been okay except when we went into the sorcery-proof room we found an Orcish Sorcerer there."

"An Orcish Sorcerer? Are you sure?"

"Of course I'm sure!"

"What was he doing?"

"Sleeping," says Makri. "But he woke up pretty damned quick. He threw this spell at me which knocked me down but I was wearing my spell protection charm which saved me, and then Hanama threw a knife at him which should have pierced his neck except he had some sort of protection as well, and then Tirini used a spell herself and he used one back and there was an explosion and the place caught fire. And this Sorcerer was strong, he kept trying to fire more spells at us with some sort of wand, and Tirini could only just manage to hold him off."

Makri pauses for breath.

"And then?"

"Then I managed to distract his attention by flinging a chair at him and so Tirini managed to knock him down with a spell. Then Hanama kicked him and he fell down and I grabbed the wand and then the place really started blazing badly and we all had to run."

"What happened to the Sorcerer?"

"Who knows? By this time the roof was coming down. Outside, the whole neighbourhood had heard the commotion and everyone was running around screaming and calling for the fire wagons and the four of us just piled into the wagon and drove here."

"Four of you?"

"Me, Hanama, Tirini and Herminis."

"Where did you take Herminis?"

Makri crosses one foot over the other and looks a little awkward.

"She's next door in your office."

"Goddammit! You said she wasn't!"

"I was going to break it to you gently."

I march from my bedroom into my office, where I find Hanama, Tirini Snake Smiter and Herminis all looking somewhat the worse for wear.

"Congratulations on a successful mission!" I say, and I mean it to sting. "Trust the Association of Gentlewomen to bungle anything they set their well-manicured hands to."

"In fairness to us," says Makri, bringing up the rear, "we couldn't really anticipate that there was going to be an Orcish Sorcerer in our safe house. I mean, what are the chances?"

She has a point, I suppose. But they'd have bungled it some other way, enemy Sorcerer or not. I round on Makri.

"What is it with you and my office? Last year you brought that exotic dancer here when the Guards were looking for her."

"She needed help."

"She turned out to be a spy for the Brotherhood. And

now you've brought this—this—condemned murderer here. It's not like upstairs at the Avenging Axe is a cunning hiding place. Captain Rallee is in and out of here every week. Why couldn't you take her somewhere else?"

"Like where?"

"Like Morixa's bakery. There must be somewhere she can hide there. Why drag me into this?"

Herminis, a slender woman of thirty or so, with fair skin and blue eyes, rises to her feet. Despite her months of incarceration, she's not in bad shape. When they lock up a Senator's wife, they give her a private suite and let her keep her own clothes, and have food sent in from home. Probably not such a hard life, till it's time to be hanged.

"I'm very sorry to inconvenience your—" she begins.

I hold up my hand.

"Stop right there. I'm in enough trouble already due to Senators' wives being polite to me. What is it with you people? You think you can just go round being well-mannered all the time?"

Herminis looks confused, and turns towards Makri. Makri's eyes flash with anger.

"Don't abuse this woman. She's been in prison for four months. I brought her here because I thought you might be able to help."

"You did?"

"Yes. After the fight we weren't thinking too clearly. None of us knew what to do."

It's rare indeed for Makri ever to admit to anything that might be construed as a failing.

"So you thought you'd drag me into your sorry mess?"

"We're all facing arrest and execution. I thought you

might have some ideas." Makri's voice rises angrily. "I should have realised you're not capable of helping a friend without going through an endless round of sarcasm, bad temper and insults. Foolish of me, I've experienced it often enough."

Makri takes Herminis's hand.

"Come on. We'll see if Morixa has any suggestions."

I bite back the dozen or so bad-tempered, sarcastic insults that spring to mind and march over to the door, blocking their exit.

"Don't go out there. You'll only make it worse. The Guards will be combing the city for you by now."

I turn to Tirini.

"Can you hide us?"

She shakes her head.

"I'm out of spells. The Orcish Sorcerer was tough."

Once a Sorcerer uses a spell she can't use it again till she's relearned it. The great Sorcerers can hold quite a few spells in their memory, but any sustained period of action will leave them drained. I take my grimoire from the shelf and hand it to her.

"This is out of date but you'll find something in it. Learn it and use it quick."

Tirini takes the book and opens it at the index. She's wearing the most expensive-looking fur cloak I've ever seen, a garment so thick and luxurious I'm not even sure what animal it's made from. Northern wolf maybe, or even the rarely seen golden bear. Her hair is bleached brilliant blonde and dragon-scale earrings dangle from her ears. Inconspicuous she's not. I'm praying no one saw them roll up outside in their wagon. At this time of night, with the snow coming down, it's possible they were unobserved.

"Did you stable the horses?"

Makri nods. "And the wagon's out of sight."

I notice that Hanama is bleeding quite badly from a cut on her leg. I hunt in my desk for the remains of the herbs that Chiaraxi the healer left here. I hand her the bundle, along with some water.

"You know how to use these?"

Hanama nods, and starts wetting the herbs and applying the damp mixture to her leg. It should stop the bleeding quickly. For all that she's quite fragile to look at, it will take more than a slashed leg to seriously trouble her.

Tirini Snake Smiter has meanwhile found a spell of hiding. I sit down next to her and read along. I'll add my power to hers. It might be enough to buy us some time. Peeping out from beneath her fur cloak is a delicate pair of silver slippers. Foolishly inappropriate footwear for this weather. She starts speaking the words of the spell. The room becomes colder as the sorcery takes effect. As soon as she's finished I do the same. It will hide Herminis for a while. Not for long, though, when they start turning their full power on the hunt.

Herminis shivers. Tirini speaks a word of power and the fire in my grate bursts into life.

"What now?" asks Makri.

"A swift trial followed by execution, most probably. We should tell Lisutaris what's happened."

I'm not just thinking about our present plight. It's an extremely serious matter that there's an Orcish Sorcerer lying low in Turai. How he got into that villa undetected I can't imagine. It suggests treachery on a high level and it bodes very ill for the city. God knows what he's been up to while he's been there, undetectable to the authorities.

"I could probably send a message to Lisutaris," says Tirini. "Just give me a moment to recharge my powers."

"No. Too dangerous. If Old Hasius the Brilliant is scanning the city he might pick it up."

Makri offers to take a horse and ride up to Thamlin but I advise against it. They were lucky not to run into a Guards patrol on their way south and it's too much of a risk to try it again. I consider making the journey myself but decide against it. I could probably bluff my way past any Civil Guard, but the streets are icy, it's freezing cold and I'd quite likely suffer some serious mishap.

"I'll send her a message."

There's an outpost of the Messengers Guild not far up Moon and Stars Boulevard. It means a cold walk along Quintessence Street but we have to inform Lisutaris. I ask Makri if she can compose a message in the Royal Elvish language. Almost no one in Turai can speak that, apart from a few senior Sorcerers who need it for spells. And Makri, who studies it at her college. In theory it's illegal for a message carried by a member of the Messengers Guild to be intercepted, but it's as well to be careful.

"What will I say?" asks Makri, taking a sheet of paper from my desk.

"Have tragically messed up the whole affair through our staggering incompetence," I suggest. "Please come and save our sorry excuse for a rescue party."

Makri frowns.

"I'll paraphrase that."

"Remember to mention the Orcish Sorcerer."

I notice the end of a dark piece of wood sticking out of one of the deep pockets of Tirini's cloak.

"His wand?"

She nods. I can feel the Orcish sorcery latent in the wand. It's quite uncommon for Human Sorcerers to use them, but some Orcish Sorcerers do channel their energies through wands. More powerful, according to them. More primitive, according to us.

I haven't had time to recharge my magic warm cloak and am consequently as cold as a frozen pixie before I reach the end of Quintessence Street. I'm alone on the streets and the man on duty in the messengers' station is surprised to see me when I struggle in, shaking off the snow.

"Must be urgent."

"Sudden birth in the family," I say, handing over the sealed letter.

"Congratulations."

By the time I'm struggling back along Quintessence Street my temper has substantially worsened. A man tries to get a good night's sleep before phalanx practice and what happens? The Association of Gentlewomen arrive uninvited in his office with a wanted criminal. I swear an oath that none of these women will ever enter my office again. If necessary, I'll procure a powerful spell from Astrath Triple Moon to keep them out. God knows what outrage Makri will commit next if I don't put an end to it. Not that this one isn't bad enough. If the authorities find out I'm giving shelter to Herminis I'll have to flee the city. Fleeing the city is extremely difficult in winter, I know from experience. If you have to annoy the authorities, do it when the weather's good.

The snow turns to sleet. By the time I reach the Avenging Axe I'm as wet as a mermaid's blanket. As I trudge bitterly up the stairs my one consolation is that at least these foolish women will now have learned their lesson. I expect them to be suitably chastened.

As soon as I open my door I'm greeted by a powerful aroma of thazis smoke and a great burst of raucous laughter. Makri is jumping round with a sword in her hand, apparently demonstrating how she fought the Orcish Sorcerer. Tirini Snake Smiter is pretending to fire spells with the Orcish wand. Even Hanama, never the most vivacious of personalities, seems close to smiling. There's an empty bottle of klee on the floor alongside a crate of ale.

"Have a drink! We were just celebrating."

"Celebrating? What?"

"Rescuing Herminis, of course."

Makri raises a tankard.

"Number one chariot at rescuing!"

Tirini, Hanama and Herminis raise their own tankards and drink deeply. I'm appalled.

"Have you all forgotten the danger we're in?"

"Pah," says Tirini, waving her hand dismissively. "No danger. I've hidden us."

She raises her tankard again. Having finished off my klee, Makri has apparently raided the bar downstairs.

"Civil Guards, prisons, Orcish Sorcerers, spells, explosions, bad weather," cries Makri. "Did it put us off? Not at all. Just rode in, grabbed Herminis and rode out again. A famous mission. Go down in history. Rode in, fought the guards, blasted them with spells, set the place on fire and rode out again."

"Beat the hell out of them really," says Hanama. Once more she almost smiles. I glare at her.

"Are you drunk?"

"The Assassins Guild does not tolerate drunkenness," says Hanama, coolly.

I grab a bottle of beer from the crate and am about to leave them to it when I suddenly sense something strange. Something I can't quite identify. I can't make it out, but something is setting off a warning, and my senses generally don't lie. Even though I've little sorcerous power left, I can always feel it nearby.

"Tirini, can you sense something strange?"

"Yes!"

"What is it?"

"A mighty victory for the Association," she shouts, and fits a bottle of klee to her mouth.

"Will you concentrate?. There's something . . . Orcish about . . ."

I place my hand on the Sorcerer's wand, trying to tell if it matches the odd vibrations I'm picking up. I don't think so, but the powerful aura that surrounds it makes it hard to distinguish anything else. Could it just be a combination of the wand and Makri?

"Makri, give me your hand,"

"What?"

"Give me your hand."

"Well, this is very unexpected," says Makri. "I mean, we've been companions for a while now but I didn't think you had those sort of feelings for me."

"I just need to check—"

"It's really quite a surprise," continues Makri. "Of course there's the age difference to think about. And can I carry on with my studies? I'd probably need my husband to provide for me when I go to the university, and then there's your relatives to consider, what with my Orcish blood—do you have any relatives?"

"Makri, if you keep this up I swear I'll kill you."

I grab her hand. Ignoring the general merriment I try and focus on the strange Orcish aura I can now feel permeating my office. As far as I can tell, it's not coming from either Makri or the wand. I draw my sword and tell Makri to draw hers.

"What for?"

"I think the Orcish Sorcerer is close."

"Nonsense," says Tirini Snake Smiter. "I can't sense anything."

"That's because you're drunk."

"So who's the proper Sorcerer here, you or me?" demands Tirini.

At this moment my outside door flies open and a dark cloud starts rolling into the room.

"Goddamn!" yells Makri, leaping to her feet, sword in hand. "Why didn't you warn us?"

The Orcish Sorcerer, garbed in black, appears in the doorway.

"You have something of mine," he says in a voice so chilling it might have been forged under the cursed mountain of Zarax. He rasps out some word of power and we're all flung against the far wall. I land painfully, and clamber to my feet with a grim expression on my face. My spell protection charm has saved me from the worst of the assault, but even so, it was a painful experience. I raise my sword and charge. He doesn't have his wand and he must have used up most of his sorcerous powers during his battle with Tirini Snake Smiter. Which means I've a reasonable chance of planting my sword in his guts before he can use another spell.

He's small for an Orc, and almost engulfed by his black cloak. He wears a black jewel on his forehead, the badge of his guild. I arrive in front of him at the same time as Makri, and we both aim blows. My sword smashes into some sort of invisible force and flies from my hand, leaving my arm numb. He's invoked a protective spell. A good one, from the way Hanama bounces off him seconds later. Tirini doesn't seem to be doing much in the way of offering resistance, either because she's been dazed by the Sorcerer's first assault or, more likely, because she's drunk so much klee she can't remember how to intone a spell.

The black-clad Sorcerer raises his hand. I brace myself for another journey through the air. He falls down dead in front of me. I look down at him, puzzled. Makri steps up and prods the body with her toe.

"I wasn't expecting that to happen," she says.

"Me neither," I admit.

"Maybe he had a weak heart?"

Lisutaris strides into the room.

"I killed him," she says.

"Another triumph," says Makri, and sits down heavily beside Herminis.

"I came as soon as I got your message. What has been happening?" asks Lisutaris.

"These idiots brought Herminis to my office. Insane behaviour."

"I meant, what has been happening with regard to this Sorcerer?"

A babble of intoxicated voices all seek to explain. Lisutaris listens intently to the tale, then kneels down to examine the body. She lays her hands on the Sorcerer's heart, then on the jewel on his forehead, before transferring her attention to the wand.

"This Sorcerer has been working continually in Turai for several months," she announces, presumably having learned this by some sorcerous means. "No wonder my own sorcery has been interfered with."

A powerful enemy Sorcerer, right in our midst. It's a neat move by the Orcish Sorcerers Guild. Sneak a Sorcerer into the city, and hide him in a room lined with Red Elvish Cloth so he can't be detected. All he had to do was leave the room for a moment, work some spell which would interfere with Turanian sorcery, then scuttle back to his hiding place before anyone noticed. The Sorcerers at Palace Security and the Abode of Justice scan the city every day for hostile sorcery, but even their sophisticated magic can't penetrate Red Elvish Cloth.

"He could have stayed there all through the war with no one noticing," says Hanama.

"Lucky we flushed him out," says Makri. "You think the city might give the Association of Gentlewomen some sort of reward?"

"We can hardly let it be known in public," says Hanama. "We were breaking a condemned woman out of jail at the time."

"It does make everything more awkward," agrees Lisutaris. "I should report this to the War Council immediately, but—"

She breaks off. Once the authorities know that an Orcish Sorcerer was hiding in the secret villa, they'll mount a full investigation, which will, of course, lead to the discovery of the Association's criminal enterprise.

"We have some major hiding sorcery to do," says Lisutaris to Tirini Snake Smiter. "We might be able to cover things up. Let them know about the Sorcerer without giving ourselves away. Tirini, are you listening?"

Tirini is slumbering gently on the couch. Lisutaris notices for the first time that her associates are somewhat the worse for wear.

"We were celebrating," explains Makri.

"Quite normal after arduous combat," adds Hanama.

"Appalling behaviour," I say.

"Thraxas," says Lisutaris. "After the last war ended you were listed among the dead because no one could find you for a week. It wasn't till they started clearing the rubble and they dragged you protesting out of the Three Dragons' beer cellar that anyone realised you were still alive."

I shrug this off.

"That was a real war. Not a minor skirmish with one hostile Sorcerer. I needed to recuperate."

Lisutaris gets busy adding her considerable powers to the hiding spells already protecting us from discovery. Makri drifts off to sleep with a thazis stick still burning in her hand. Hanama removes it from her fingers and smokes the rest of it herself before also closing her eyes.

Herminis yawns, and asks Lisutaris if it's safe for her to remain here.

"For now, yes. Providing Thraxas doesn't object."

"I object."

"He's fine with it," says Lisutaris. "Because he knows I'm about to do him a favour."

"What favour?"

Lisutaris has completed the hiding spell. My office is now shielded securely from the prying eyes of Old Hasius the Brilliant, Lanius Suncatcher and any other nosy government Sorcerer. Not the first time my office has had to be protected in this way, I reflect.

"What's the favour?"

"That Sorcerer has been interfering with all sorcery in Turai. Very subtly. Too subtle to detect at the time. But now he's dead, I can feel a difference. I'm grateful for your help. Perhaps I might be able to find something new on the case you're investigating."

Lisutaris takes a small phial from a pocket in her robe. Kuriya. I hand her a saucer and she pours in enough to make a small picture. She waves her hand over the saucer. I study the results. It's a lot clearer than before. Rittius, Kalius and Bevarius can be seen in the corridor as before. After they've departed, Lodius appears, next to a trolley of food. He picks up a pastry and puts it back on the trolley. I haven't seen that before. It doesn't look good. Another Senator appears, someone I don't recognise. Lodius talks to him for a while. Slightly furtively, it seems, though it's hard to be sure. The image fades.

"Wait," says Lisutaris. "There's a little more."

As we watch, Consul Kalius reappears in the corridor. I

haven't seen that before either. The same Senator who was talking to Lodius now meets the Consul and they confer. After this the pictures fade.

"Any help?" asks the Mistress of the Sky.

"Maybe. A few things for me to think about."

Who was that Senator? Why were Lodius and Kalius talking to him? And why has neither of them mentioned it before? Now I've seen Consul Kalius hanging around in the corridor next to the food trolleys. And Kalius's assistant Bevarius hired a man to kill me, if I can believe Kerinox, which I think I can. Everything points towards the Consul's office. That's going to be awkward for me.

Lisutaris wishes to remain here for the night. I leave them to it, and retire to my bedroom. As I leave, the Mistress of the Sky is rolling a stick of thazis from her own superior supply, and staring deeply into the fire, considering the matter of the Orcs, and the rescue of Herminis, neither of which is over yet.

CHAPTER EIGHTEEN

It's exactly a year since Deputy Consul Cicerius made me a Tribune. Today is my last day in office. Having spent the year using the powers of the tribunate as little as possible, I decide to go out in style. It's time to throw some official weight around. I want to speak with Consul Kalius and his assistant Bevarius, and I'm not about to be put off.

"Tribune Thraxas to see Consul Kalius."

The guard at the gate tries to brush me off.

"Do you have an appointment?"

"Didn't you hear me?" I bark. "I said Tribune Thraxas. As in Tribune of the People. As in a man with the power to have you arrested for interfering in official business if you don't open the gate this instant."

I sweep my way imperiously past guards, clerks, minor officials and state Sorcerers on my way to Kalius's inner sanctum, stopping for nothing except a plateful of spicy yams. Once more they're excellent, and a credit to Erisox's talents. Outside the final door I'm confronted by an official in a toga.

"The Consul is busy."

"Then unbusy him. This is Tribunes' business."

He wants to resist. Unfortunately he knows the law.

"You may see the Consul after he has finished his business with Coranus—"

"Can't wait," I say, and force my way past.

Kalius is startled as I march into his office, as is Coranus the Grinder. The Sorcerer, legendary for both his power and his bad temper, leaps to his feet in agitation.

"Who dares—"

I hold up my hand.

"I do. Thraxas. Tribune. With some questions for the Consul that can't wait."

"Do you realise the importance of this meeting?" roars Kalius.

"No. But you can get right back to it after you answer some questions about who you were talking to at the food trolley right before Galwinius was murdered."

Kalius's face turns red with fury. He orders me out of his office. A waste of time. I inform him that I've just seen some better sorcerous pictures of events.

"So unless you want me to go forth and blab to the Senate, you'd better come up with some answers."

Coranus is looking wryly amused. He's never been that much of a friend of the city's hierarchy and doesn't seem to mind seeing the Consul discomfited. He rises gracefully. He's pale-skinned, with sandy hair, not a tall or imposing man. There's little about his looks to suggest the great power he wields.

"Perhaps I should leave you, Consul. I have an appointment to see Lisutaris, Mistress of the Sky. I'm sorry I have not been able to help you in the matter of Herminis. Perhaps the Mistress of the Sky will be able to pierce the gloom which surrounds the affair."

Apparently the Consul has just been discussing the escape from prison of the Senator's wife, in which I am now deeply implicated. For a moment I expect the powerful Coranus to denounce me on the spot. Was there something in the way he mentioned Lisutaris's name? Are they suspicious already?

Coranus pauses at the door. I wait to be denounced.

"Be sure to pass on my message to Prince Dees-Akan that he is a fool of the highest order to remove Lisutaris from the War Council."

The Consul nods stiffly. If he passes on the message I doubt he'll use those exact words. Coranus looks at me quite affably before sauntering out. I think I made a good impression. The door closes. Kalius turns to me.

"You will regret this. When you were made Tribune there was never any intention that you should interfere in the governing of Turai."

"No. Just an intention that I'd help Turai cheat to get Lisutaris elected head of the Sorcerers Guild. And now I'm here with some awkward questions for you. Funny how these things work out. What were you doing in the corridor before Galwinius was murdered?"

"I have already explained that I was in conference with Rittius and Bevarius."

"Not then. After. You all walked down the corridor. But you walked back alone, which you never mentioned before. And then you talked to someone at the food trolley. A Senator I didn't recognise. Who was it?"

"Do you think you can barge into my office and bully me? The Consul of Turai?"

I lean over the desk.

"You think that's bullying? How about this. You're badly in debt. Creditors are chasing you and if you don't get some money soon you're going to find yourself in the bankruptcy court, disbarred from office. No fancy carriage and seat in the Senate. No big house in Thamlin. No cosy relationship with your lady friend Tilupasis. Even your buddy Capatius won't cover your bills. But then Prefect Galwinius dies and suddenly you've come into a very fat inheritance. Nice for you. But I'd say it makes it fairly suspicious that you didn't mention to anyone that you were alone in the corridor and then talked to someone right beside the food trolley. Quite an omission, in the circumstances. It will all make for a good report to the Senate."

"I'll have you thrown out of the city!"

"Not before I've made a report."

Kalius hesitates. He's wondering if I've really seen some better sorcerous pictures of the events or if I'm bluffing. As Consul, he's been privy to all the findings of government Sorcerers so far. None of these showed him doing anything suspicious. And now here I am, spoiling things. Kalius is struggling. There's something on his mind he really doesn't want to admit.

"You might as well tell me. I'll find out in the end. I generally do. Politicians threaten me and thugs attack me and I just keep going. It's annoying for other people, but it's what I do."

"You expect me to reveal anything to a man who is working for Lodius?"

"I'll keep it private. Unless you did kill Galwinius. You don't have a choice. It's me or a Senate committee."

Kalius gives up the struggle.

"Very well, Investigator. I was called to meet with Senator Cressius. My talk with him was not something I wished to make public."

"Why not?"

"Because Senator Cressius is a moneylender. My debts are such that I was left with no choice. No bank in Turai will do business with me."

I chew this over for a few seconds. I'm aware of Cressius's reputation though I've never encountered him. I didn't know he was a moneylender but it fits with what I've heard about him. He's one of our more disreputable Senators and not a man the city's Consul should be associating with. Kalius would certainly want to keep it quiet. The only strange thing is that they were talking in such a public place.

"I had not arranged the meeting beforehand," explains the Consul. "But on that morning a note arrived from my banker informing me that he was about to foreclose on my mortgage. I therefore instructed my assistant to approach Senator Cressius at the meeting and arrange an impromptu discussion. And now, Investigator, you will leave my office, and never enter it again. I told you that you were finished in this city, and I intend to make that happen."

I leave the Consul's office deep in thought. It's possible that Kalius is telling the truth about Cressius. He needed money badly enough to approach him. Much the same would apply to Senator Lodius. Another man badly in need of funds. Maybe there was no more to the events in the corridor than two aristocrats both needing a loan. I'm still uneasy. Lodius and Kalius both stood to gain from Prefect Galwinius's death. Was borrowing money all they were discussing in the corridor with Cressius?

It's time to confront Bevarius. His secretary informs me that the Consul's assistant is not in the building today so I set off towards his home. Bevarius is unmarried and lives in a house of moderate size on the outskirts of Thamlin. On the way there I'm so deep in thought I hardly notice the cold. There's no one around except for a few hurrying servants, out buying provisions, as I walk up to Bevarius's modest dwelling. Not cheap—nothing is in Thamlin—but suitable for a young man whose parents never rose far in Turanian society. A few large rooms, small private temple, couple of servants, nothing more.

There's no answer when I knock on the door. I apply some weight. Nothing happens. I try a minor word of power for opening locks and the door swings open. The Consul's assistant should take more care. The hallway is bright, white walls, little furnishing. Likewise the main room. Bevarius obviously isn't a man given to luxury. I turn round to find him standing in the doorway pointing a small bow at me. He takes a step forward. I don't like the weapon he's carrying. It looks powerful and there's an arrow pointed at my heart. Bevarius notices my gaze.

"Specially issued to all cavalry commanders," he explains. "Small and light for using on horseback. Made from the horns of the arquix. Almost as powerful as a crossbow. The arrow will pin you to the wall."

"I didn't know you were a cavalry commander."

"Just commissioned. What are you doing in my house?"

"Investigating."

"Investigating what?"

"Kerinox."

"Ah, Kerinox," says Bevarius, calmly. "The man I hired to kill you."

"That's the one."

Bevarius comes further into the room. I'm looking for a chance to jump him but he's careful not to come too close.

"Why did you want me killed?"

"I'm sure you must know already, Investigator. You were coming rather too close to finding out the truth about Galwinius's death."

Bevarius is making no attempt to lie, which can only mean that he intends to kill me. No reason why he shouldn't. It's the smart thing to do, in the circumstances. Gets me out of the way, and the Civil Guards won't be too upset with the Consul's assistant for killing an intruder. I try to buy some time.

"Why did you kill Galwinius?"

"He found out about the Orcish Sorcerer. An informant told him. We couldn't let him give us away."

"How did you manage to frame Senator Lodius? He could have handed that pastry to anyone, or eaten it himself."

Bevarius looks amused.

"You're no better at investigating than the Civil Guard, and God knows, they're bad enough. Galwinius wasn't killed by the pastry from Lodius's tray. The poison doesn't act that quickly. Unlike carasin, it takes a minute or two to take effect. I fed the poisoned item to Galwinius before the Consul entered the room. It was just good fortune that Galwinius keeled over when he did. Made Lodius the prime suspect. In the confusion, I dropped a little more poison on to the pastry he'd eaten. Enough to fool the Sorcerers."

"That was smart."

"It was."

"The Orcs must have paid a lot for the services of a smart man like you."

Bevarius's eyes narrow.

"Maybe they did. And I think we've talked long enough."

He's about to loose the arrow.

"So who were you working with? Kalius?"

Bevarius frowns. Then he gasps, and sags forward. His finger lets go of the arrow and it thuds into the floor in front of him. He grasps at his neck then crumples to the floor. I dash to his side. There's a dart sticking in his neck. I look round wildly, unable to fathom where it came from. One of the front windows is open a few inches. It doesn't seem possible that anyone could have fired a dart through the gap so accurately as to kill Bevarius, but there's no other solution. Someone very adept in the use of weapons has just assassinated him. There's no one in sight. His killer will be long gone by now, disappearing into the snow.

I return to the corpse. Blood is pumping from Bevarius's neck. I put my hand inside his toga, looking for the concealed pocket that these awkward garments always contain. I pull out a few papers. A betting slip, from the look of it, and something larger. I frown. The larger piece of paper is now stained with blood but I can still make out some of the letters. They're written in Orcish. There's a noise outside. I look out the window. Two servants, coming home laden with goods. I make quickly for the back door and exit as they go in the front. I'm hurrying along the road by the time I hear someone screaming that Bevarius has been murdered.

The snow is falling more heavily. I keep my head down and hope that no one will pay enough attention to me to give the Civil Guards a good description when they arrive to investigate. I'm keen to get back to the Avenging Axe as quickly as possible to examine the Orcish writing. I have a fair knowledge of the common Orcish tongue and Makri's is better.

I find her in her room, studying some old books. Makri has very few books. She'd like more, but they're expensive items.

"Makri. I did swear never to speak to you again after the Herminis debacle but I need your help translating this Orcish document."

"Okay," says Makri, quite brightly.

"New books?"

"Samanatius gave them to me. I went along to his academy to say goodbye."

"Is he leaving town?"

"No, he's going to fight the Orcs."

I can see why Makri was saying goodbye. I can't see the elderly philosopher lasting long on the battlefield.

I spread out the sheet of paper on the floor for Makri to examine. It's torn and stained with blood. Makri purses her lips and says that it's not a form of Orcish she's familiar with.

"I can make out some of it. But there are words I've never seen before. I can probably work it out given time; it looks like some old form of the dialect they speak in Gzak. Like the Orcish their Sorcerers use, I think."

"Okay. But what about the bits you can read? Does the heading say something about feeding dragons?"

"Not feeding," says Makri. "Transporting."

"Transporting?"

With an Orcish army on the way, anything about transporting dragons can't be good news.

"Where did this come from?"

I tell Makri about Bevarius. Makri asks if the Consul's assistant was working alone. I admit I'm not sure.

"Someone killed him before I could finish my interrogation."

I examine the betting slip. Not an official slip from one of Turai's bookmakers but the sort of note a man might make to record some bet between friends, or maybe a note to remind him who was gambling on what when he went to place the bet. Might not be important. All classes in Turai place bets on the races.

"You were right about the poison. It wasn't carasin. Something similar, but slower working. Bevarius poisoned the pastry in—"

I stop. Where did Bevarius poison the pastry? Not in the kitchen. The cook said no one entered the kitchen. In the corridor? Maybe. But if he did, it didn't show up in Lisutaris's sorcerous reconstruction of the scene, even with her improved pictures. Maybe the Consul did it.

He was definitely around the food trolleys. But somehow I can't see Kalius injecting poison into a pastry in the corridor, not when he was due to negotiate a loan from a moneylender. Kalius isn't cool-headed enough to do all that. Everything seems to be pointing towards the Consul but I'm hesitant. I just don't see him as a murderer. Incompetent, yes. Greedy, to an extent. But not murderous. The whole affair sounds much more like the work of a ruthless man like Rittius. There's a man who'd have no qualms about organising a few deaths. And I could easily see him betraying the city for money. Unfortunately nothing points in his direction, and he was never in a position to poison the pastry. Now I think about it, he was alone in the corridor with Bevarius for a while. Neither of them was near the food though. Bevarius's partner in crime has to be someone else.

I ask Makri where Herminis is and she says they've moved her to a secret location.

"Is that secret location my office?"

"No."

I leave her to translate the Orcish paper while I go downstairs and get myself outside a substantial helping of everything on the menu. It takes more than a brush with death to affect my appetite. Viriggax and his mercenaries are drinking steadily at a table nearby. Young Toraggax is pouring a huge flagon of ale down his throat, urged on by his companions. Being new to the brigade, he doesn't want to lag behind in the drinking, but he's looking a little the worse for wear. As he finishes the tankard, Viriggax claps him heartily on the back and pushes another one into his hand.

I find myself nodding off in the chair, so I take myself off to my room, drink a last beer, then fall asleep.

Deep into the night I'm woken by noises outside. Someone is clumping around in the corridor. It's long past the hour when anyone in the tavern should be awake. I throw on a tunic, grab my sword and whisper a word to my illuminated staff, bringing forth a dim light. I open my door carefully, wary of attackers. Some way along the corridor I find Makri in the process of hauling an unconscious Toraggax out of her room. Makri's a lot stronger than she looks but she's having some difficulty in moving the huge mercenary.

"Need a hand?"

Makri spins round and looks guilty.

"No," she replies.

I look down at the unconscious man.

"What happened? You slug him when he tried to sneak into your room?"

"He didn't sneak in. He knocked on the door and I let him in."

"And you slugged him when he started getting amorous?"

"I didn't slug him at all," replies Makri. "He just fell over drunk."

I nod.

"Too much beer. He was trying to keep up with Viriggax."

I'm puzzled.

"Why did you let a drunken mercenary into your room without punching him?"

Makri shrugs.

"No reason."

"So what happened?"

"What do you mean, what happened? He came in, then he fell over unconscious. What's it got to do with you anyway?"

"Nothing. If you want to start inviting mercenaries into your bedroom it's your affair."

"I didn't invite him into my bedroom. He just arrived."

Makri suddenly glances over my shoulder. I look round to find that Hanama has arrived on the scene, quite noiselessly. The Assassin looks slightly confused at the sight that greets her.

"What are you doing here?" I demand. "How did you get into the tavern?"

"I picked the lock. What's happening?"

"Nothing," says Makri.

"She's just evicting a drunken mercenary," I explain.

"Did he try to break into your room?"

"No," I say. "She invited him in."

Hanama frowns.

"You're inviting mercenaries into your room? When did this start?"

"Nothing has started," says Makri, raising her voice. "He just knocked on my door and I let him in. I don't see anything strange in that."

"I think it's very strange," says Hanama, who, for some reason, is not sounding at all pleased. "You've never done it before."

"She's right," I agree. "It's not like you at all. Usually you'd just punch the guy."

"Or maybe kick him," says Hanama.

"Or even stab him."

"Shut up," says Makri crossly. "It's none of your business."

I notice a few leaves projecting from Hanama's winter cloak.

"Are those flowers?"

"No," says Hanama.

"Yes they are."

"Well so what if they are?"

Assassins are trained from a young age to hide their emotions. Even so, for the briefest of moments I'd swear a look of embarrassment flickers across Hanama's face.

"Did you bring them for me?" asks Makri.

"No," says Hanama. "I just had them on me."

She pauses.

"Unless you want them. You can have them if you want."

"Thank you," says Makri.

"Of course," says Hanama, "if you're too busy with the mercenary . . ."

"I'm not busy with anything."

Hanama suddenly looks cross.

"I do think it's very strange that you're suddenly inviting northern mercenaries into your room late at night. Did you really think about the consequences?"

"Goddammit," explodes Makri. "I didn't know I had to ask permission before I had visitors!"

Heavy footsteps on the stairs announce the arrival of Gurd. He walks up, torch in hand, wondering what all the noise is.

"What's going on?"

"Nothing," says Makri.

"She has drunken mercenaries in her room," says Hanama, quite sharply.

"Is this true?" demands Gurd.

"Only partially," replies Makri.

Gurd looks down at the unconscious figure of Toraggax. "Did you punch him?"

"What is this with me punching people?" demands Makri. "You all seem to think I spend my whole time punching everyone."

"Well you do," says Gurd.

"She didn't have to punch him," says Hanama. "She just invited him right into her room."

"What for?"

"We're not exactly clear about that," I say.

There are some softer footsteps on the stairs. Tanrose has arrived. She's clad in a very fancy robe, embroidered with yellow roses.

"What's happening?"

"Makri punched a mercenary," says Gurd, who hasn't quite got the picture yet.

"I didn't punch him," protests Makri. "I invited him in."

"So you just come right out and admit it?" says Hanama.

Gurd suddenly becomes suspicious, and looks at Makri and Hanama.

"Are you having a meeting? You know I told you you couldn't have meetings of the Association of Gentlewomen in my tavern."

"It's not a meeting," says Makri.

"Because I absolutely forbid it."

"Yes, I heard you the first time," says Makri, testily.

"Why can't they have meetings?" says Tanrose.

"Why? You expect my tavern to become a meeting place for these appalling women with their constant complaints? I will not put up with women who hate men."

"How can you say that Makri hates men?" objects Tanrose. "She's just told us that she's been inviting mercenaries to spend the night with her."

"Has Makri been inviting mercenaries to spend the night with her?" says Dandelion, appearing in a nightrobe so bright it would serve as a beacon. She looks at Makri.

"Is that wise? Did you really think about the consequences?"

"That's exactly what I said," cries Hanama.

"Hello, Hanama," says Dandelion. "Those are nice flowers. Did you bring them for Makri?"

"No," says Hanama, sharply. "I just found them outside."

Dandelion looks down at the prone figure of Toraggax.

"If you invited him to spend the night with you, why did you knock him unconscious?"

"I didn't knock him unconscious," says Makri.

Dandelion looks troubled.

"Did you stab him? Is he dead?"

"Could everybody just leave me alone?" demands Makri.

"Well of course," says Hanama, icily. "I wouldn't have visited if I'd known you were engaged in a secret rendezvous with the virile young Toraggax."

"I was not engaged in anything!" roars Makri.

"Is this a meeting?" asks Dandelion, eagerly. "Will you let me join the Association of Gentlewomen now?"

It isn't the most helpful thing Dandelion could have said. The corridor seems to erupt in a very loud series of accusations, counteraccusations and general bad temper. Gurd, Tanrose, Makri and Hanama yell at each other while Dandelion stands there grinning like an idiot. Realising that pre-war dementia has now set in and there's nothing to be done about it, I retreat back to my rooms. At least no one seems to be yelling at me. Which should make me feel good, I suppose, though I don't seem to be in the best of moods as I climb back into my bed.

CHAPTER NINETEEN

The landus making its way slowly along Moon and Stars Boulevard contains three rather moody passengers. Gurd, Makri and I sit in silence as the driver negotiates his way through the icy streets. Our phalanxes are scheduled for practice. The weather is far too severe but the Consul has decreed that it must go ahead anyway. As for Makri, she's on her way to Lisutaris's villa. The Sorcerers Guild are due to appear on the field later today and Makri is required to take up her duties as bodyguard. She's carrying her armour in a bag on her lap. Also in the bag is the paper I took from Bevarius. Makri has been unable to translate some of the Orcish sorcerous terminology but it seems to concern the magical transporting of dragons, so Lisutaris should examine it.

Gurd has hardly spoken a word since we climbed into the landus. I presume this is due to last night's disagreement with Makri, though it's unlike Gurd to bear a grudge. Our landus is halted by a road block. The Civil Guards are checking every carriage, looking for Herminis. A guard pokes his head inside, then waves us through. Though the city is already in crisis, the sensational prison breakout of the Senator's wife has not failed to grip the public's imagination. The Chronicle is reporting that an armed gang, aided by Sorcerers, freed the woman from her place of captivity and are currently being hunted by every Civil Guard in town.

"You've really landed me in it this time," I mutter to Makri, softly, so that Gurd won't hear.

"There's nothing to worry about," whispers Makri. "Lisutaris and Tirini have got everything hidden."

"I'm not ready," blurts out Gurd, unexpectedly.

"What?"

"I'm not ready to get married,"

Not feeling that it is quite the time to discuss this. I make no reply, but Gurd seems insistent. He grabs my arm.

"You saw how Tanrose took Makri's side against me last night. How can we get married? Why did you talk me into it?"

"What?"

Gurd looks pained.

"Why did you insist that I married Tanrose? I'm not ready."

"I didn't—"

"I saved your life at the Battle of Ekinsbrog!" says Gurd. "And this is how you repay me!"

I shake my head. He's a sorry sight.

"Don't worry. We'll all be dead before the ceremony."

"What if we're not?" says Gurd. "If I survive the war I'll still have to get married."

"Yes, no happy solution there," says Makri, icily. "Maybe you should just ask Tanrose if she wouldn't mind cooking and cleaning for you for the rest of your life and just forgetting the marriage bit."

"Don't you take that tone with me!" says Gurd, angrily. "And how dare you have these meetings in my tavern. And steal beer from the cellars!"

Makri looks accusingly at me.

"You told him about that?"

"He didn't need to!" yells Gurd. "You think I didn't notice?"

"If you'd pay me better I'd be able to buy my own beer," says Makri.

"You're fired!"

"Fine. I quit anyway. Remind me never to enter your disgusting tavern again."

"You will never be allowed in my disgusting tavern again."

Makri looks balefully at me.

"You just had to run and tell tales, didn't you?"

"Tell tales? You think that's bad?" I retort, with some justified outrage. "After the catalogue of appalling behaviour you've involved yourself in recently? What a curse it was the day you walked into the Avenging Axe."

We lapse into a brooding silence. As the landus passes through Thamlin, Makri departs towards Truth is Beauty Lane, home of the Sorcerers. She doesn't say goodbye. We turn east towards the Superbius Gate. Progress soon becomes impossible as we find ourselves mingling with a horde of part-time soldiers on their way to the practice fields. We leave the landus and join the throng. The snow is falling heavily. Visibility is poor. A few boisterous souls among the crowd attempt to cheer their friends by shouting encouragement, but mostly the citizens trudge along quietly. No matter what happens in the war, a lot of these men won't be around next summer.

Rumours in the city are rife. The Elves won't be able to sail because all the young Elves have become addicted to dwa. The Simnians won't come because they've decided to defend their own borders instead. The Niojans are doing a deal with the Orcs to sack Turai and split the booty. Queen Direeva has done a deal with the Orcs to provide them with a squadron of fresh dragons in return for leaving her kingdom alone.

The rumours are not all negative. Last week we heard a report that Prince Amrag had been killed in a feud arising from bad feelings among the Orcish nations over the rumour that the Prince's blood is tainted by a Human ancestor. There's little likelihood of this being true. The Prince has already shown himself capable of subjugating all opposition.

Before we reach the city gates we're forced to the side of the road by an official cavalcade. It is the Consul riding out with his retinue. As he passes in his liveried carriage it strikes me how ridiculous my investigation has become. It's brought me to the verge of accusing the Consul of conniving in the murder of Prefect Galwinius. How can I possibly pursue such a notion at this time? Even if I had proof, what could I do about it? Interrupt the War Council to accuse the Consul of murder? Hardly. At best

I'd be ignored. At worst I'd be quietly got rid of. No one wants to hear the truth behind the murder of Galwinius.

More official carriages delay our progress. This time it's Prince Dees-Akan and various members of the War Council. Today will be a major event, with the whole of our forces arrayed on the field.

Once outside the gates I hurry along to join up with my phalanx. Our spears have been brought here by wagon and I supervise my troop as we get into position. The line of spears projects almost twenty feet from the front of the phalanx. As corporal in command of my section, I'm in the third row. The first row is made up of the youngest and strongest men. They have to carry large shields, and bear the brunt of an enemy attack. I know from experience that it's not a comfortable place to be. When I find myself screaming at some of the more incompetent soldiers under my command it's really because I know that if we don't do our job properly, the young men in front will be the first to die.

I can't see Gurd's phalanx; it's some way to the left of us. I regret that we argued this morning but no doubt by tonight he'll have got over his dread of marriage. Or at least he'll have got over blaming me. Gurd is too old a companion for us to really argue; we've been through too much together.

Senator Marius gives an order and the centurions start barking at us. We walk up the field, turn and come back again, more or less in formation. No one falls over. It's progress. We even manage to draw up alongside Praetor Capatius's phalanx without bumping into them. The mercenary companies have emerged from the Stadium

Superbius to join in the drill. Intent on their own manoeuvres, they're no longer mocking us. I can hear Viriggax as he bellows at his men. Must be making young Toraggax's head hurt, after his experiences of last night. I'm annoyed that Makri let him into her room. I don't know why. None of my business, as she said.

After an hour or so of manoeuvres the Senator draws us up in ranks.

"Prepare to meet the Prince."

Prince Dees-Akan trots up on his horse. It's a fine-looking stallion and the young prince makes for an impressive war leader in his shining chainmail and gold-plated helmet. He pushes the helmet back on his forehead and begins to address us. He's a good speaker and I can sense that the men around me are heartened by his words of encouragement. I'd be more heartened if the Prince had ever led an army into battle, but at least he looks the part.

After a nice build-up, he's exhorting us to stand firm when he's interrupted by the sound of galloping hoofs. Heads turn. Lisutaris, Mistress of the Sky, is approaching fast, riding a white horse. The Sorceress is wearing a man's tunic and leggings, something I haven't seen her in since the last war, and there's a sword at her hip. Behind her comes Makri on a black horse, dressed in the light body armour she brought with her from the Orcish lands, made of black leather and skillfully wrought chainmail. There's no sign of the rest of the Sorcerers Guild. Obviously Lisutaris has come in haste. She leaps from her mount and hurries towards the Prince.

I'm close enough to hear the conversation. It starts badly. Prince Dees-Akan, showing little respect for

Lisutaris's rank, rudely demands to know what the Sorceress is doing here. Lisutaris informs him that she has some urgent news. The Prince tells her that any news she has can wait till he's finished inspecting the troops. Lisutaris replies that it can't wait. Voices are raised. In front of the soldiers, it's an unseemly sight.

"You are no longer even a member of the War Council. Leave the field."

"I will not leave the field until I've informed you of my latest findings."

General Pomius, next in command after the Prince, shifts his stance uncomfortably, not at all enjoying the spectacle of his commander ordering Turai's leading Sorcerer from the field. There are murmurings from the troops and the mercenaries. It's bad for the city to have our commander and our main Sorcerer on such poor terms. Finally Lisutaris gives up on the Prince and turns to General Pomius.

"General. The Orcs are coming. Soon. They've sent an army to Yal and they've been marching from there through the winter. Sorcerous interference in Turai has prevented us from tracking them. Worse, they've learned how to teleport dragons. They could be here any second."

"Surely you—" begins the General, but Prince Dees-Akan angrily waves him quiet.

"I forbid you to speak to this woman. Lisutaris, if you do not withdraw I will have my guard remove you."

Makri is nearby, with the horses. As the Prince threatens Lisutaris I notice Makri's hands drift towards her twin swords. Another horseman appears through the snow. It's Harmon Half Elf, with his cloak askew. He looks like a

Sorcerer who's dressed in a hurry. Immediately after him comes Coranus the Grinder, wearing his habitual scowl. The Sorcerers address the leader of their guild.

"We received your message and came immediately. The others are following."

"What is this?" demands the Prince. "You have summoned the Sorcerers Guild without consulting me?"

Coranus eyes the Prince and speaks harshly.

"Have you not yet acted on Lisutaris's warning?"

Three more horses pound on to the scene, mouths foaming, bearing younger members of the Sorcerers Guild. Anumaris Thunderbolt, too young to have been in combat before, leaps from her horse and looks around her wild-eyed, her hands raised, as if expecting to confront a dragon this very moment. When Old Astrath Triple Moon rolls up with the appearance of a man who's very glad to be back in the saddle, the Prince erupts in fury.

"How dare you disregard my orders!" he roars.

"Perhaps we should hear her out," suggest General Pomius. He doesn't want to go against the Prince but he's too wise a soldier to ignore the Sorcerers Guild.

"Hear her out? The Orcs are marching? In this weather?"

"The force is made up of northern mountain Orcs," says Lisutaris. "They're used to the weather."

"And are they used to transporting dragons by magic? Do you see any dragons?"

"Yes," says Makri. "There's one right there."

We look up. Through a thin grey cloud, masked by the falling snow, an ominous shape is just visible, circling in the sky. It's joined by another, and another. Suddenly the shapes become clearer, as the war dragons begin to swoop

from the clouds. At this moment there's a great shout from
the eastern side of the field, a shout that extends into a
prolonged series of screams and the clash of weapons. As
the dragons hurtle down towards us, Orcish troops smash
into the left flank of our unprepared army.

CHAPTER TWENTY

The noise, chaos and confusion are indescribable. Appearing unseen from the banks of snow, the Orcish phalanxes mow their way through the unprotected flanks of the Turanian soldiery. Simultaneously the dragons pour down fire on our heads. I'd be dead already if it wasn't for the instantaneous protection thrown out by the assembled Human Sorcerers, most of whom have now arrived on the field, thanks to Lisutaris's alert.

In the overwhelming confusion Senator Marius tries to form up the phalanx and turn to face the enemy but it's not easy. Men are panicking, and with the phalanxes on either side marshalled to hear the Prince, there's not enough room to manoeuvre. Spears, shields, arms and legs become tangled up as another phalanx collides with us. The snow is falling thicker than ever and we can't yet see our enemy, though we can hear the screams of the battle in progress. Soon our ranks are further disrupted by streams of fugitives from the fighting, remnants of the troops on our left flank who, I can readily guess, have been swept aside in an instant.

All the while the dragons above, twenty or so, keep up the attack. Each dragon carries a rider, a Sorcerer and perhaps ten more Orcs, who shoot bolts into our ranks with crossbows. Their Sorcerers pound us with spells, attempting to break through the protective barrier set up by Lisutaris and her companions. Shafts of fire pierce the sky as our own Sorcerers return the fire.

In the deafening confusion no one can hear Senator Marius's orders. His centurions struggle to bring the men into line. Noise and confusion are always present on the battlefield. A well-trained phalanx could cope. We're not a well-trained phalanx. By the time we're turned to face the attack there are gaps in our ranks and our whole right flank is lagging behind. I scream at the men around me, ordering them to get in line and bring our long spears into position. There's frantic movement on all sides but we're nowhere near organised when an Orcish phalanx looms out of the snow, marching in good order towards us. With their craggy features, black clothes and dull armour, it's a sight to unnerve the novices around me.

The instant they appear I know we're doomed. Whatever we might have believed about the Orcish army's lack of organisation was wrong. This phalanx is fearsomely well organised. As soon as they see us, horns blow and the long spears that point to the sky are lowered towards us, forming a sharp and deadly wall. The Orcish phalanx breaks into a slow run, picking up speed as they advance. Each man around me grasps his short spear, preparing to hurl it at the enemy, hoping to break their ranks. This doesn't work as well as it should. The whole of my phalanx should toss their spears in unison, raining a blizzard of steel on to the enemy. Men all over the line, unable to hear their orders and forgetting their training, let go of their spears far too early. Most of the missiles fall short. Meanwhile the disciplined Orcs have held their fire. Without pausing in their stride, they let go with their own short spears. A lethal barrage of pointed metal rains down around our heads. All our Sorcerers are engaged with the dragons and we have no protection from the enemy spears. Every man here wears a breastplate and helmet, but a sharp, heavy spear, falling from above, can penetrate the sort of armour worn by a common soldier. Even if your armour turns the spear away, the next one is as likely to hit an arm or a leg, causing terrible, incapacitating wounds. Men on either side of me crumple to the ground. I've raised my shield over my head. A spear catches it, piercing it, and scraping my helmet. Fortunately it doesn't penetrate far enough to wound me.

By now the front line of my phalanx has yawning gaps which grow larger as a supporting unit of light Orcish infantry, running alongside their phalanx, pelts us with spears and arrows. I scream at the men behind me to advance, to fill in the gaps, but it's useless. Panic is setting in. Many of the long spears, which should bristle from the front of our formation, are either lying on the ground or pointing at the sky as men struggle to keep some sort of shape in the face of the onslaught. The man in front of me falls to the ground with an arrow in his eye. I step forward into his place. I'm now in the ragged front line. The Orcs are forty feet away, running towards us at great speed. Their long spears are held rigidly in line as they charge. I grab the lance that's waving above my shoulder, held there unsteadily by the men behind me, point it firmly at the Orcs, and wait for their phalanx to strike. As I do so I mutter a prayer which, I'm quite certain, will be the last words I ever say.

The dark Orcish phalanx crashes into us. My spear goes through the throat of an Orc but few others do. Our front line crumples on impact and the Orcs mow us down. I'm on the ground with bodies piling on top of me, feet trampling us into the snow, my face covered, unable to breathe. I use my strength to fight my way to my knees. My helmet is gone, I can't free my arms and an Orc from the middle of their phalanx draws back his sword to cut my head off. I yell out the spell I've been keeping in reserve, a spell for killing Orcs I learned a long time ago. My assailant falls silently to the ground, slain by magic. Three or four Orcs around us fall with him. By now I've freed my arms and drawn my sword but my situation remains hopeless. My phalanx is broken, I'm isolated from my troops and I'm surrounded by hundreds of Orcs. I can use my spell one more time before it vanishes from my memory. I do so. The three closest Orcs fall dead. That's it. My magic is used up. I've killed eight Orcs. Not so bad for a death stand. I raise my shield as they come in swiftly from all sides.

Suddenly there's a violent flash and the air around goes green. I'm thrown down and find myself once more lying in the trampled snow. When I hoist myself to my feet I'm the only one that does so. All around me, dead Orcs lie in twisted heaps. Somewhere a Human Sorcerer has come to our aid. Needing no more encouragement, I sling my shield over my shoulder and set off at a run, hurdling bodies and weapons as I rush through the falling snow, looking for any company of armed Humans. As generally happens in battle, I have little idea of what's happening. I'm guessing things aren't going so well for Turai.

About a hundred yards on I run into the remains of my phalanx. They're hurrying along under the protection of young Anumaris Thunderbolt, recent recruit to the Sorcerers Guild. She's lost her horse and her rainbow cloak is in tatters but whatever she's suffered she's managed to rescue a group of men from my phalanx.

"Good spell," I say. "Any left?"

"Just one," she replies.

There are around forty or so men here, many of them wounded. No sign of Senator Marius, or any of his centurions. Not even a corporal. I take command, ordering the men into four lines of ten. We set off towards the city walls, though they are now invisible, hidden by snow and smoke from the Sorcerers' spells.

Above us dragons are still raging in the sky, though some have been killed, and some have landed to set down more troops and Sorcerers to press their attack. I'm quite clear as to the Orcs' intentions. Prince Amrag wants to seize Turai to use it as a bridgehead against the west. He's taken the risk of attacking us in winter before our allies arrive, and the risk might pay off. Knowing that the battle is lost, it's the duty of all Turanians to get back inside the city to defend it. I lead my men towards the gates. The main body of Orcish forces has passed on by. If the slaughter of Turanian troops has been everywhere as bad as on this part of the field, we'll have little chance of reaching the city in safety.

I urge my small squadron onwards. Anumaris jogs alongside us. Her face is deathly white and I can tell that she's profoundly shocked. She's never seen rows of corpses before, never had to run over a carpet of dead men and blood-spattered Orcs. I check on her as we progress. The young Sorcerer saved my life and if necessary I'll carry her back to Turai.

The Stadium Superbius looms large on our right, a huge building covered in snow. All around the entrance are the bodies of slaughtered fighters, killed by the dragons and Sorcerers as they rushed from the stadium to join in the fray. I wonder if Viriggax is among the dead.

Through the blanket of snow, I catch sight of a large body of Orcs. I hold my hand up, halting my troop. I hesitate, uncertain what to do. If I was with Gurd and a trusty group of warriors, I'd charge. My companions are mostly young recruits, some of them wounded, most of them scared. I don't give them much chance of hacking their way through any sort of opposition. A gust of wind clears the snow, allowing me to make out the shapes in front of us. There, on a small knoll, Makri is standing with her weapons raised. Lisutaris, Mistress of the Sky, lies dead or unconscious at her feet. Makri is protecting the body from a force of around one hundred Orcs. Makri's face is covered by her helmet but she's easily recognisable from the hair which billows from underneath, and from the weapons she bears: one dark Orcish sword and one hefty silver axe. The Orcs close in on her from all sides.

I order my men forward. My orders are met by some very hesitant faces. I've no time to persuade and no time even to threaten. Makri will be dead in a few seconds. I set off at a run towards her and hope my men follow me. As I sprint for the raised mound I get the curious feeling that time is passing extremely slowly, and everything around me is unusually clear. I run past the body of a huge dragon, dead on the ground, and it seems to take forever. I can see Makri engage her assailants but though my feet are moving I don't seem to be getting any closer. I watch as the Orcs attack. Their swords and spears come at her from every direction at once. I've seen Makri fight on many occasions, and I've seen her fight in difficult circumstances. But I've never seen Makri, or anyone else, engage in combat in the way she does now. She spins and weaves in a manner which seems impossible, and as she does so she cuts, thrusts, and deflects oncoming blades with a speed which is barely credible. She cuts down an opponent in front of her while another thrusts a spear directly at her back. Somehow she manages to block the blow, deflecting the spear without even looking at it, sliding out of range of another two blades, spinning round to thrust her blade into the face of the spear carrier then back again to hack off the sword arm of another Orc. She leaps over a sword that hacks at her legs and before she lands, her axe has severed the head of her assailant. I'm still running towards her and the thought goes through my mind that if these few seconds were the only time I ever saw Makri in combat, I'd still know for certain that she was the greatest sword fighter who ever lived.

My heart is pounding. I can't run any faster. It's taking

me too long to get there. Makri can't hold off the Orcs for much longer, no matter how skilful she is. Not with a hundred opponents and nowhere to seek cover. Already her chainmail is in tatters and several arrows project from her leather leggings. Bodies are piled up around her feet but the Orcs fly in relentlessly. I'm no more than twenty feet away when she takes a blow to the head and stumbles. There are four rows of Orcs between me and Makri. I'm on my own, I've outdistanced my companions. I crash into the rear of the Orcs like a one-man phalanx, breaking through their ranks and scattering them. Makri is on her knees, still fighting. I kill an Orc who's about to stab her, then slash wildly at his companions. The Orcs, temporarily surprised, fall back a few paces. Makri is already on her feet, weapons raised, blood seeping from under her helmet.

"It's good to see you again, Thraxas," she says.

"And you," I reply.

The Orcs, realising that I'm a lone rescuer, hesitate no longer. They rush us from all directions. Makri stands on one side of Lisutaris's body and I stand on the other and we prepare to meet our fate. Suddenly the air flashes with green flame and the Orcs crumple to the ground. Once more I've been saved by Anumaris. She's finally caught up, and unleashed her last spell. I should feel grateful: I wish she'd got here earlier. I sink to my knees. I've run too far, too fast, and I'm wounded in the shoulder. I need to catch my breath.

"Have a nice rest," says Makri. "Why don't you have a beer while you're down there?"

I draw a small flask of klee from inside my breastplate.

"Next best thing."

I take a slug and pass the flask to Makri, who does the same. Anumaris Thunderbolt is bending over Lisutaris.

"She's still alive."

"Of course I'm still alive," snaps Lisutaris, opening her eyes. "What the hell happened?"

"You got hit by a dragon's tail," says Makri.

"What happened to the dragon?"

"You killed it."

"Good."

Lisutaris looks around the frozen battlefield.

"We must get back inside the city."

We set off, a force now of forty soldiers, two Sorcerers and one Sorcerer's bodyguard. As we near the city the wind blows fiercely from the east, again clearing the air of snow. The gates are closed. There's a battle going on in front of them as the victorious Orcs press their assault on the last remnants of Turai's army, no longer a force in any sort of order but a ragged band of soldiers and mercenaries desperate to escape, with nowhere to go.

Lisutaris suddenly halts, takes stock of her surroundings, then calls out.

"Harmon? Coranus?"

Harmon Half Elf and Coranus the Grinder stride out of the white gloom.

"Lisutaris. I thought you were dead."

"Still here."

"We brought down many dragons," says Harmon. "But we couldn't save our troops."

Both of the powerful Sorcerers are unharmed. A small blessing for Turai. When the Sorcerers responded to

Lisutaris's urgent alarm, most of them arrived without their bodyguards. Their continuing survival is probably the only chance for Turai, but it's not going to be easy getting them back into the city. They've expended their magic and the Orcish army stands between us and the gates.

Only two or three dragons remain in the sky. Some have fallen to our Sorcerers. Others may just have flown off to rest, away from the battle. Dragons are never as efficient in winter and can't match the endless intensity they're capable of in warmer weather. By now the great beasts that remain will be running low on fire. The Sorcerers they bear may well have run out of spells. If the city can just prevent the Orcish army from entering, we might still be able to defend the walls.

"We should head south," I advise. "Avoid the Orcs and make it to the gate on the shore."

"And avoid the battle?" protests Makri.

"We have to get the Sorcerers back inside so they can recharge their spells."

It's possible we might creep past, hidden by the bad weather. It means abandoning the men defending the East Gate, but I don't see what we can do for them anyway. Lisutaris considers our options. She doesn't like the thought of ignoring the plight of the Turanian soldiers at the gate. I shrug, and draw my sword.

"Okay," I say. "Then we'll attack."

I start marshalling my forty men, ready to advance on the thousands of Orcs that stand between us and the city walls.

"Walk behind me," says Lisutaris. We follow her towards the battle. Several hundred Turanians are trapped beneath the city walls, fighting a hopeless rearguard action. They're using overturned wagons for shelter. Up on the walls, men are hurling missiles towards the Orcs, and other Sorcerers on the ramparts send down spells. But the Orcs have Sorcerers of their own, who protect their forces, and send back fire. Meanwhile the Orcish troops pour arrows into the huddle of men. An Orcish phalanx swings into view. Fresh troops, from the look of them, making ready to mop up the Human survivors. After which they'll attempt to force the gate. The Orcish army isn't equipped with siege engines but after destroying the Turanian forces on the field, and making our Sorcerers expend all of their power, they might not need siege engines to force their way into the city. A battering ram and a few spells will probably do it.

We walk behind Lisutaris, who's limping. Makri supports her. Makri has removed her helmet. Her neck is caked with blood and her hair is streaked with the congealing liquid. When we're about one hundred yards from the Orcs, Lisutaris halts.

"Any spells?" she asks, turning to Harmon Half Elf and Coranus the Grinder. They shake their heads. Neither they nor Anumaris have so much as a single spell left between them. Lisutaris nods. She's weary and in pain from her wounds. Being struck by a dragon's tail is no light matter. She fishes around in her tunic and pulls out a rather crumpled thazis stick, igniting it with a word. She inhales deeply. Above our heads two dragons swoop towards the battle, ready to burn the defenders outside the gate. As the same time, the Orcish phalanx lower their long spears and break into a run.

Lisutaris hands the thazis stick to Makri. Then the

Sorcerer raises her arms in the air, one hand pointing at each dragon, and starts to intone a spell. It's not one I'm familiar with. Though I've a reasonable knowledge of most magical lore, it's not even a language I'm familiar with. It's a harsh, guttural incantation, and as she recites it Harmon Half Elf looks very uncomfortable and Anumaris Thunderbolt seems surprised. Coranus the Grinder nods in approval. I'd guess that this spell is something particularly unpleasant that the Sorcerers Guild would normally leave in the vaults. Something that Lisutaris would only dredge up in the direst emergency.

It's already as cold as the Ice Queen's grave. As Lisutaris chants the spell, it somehow becomes colder. The Ice Queen's grave seems to open up and engulf us in a freezing void. There's a great roar of rushing wind, and two shafts of dark purple light fly from Lisutaris's hands up into the sky, one striking each dragon. Their cries of rage and pain are terrible to hear, drowning out even the roar of battle. The dragons halt in mid air, writhing, before Lisutaris draws her hands downwards, pulling them from the sky. As she does this, several bolts of light fly through the air towards her. The dragons are carrying Sorcerers and they're fighting back. Their bolts strike Lisutaris, shaking her, but she remains upright, still supported by Makri. For a moment time stands still. The dragons are motionless in the sky as Lisutaris strives against their own colossal strength and the sorcery of their Orcish riders. Then something gives, and the dragons cease to beat their wings. They plummet towards the earth, heading straight for the Orcish phalanx. As they hit the ground, both dragons explode in flames.

"That's not something you see every day," mutters Makri.

The Orcish phalanx is destroyed by the force of the explosion. The remaining Orcish troops scatter before the flames. Lisutaris falls to the ground. I pick her up, sling her over my shoulder, and order my men forward.

CHAPTER TWENTY-ONE

The Orcs have scattered in confusion. I lead my company directly between the flaming corpses of the dragons. Thick oily smoke pours from the bodies of the beasts, now burning with some evil sorcerous fire conjured up by Lisutaris. We're no more than fifty yards from the gates and I'm praying that someone inside the city will seize the opportunity of opening them and letting us in before the Orcs can regroup.

Lisutaris weighs heavily on my shoulder but I keep going. If we miss this chance we're not going to get another. The gates open. The trapped Turanian troops leave the shelter of their wagons and run towards the city. We follow on. We're still some way from the walls when I sense a hostile spell on its way. The ground shakes beneath my feet. I'm hit by what feels like a hammer to the back of the head. My protection charm keeps me alive but it doesn't stop the pain. I sag to my knees, dropping Lisutaris. It's a terrible struggle getting up again. Even Makri is slow to rise.

"What the . . . ?"

Harmon, Coranus and Anumaris help each other to their feet. The Sorcerers are wearing spell protection charms, as are Makri and I. They're rare items. My troops didn't have them. None of them are rising to their feet. As my head slowly clears I find that we're not alone. We're faced by twelve Orcs. Three Sorcerers, seven warriors and two who look like they might be officers. One of the Sorcerers is Horm the Dead. Lisutaris stirs at my feet. Horm glares down at her.

"You killed my dragon," he says, sounding pained. "It was my favourite."

He shifts his gaze to Makri. Rather longingly, I think. If he offers her flowers again I'll kill him with my bare hands. But if Horm is about to speak further, he halts himself as one of the officers steps forward. A tall Orc, not bulky, but strong-looking, with fine black armour, long black hair, and a small circlet of gold on his brow. Not quite as craggy as his followers. I realise that it's Prince Amrag himself.

He regards us for a few seconds. Then he looks curiously at Makri. Lisutaris hauls herself upright. Prince Amrag's guards step forward anxiously, to protect their leader from the Human Sorcerer. Amrag glances questioningly towards Horm.

"They have no sorcery left," says Horm.

"And neither have you," responds Lisutaris.

"Regrettably, no," admits Horm. "We were obliged to expend all our efforts in saving our lives when you brought us down from the sky."

Even here on the battlefield, Horm, with his pale skin, languid manners and long cloak, cuts an unusual figure.

"But we do have an army," adds Horm, and gestures behind him to where around a thousand Orcish warriors are charging towards us. I push Lisutaris in the direction of the city wall.

"Go," I say, "now," and gesture for the Sorcerers to flee. Harmon and Anumaris need no encouragement. Lisutaris hesitates, but Coranus the Grinder grabs her tattered cloak and drags her off. Makri and I draw our swords, planning to sell our lives gaining the Sorcerers the few seconds they need to reach the city. The thick smoke from the flaming dragons is still billowing around our heads. I'm expecting Prince Amrag to order his bodyguards to set off in pursuit. Seven warriors. Makri and I can hold them till the rest of the army arrives. The Prince, however, issues no orders. He looks at Makri again, then speaks, this time in the common Human tongue, which few Orcs know.

"Hello, sister."

"Hello, brother."

"I admired your progress. Champion gladiator."

"You left me in the slave pits to die," says Makri.

Prince Amrag shrugs.

"And now you fight for Turai?"

"I do."

"Would you wish to join my army?"

Makri spits on the ground.

A small chuckle escapes from the Prince's lips.

"The unclean Elvish blood. It always caused problems." He glances over our shoulders.

"They're closing the gates. If you wish to re-enter your city, you had better leave now. I'll be joining you inside soon enough."

Makri dithers, as if about to say something more. I grab her and drag her after me, through the thick smoke, through the still falling snow, towards the great East Gate. It's swinging shut as we arrive. I let out a series of the foulest and loudest curses. Mercifully someone takes heed. The gate opens a few inches, we squeeze though, and then it's closed. Heavy bolts are drawn and huge metal bars descend to reinforce it. We're the last people back in Turai. I turn to Makri.

"Hello, sister? Sister? Prince Amrag is your brother?"

"Half-brother. Same father, different mother. He has no Elvish blood."

"Have you known this all along?"

Makri shakes her head.

"I never knew what became of him after he escaped from the slave pits."

All around us is confusion. There's no sign of Lisutaris.

"What do we do now?" asks Makri. "Man the walls?"

"A good question."

I don't really know what to do. No one has prepared for this eventuality. There's no designated meeting point for defeated soldiers straggling back into the city. I've no idea where to go. Some battalions of soldiers, still intact, are already on the walls. Others are rushing up the steps to take up positions. I should join them somewhere but I don't know where.

"I should find Lisutaris," says Makri.

I walk along after Makri. It's a long time since I've felt

quite so unsure of myself. Perhaps I should head back to Twelve Seas, climb on to the nearest bit of the wall, and wait for the Orcs to attack. Or maybe I should wait nearer the East Gate in case the Orcs break through here first. I don't know.

Just inside the eastern wall lie the pleasure gardens. The ponds are frozen over and the trees are covered in snow. The frozen ground is littered with dead and wounded, soldiers who've been helped back into the city by their comrades. Turai has not made provision for so many casualties. Doctors, herbalists and apothecaries were not yet prepared for this. Wounded men lie in the trampled snow, unattended.

"You were right about being in battle," said Makri. "From the moment it started I had no idea what was going on."

"Me neither. Except we were taking a beating."

"Is Gurd still alive?"

I shake my head. I don't know.

We come across a familiar figure, kneeling on the ground. It's Erisox, the Consul's cook. The poor guy was caught outside the city walls. He must have scuttled back inside quickly enough, because he's still got his little cart with him, and the portable oven. He's got an arrow in his calf and is trying to draw it out. I bend down to help. The arrow isn't embedded very deeply and won't cause too much damage when it comes out. I yank it free. Erisox screams and faints.

"Didn't do too much damage," I say.

I look at the little oven. I haven't eaten for a while. I prise open the door, just in case there's anything left. There's a pastry inside. I take it out and offer half of it to

Makri. She refuses and I swallow the pastry in a single bite.

"Erisox. He's a master of the art. I doubt there's a finer cook in the whole city. That pastry was superb."

"Really," says Makri.

"Yes. Perfect. And think of the difficult circumstances it was made in. Portable oven, snow falling, Orcs attacking, dragons flying overhead. Still the man makes a perfect pastry. Nothing seems to put him off."

I halt. It's just dawned on me that Erisox has been lying to me. He moans. I help him sit upright. The wound in his calf isn't so bad.

"Erisox. The whole time I was investigating Galwinius's murder the one person I trusted was you. Because you're such a great cook. But you were lying, weren't you? You told me no one entered your kitchen, and you were there all the time. That wasn't true, was it?"

Erisox immediately looks forlorn. Having just come off a battlefield with an arrow in his leg, he's not in the mood to put up too much resistance.

"No. Bevarius came in with Rittius. Then I went to the storeroom with my assistant and Bevarius."

"What for?"

"To make bets on the races. The whole kitchen staff at the Consul's offices usually give their money to Bevarius's cook and he places our bets."

"So why did Bevarius take the money instead?"

"He said his cook was sick. We thought it was strange, a Senator taking bets instead of his cook, but who knows, these Senators all like to bet anyway."

I nod. Bevarius just found a convenient excuse to get

the chef and his assistant out of the way for a few moments.

"Why did you need to go into the storeroom?" I ask.

"Just being discreet. The Consul doesn't like it if his staff are placing bets during work time."

"So where was Rittius all this time?"

"He was on his own in the kitchen."

Rittius was alone in the kitchen. Using a little poison, no doubt. I was so busy thinking about why the Consul came back along the corridor on his own, I never checked where Rittius and Bevarius went. They went into the kitchen. Erisox lied to me. I help him bandage his calf. His lies made my investigation difficult but I can't really hate a man who has such a command of the pastry oven.

The Orcs are at the gate. I should be doing something warlike.

"How did you know I was lying?" asks Erisox.

"From the excellence of your cooking. I've eaten pastries made by you in the Consul's office, on the military training grounds, and I just ate one you made while the Orcs were attacking. Each one perfect. You can cook a perfect pastry no matter how difficult the circumstances. But I just remembered that on the day Galwinius was murdered, I bit into one which was slightly undercooked. The only explanation for that is that you'd left the oven unattended."

Erisox casts his eyes down.

"A whole batch, too soft in the middle. I should never have left the kitchen."

"Don't feel too bad. A man needs to get his bets down while he can."

"Thraxas!" bellows the loudest voice in the west. It's Viriggax, not looking in such bad shape.

"Hell of an affair, that! Since when could dragons fly here in winter? Half my troop were killed before we got near the Orcs."

Viriggax and his remaining mercenaries have carried their wounded companions inside and are now searching for some medical help before heading back to the walls. Some of the men they've carried in are badly wounded and a few have died.

"Is that Toraggax?"

Viriggax nods.

"Poor boy. First battle and he gets killed."

Makri steps over to the body. It's quite badly mutilated. She looks at it expressionlessly. Not even a frown.

"You know your Prince is dead?" says Viriggax.

"I didn't."

"He was a bad leader."

He was. It wasn't entirely his fault that the Orcs took us by surprise but he should have trusted in Lisutaris's warnings.

Makri moves away from Toraggax's body.

"Was someone responsible for this? I mean, the Orc Sorcerer in Turai, the surprise attack? Did someone betray the city?"

"Rittius, I think," I mutter, softly, so no one else can hear. Makri nods.

Horses sweep into the pleasure gardens. It's General Pomius, Lisutaris and various other officials. There's no sign of the Consul. I wonder if he's dead. Officers, taking orders from the General, hurry this way and that around the gardens, issuing commands, organising the scattered troops.

"Is that Rittius's carriage?" Makri asks, indicating a vehicle to the rear of the General's.

"Looks like it."

Makri sets off. I follow on after her. In the aftermath of the catastrophic battle, it's not a time to be investigating a murder, but I'd like words with Rittius anyway. I force my way through the crowds of soldiers and officials that surround the General's carriage. No one pays me much notice. There are a lot of soldiers wandering aimlessly around the field, shocked by their experiences. Makri pulls open the door of Rittius's carriage and leaps inside. I hurry after her, closing the door behind me. Rittius is sitting on his upholstered seat, looking at Makri in surprise.

"Rittius, you dog," I begin. "I know you're a traitor—"

I stop. There's more I want to say but Makri chooses this moment to stick a dagger in Rittius's heart. I stare at Makri, then back to Rittius.

". . . and after due process of law you'll answer for your crimes in court."

Rittius slumps forward, dead from his wound. I turn to Makri.

"You couldn't even wait till I made a speech?"

"What for?"

"I had things to say."

Makri shrugs.

"Nothing important."

"You know I only suspected Rittius? I haven't gathered any proof. We generally don't execute people merely on my suspicions. We wait till after the trial."

"There's never going to be another trial in this city," says Makri.

"You're probably right. We should get out of here."

We slip out of the door on the far side. In the confusion, no one takes any notice of us. I'm not exactly sorry that Makri killed Rittius. He's been my enemy for a long time and I'm sure enough he betrayed the city, not to mention poisoning Galwinius. And he was probably responsible for the death of Galwinius's informer, and Bevarius too, to cover his tracks. But I do have a feeling of dissatisfaction. There were things I wanted to say. Makri might have waited till I'd got a few sentences out.

We find ourselves only a few feet away from Lisutaris, Mistress of the Sky. I whisper to Makri.

"Don't say anything about what just happened."

"Lisutaris," says Makri. "I just killed Rittius because he betrayed the city."

The Sorcerer looks surprised.

"Pardon?"

"Thraxas can give you more details."

"The details will have to wait," says Lisutaris. "I'm needed at the East Gate."

She isn't looking in such good shape.

"You don't look fit for more fighting," I say.

"I'm not," replies Lisutaris. "That last spell took it out of me."

Tirini Snake Smiter, in excellent shape, appears beside her, still glamorous. She holds a scented handkerchief in her hand which she dabs around her nose as if to keep away the stench of death.

"Tirini is assisting me," says Lisutaris, drily. "She's

still full of spells. Having not actually made it to the battlefield."

"I told you, I was having my hair done," says Tirini, defensively.

They walk off. The Orcs don't seem to be storming the city at this moment but I can smell burning coming from somewhere. Makri lingers for a moment.

"Don't tell anyone Prince Amrag is my brother."

"I won't."

She hurries off after Lisutaris.

A centurion strides up to me and demands to know what I'm doing, standing uselessly in the middle of the pleasure gardens. I tell him my phalanx was destroyed outside the walls.

"So?" he barks. "Are you just planning to stand there? Get down to the South Gate and report for duty on the walls."

I wrap my cloak around me and set off. From the lack of dragons flying overhead and the absence of noises of battle it seems like the Orcs are not immediately pressing their attack on the city. The aroma of burning gets stronger as I head south. Though the dragons didn't try to raze the city, it seems like they did target several buildings. The grain stores at the harbour are burning furiously. Fire wagons race past me as I trudge towards the gate. I find an officer and report for duty. He sends me up on the walls, where I look out on to the cold shore. It's dark, snow is falling, but there's no sign of an attack. I'm hungry.

"Still here?" comes a familiar voice.

It's Gurd. I'm so relieved I could throw my arms around him. But I'm not really a throwing-my-arms sort of person, so I nod.

"Still here. Last survivor of phalanx number seven."

Gurd shakes his head wearily.

"Mine crumbled at the first attack. God knows how I survived."

I know how Gurd survived. By hewing off the head of any Orc who came near him. We wait for the night to pass. On the cold, exposed walls, the mood is grim. Turai's army has been destroyed. Prince Dees-Akan is dead, along with many of our commanders and countless troops. There's an Orcish army outside the gates and no prospect of relief. You don't have to be sharp as an Elf's ear to know we're in serious trouble.

When I reflect that today I've solved my case, and a perplexing one at that, I almost manage to smile. Who cares now who killed Prefect Galwinius? No one at all. We'll all be dead soon enough.

CHAPTER TWENTY-TWO

Three days later I'm still on guard duty on the walls. The Orcs have not yet pressed home their attack but neither have they withdrawn. The main bulk of their army has taken shelter in the Stadium Superbius and the buildings around it. Others have been deployed to watch the city gates, making sure that no one enters or leaves. The city is now under siege.

It took two days to put the fires out at the grain warehouses. As a result of this well-directed assault by the dragons, our food stores are already badly depleted. Our army has been all but destroyed. The mercenaries didn't fare much better. All over the city men are still dying. Turai is well supplied with healers, herbalists and doctors, some of them aided by sorcery, but for many of the terrible wounds inflicted by Orcish weapons, there's no cure.

If it was Prince Amrag's intention to seize Turai in winter and use it for a bridgehead for his assault on the west next summer, he didn't quite succeed. We held them off and shut the gates. But the Prince hasn't gone away and no one is expecting him to. Whether he's waiting for reinforcements or siege engines, or just working on another plan for taking the city, nobody knows, but few people can sleep easily with the Orcs outside the walls. No Human nation will march to our aid till the spring. The Elves can't set sail in this weather. Even if Turai still stands when winter draws to a close, the city might not be relieved. The armies of the west might decide to defend the line elsewhere.

My guard duty ends at midnight. I make the long descent from the walls and am surprised to find a carriage waiting for me. It's Lisutaris. As a member of the War Council, to which she has now been reinstated, Lisutaris is allowed to use her carriage at night. Inside it's warm, with a comforting aroma of thazis.

"So why the lift home?"

"The Orcish spell you found on Bevarius. It was for transporting dragons. Do you know why he had it?"

I admit I don't.

"It was a target. The dragons couldn't have flown so far in such cold weather. Teleporting them was a brilliant piece of sorcery but it wouldn't have worked if they hadn't had agents already in Turai. The Orcish Sorcerer set things up and the spell itself acted as a beacon. Bevarius actually brought the dragons to Turai."

Lisutaris wants to know who Bevarius was working with.

"Just Rittius, I think," I tell her.

"Are you certain?"

"No. But I haven't found anything that points to any other accomplices."

"Such foul treachery," says Lisutaris.

"I'd guess our head of Palace Security was in the pay of the Orcs for years. If the authorities dig around enough I reckon they'll come up with a lot of money stashed away somewhere."

"I'm glad you killed him," says Lisutaris.

"Makri killed him," I correct her.

"I believe she was upset over the death of Toraggax."

"Probably. It's lucky her hero Samanatius survived or she'd probably have slaughtered the whole government."

"You do not approve?"

"No. Everyone deserves a trial, even Rittius."

Lisutaris makes no reply. At least we don't have to worry about any Sorcerer at the Abode of Justice looking back in time and finding out how Rittius was killed. With so many dragons in the vicinity, there's no chance of a Sorcerer seeing any pictures of past events. Dragons are very disruptive to sorcerous investigations.

"Who killed Bevarius?" asks Lisutaris.

"A member of the Assassins Guild, I presume, hired by Rittius. Only a skilled artist could have thrown a dart so lethally through that gap in the window. And when you hire them, they don't ask questions and they don't tell tales."

"Why did Rittius want Bevarius dead?"

"To cover his tracks. Rittius knew that Bevarius couldn't stand up to a prolonged interrogation from a man like myself. You see, Galwinius had got wind of Rittius's treachery and brought a scroll containing evidence to the meeting to give to the Consul. Unfortunately for Galwinius, his assistant Bevarius was in league with Rittius and warned him. So Rittius poisoned the Prefect. Fortunately for him, suspicion fell on Senator Lodius. Later that day Rittius and Bevarius had Galwinius's informer murdered, and when I started asking questions they tried to have me killed too."

"Have you reported all this to the Consul?"

"I can't get near him."

"No one can get near the Consul," says Lisutaris.

"So he was badly wounded in the battle?"

The Sorcerer shakes her head.

"A slight injury only. Unfortunately he has now suffered a mental collapse and is incapable of action. As is Prince Frisen-Akan, who's been in a state of advanced intoxication since the Orcs appeared."

"How about the King?"

"Practically bedridden. Cicerius has taken over the reins of government. I have some regard for Cicerius, but he's not a war leader. It's fortunate that General Pomius survived."

Lisutaris muses for a moment or two.

"Rittius's treachery has cost us dearly. I now understand who was spreading rumours to discredit me in the eyes of the War Council. Worse than this, the Orcish Sorcerer managed to block almost all of our seeing spells. No one apart from me saw the Orcs gathering in Yal. And no one could have foreseen that they'd manage to bring dragons here in winter."

I ask what the War Council know of the Orcs' intentions.

"Nothing. Possibly Prince Amrag is waiting for more dragons. With his own Sorcerers in the Stadium Superbius it seems possible he can bring them here. Our Sorcerers are working to prevent it. He's brought a lot of northern Orcs with him. They can stand the cold. They're dug in outside every gate."

She pauses to light a thazis stick.

"You solved another crime. Congratulations."

I'm not sure if there's something ironic in her voice. It would have helped if I'd solved it earlier. The carriage turns into Quintessence Street.

"One other thing," says Lisutaris. "Herminis. It's unlikely, at a time like this, that the authorities will expend much energy in looking for her, but we have to be careful. It would not do for the story of her escape to be made public."

"Why wouldn't it do?"

"Because I am vital to the War Council," replies Lisutaris. "I can't be distracted by accusations of helping a convicted woman to escape."

"No matter how true those allegations might be."

"No matter how true those allegations might be. I want your help. It will require some sorcerous power to keep her safely concealed—"

"One moment," I interrupt. "Is this going to end by you telling me Herminis is in my office?"

"Of course not. Do you think I am entirely lacking in sense?"

"Just checking. What do you want me to do?"

The carriage pulls up outside the Avenging Axe. Lisutaris alights with me and accompanies me up the stairs to my office. I'm surprised when my door swings freely open. Someone has interfered with my locking spell. A great gust of thazis smoke hits me in the face as I enter. Makri and Herminis are sprawled around the room.

"Goddammit, Lisutaris, you said she wasn't in my office!"

"I was intending to break it to you gently," says Lisutaris.

Makri rises unsteadily to her feet. From the size of her pupils and the uncertainty of her step I'd say she'd been indulging in dwa. A killer drug, which she's sworn off, in theory.

"It's Thraxas. Number one chariot at investigating. Solved a crime just by eating pastry!"

Makri sits down heavily. I inform Lisutaris roughly that I'm on guard duty every day and will not be able to help in any sorcerous matter concerning Herminis.

"Of course you can," says Lisutaris. "One simple incantation every morning to boost my hiding spell."

"Get someone else to do it."

"There is no one else. Every other Sorcerer in the Guild is fully engaged in war work."

It's true. Every Sorcerer has been thrown into action. Astrath Triple Moon is back, and Kemlath Orc Slayer has been recalled from exile. Even Glixius Dragon Killer, a criminal Sorcerer of very dubious loyalty, has been brought into the fold.

"What about Tirini Snake Smiter? You're not telling me she turns up for war duty before midday."

"She doesn't. But Tirini couldn't be relied on to speak

the incantation every morning. Mornings are a busy time for her, with her hairdresser and her beautician, and her masseuse. And one or two others. You know—shoes, jewellery, that sort of thing."

"Well, I'm glad she's looking her best. Let's hope she doesn't break a nail when the Orcs storm the walls."

"Tirini will do her part," states Lisutaris. "And it really would make my life easier if you would do me this favour."

"I refuse to aid you in any way."

There's a brisk knock on the outside door. I open it to find Senator Lodius standing there with a scowl on his face. He makes no attempt to enter my office, preferring to remain on the outside step, in the snow.

"You seem to have cleared my name."

"I seem to have."

Not officially, yet. But my findings will soon be known to the Senate. Lodius will not be tried for the murder of Prefect Galwinius. The Senator hands me a purse.

"Thirty gurans for every day you were engaged on the case. If you have additional expenses, send me a bill."

He turns and leaves. He didn't thank me. But he did pay. The moment I close my outside door there's a light tap on the inside door. Not liking the way my office is again becoming a late-night rendezvous for Turai's outcasts, I open it with a frown. The frown deepens at the sight of Hanama.

"How did you get in?"

"I picked the lock."

"Did it occur to you that Gurd might not like you breaking into his tavern every night?"

"You exaggerate," says Hanama, and slips past me into

the office. She hands a piece of paper to Lisutaris. The Sorcerer glances at it.

"Excellent," she mutters. "Thraxas, this is a full retraction of the accusations of cowardice made against you by Vedinax. He admits he was lying and that you never threw your shield away."

"How did you get that?"

"Though private means."

"Threats and bribery?"

"That, and my friendship with Praetor Capatius, Vedinax's employer. You can have this paper if you agree to my request."

I take the paper. The accusations of cowardice have been a burden. I want them lifted.

"Okay, I'll work your damned spell for you."

"What's that under your cloak?" Lisutaris asks Hanama.

"Nothing," replies the small Assassin.

"Yes it is," says Lisutaris. "It's a bunch of flowers."

"So what if it is?" says Hanama.

"Since when did you pick flowers?" demands Lisutaris.

"I didn't pick them. They were just lying in the street."

"Are they for me?" asks Makri, her voice sounding slurred.

"No. I just found them outside. I don't even know why I picked them up. They're not for anyone. Unless you want them. Do you want them, Makri? You can have them if you want."

"Did Rittius hire your foul guild to assassinate Bevarius?" I demand.

"The Assassins Guild does not discuss its affairs in public," replies Hanama.

By now Lisutaris is starting to construct a thazis stick of massive proportions. Not wishing my office to again be full of intoxicated members of the Association of Gentlewomen, I throw them out, banishing them to Makri's room, where they can do what the hell they like. I drag a bottle of klee from its new hiding place, as yet undiscovered by Makri, and drink deeply.

No more accusations of cowardice. That's good. Solved the case of Prefect Galwinius, and got paid, also good. Orcs outside the walls, not so good. City about to fall. Very bad.

Makri is half-sister of Prince Amrag. That's too puzzling to think about right now.

Since the Orcs attacked I haven't been sleeping well. It takes half the bottle of klee and several thazis sticks before I manage to nod off, and I'm far from refreshed when I wake the next day. I take a cold breakfast downstairs in the early light. Makri intercepts me before I leave the tavern. She stands awkwardly for a moment, then hands me a cloak.

"I brought you this. Lisutaris put a warming spell on it. It will last much longer than your own."

"Thanks, Makri."

Maybe I should make an apology for the abuse I've heaped on Makri's head recently. She turns and leaves before I get the chance, so I drape the cloak round my shoulders and head for the walls.

Epic Urban Adventure by a New Star of Fantasy

DRAW ONE IN THE DARK

by Sarah A. Hoyt

Every one of us has a beast inside. But for Kyrie Smith, the beast is no metaphor. Thrust into an ever-changing world of shifters, where shape-shifting dragons, giant cats and other beasts wage a secret war behind humanity's back, Kyrie tries to control her inner animal and remain human as best she can....

"Analytically, it's a tour de force: logical, built from assumptions, with no contradictions, which is astonishing given the subject matter. It's also gripping enough that I finished it in one day."

—Jerry Pournelle

1-4165-2092-9 • $25.00

IF YOU LIKE...
YOU SHOULD TRY...

DAVID DRAKE
David Weber

DAVID WEBER
John Ringo

JOHN RINGO
Michael Z. Williamson
Tom Kratman

ANNE MCCAFFREY
Mercedes Lackey

MERCEDES LACKEY
Wen Spencer, Andre Norton
Andre Norton
James H. Schmitz

LARRY NIVEN
James P. Hogan
Travis S. Taylor

ROBERT A. HEINLEIN
Jerry Pournelle
Lois McMaster Bujold
Michael Z. Williamson

HEINLEIN'S "JUVENILES"
Rats, Bats & Vats series by Eric Flint & Dave Freer

HORATIO HORNBLOWER OR PATRICK O'BRIAN
David Weber's Honor Harrington series
David Drake's RCN series

HARRY POTTER
Mercedes Lackey's Urban Fantasy series

THE LORD OF THE RINGS
Elizabeth Moon's *The Deed of Paksenarrion*

H.P. LOVECRAFT
Princess of Wands by John Ringo

GEORGETTE HEYER
Lois McMaster Bujold
Catherine Asaro

GREEK MYTHOLOGY
Pyramid Scheme by Eric Flint & Dave Freer
Forge of the Titans by Steve White
Blood of the Heroes by Steve White

NORSE MYTHOLOGY
Northworld Trilogy by David Drake
A Mankind Witch by Dave Freer

ARTHURIAN LEGEND
Steve White's "Legacy" series
The Dragon Lord by David Drake

SCA/HISTORICAL REENACTMENT
John Ringo's "After the Fall" series
Harald by David D. Friedman

SCIENCE FACT
Kicking the Sacred Cow by James P. Hogan

CATS
Larry Niven's Man-Kzin Wars series

PUNS
Rick Cook
Spider Robinson
Wm. Mark Simmons

VAMPIRES
Wm. Mark Simmons